Too Much of a Good Thing

By Kimberla Lawson Roby

Too Much of a Good Thing
A Taste of Reality
It's a Thin Line
Casting the First Stone
Here and Now
Behind Closed Doors

And in Hardcover

The Best-Kept Secret

Too Much of a Good Thing

KIMBERLA LAWSON ROBY

WILLIAM MORROW
An Imprint of HarperCollins*Publishers*

A hardcover edition of this title was published by William Morrow in January 2004

FIRST EDITION

Designed by Diahann Sturge

The William Morrow hardcover edition contains the following Library of Congress Cataloging-in-Publication Data

Roby, Kimberla Lawson.
Too much of a good thing / Kimberla Lawson Roby.—1st ed.
p. cm.
1. Married women—Fiction. 2. Spouses of clergy—Fiction.
3. African American women—Fiction. 4. African American clergy—
Fiction. I. Title.

PS3568.O3189T66 2004
813'.54—dc22

2003058213

16 JTC/RRD 20 19 18

For my husband, Will.

Life would not be the same without you.

Too Much of a Good Thing

Prologue

Curtis raised the volume on his big-screen TV, slouched farther into the sofa, and sighed with much frustration. He hadn't slept peacefully in weeks. But he knew it was all because he'd been tossing and turning, night after night, trying desperately to dismiss the voice he kept hearing. It was a voice that demanded his return to the ministry.

For four long years he'd been trying to appreciate the fifty-thousand-dollar salary he earned as director of a delinquent teens facility, but it just wasn't working. It wasn't working because during his pastoral reign at Faith Missionary Baptist Church, he'd become completely accustomed to earning three times more than that—not to mention the thousands of dollars he received in love offerings. He could still remember how most of the members had worshipped the ground he walked on and how loads of women in the church had openly thrown themselves at his mercy. He'd tried to fight them off as best he could, but it wasn't long before he'd given in to Adrienne Jackson, the wife of one of the deacons. Then there was Charlotte, who was all of seventeen when he'd first begun seeing her and only eighteen when she gave birth to his illegitimate son. But he regretted nothing the way he regretted being caught on videotape having sex with two women he didn't know. He'd met them at a convenience store and taken them straight to a hotel, but what he hadn't counted on was their setting him up to be blackmailed. Monique, his disgruntled church secretary, had masterminded the entire scheme, and Curtis had lost everything: his tax-free six-figure income, three-thousand-plus congregation, custom-built dream house, and, most important, his wife and daughter to another man.

Curtis cringed at his latest thought, and then returned his attention to BET's morning inspiration segment. A world-renowned TV evangelist danced across the pulpit. Curtis had watched four others do the same thing every hour on the hour, and wished he could trade places with any one of them. He watched one massive audience after another rising to their feet, clapping, screaming, and giving high praises to God and the minister who was speaking before them. He watched so intensely that he was now drunk from all the excitement. These people on television reminded him of his own flock, the one he used to have, and he missed having them praise him in the same fashion. He missed the emotional high he always felt whenever he stood before his loyal congregation.

He continued watching the program and envied the evangelist, who wore the same type of suit he'd once worn himself. It had been a long while since he was able to buy anything that cost a thousand dollars, but that was finally about to change. He'd recently been approached by the deacon board of Truth Missionary Baptist Church. Truth was a church that had been founded by approximately one thousand of his former members, right after he was ousted. They were members who either hadn't believed the rumors they'd heard about him or who merely felt that he deserved to be forgiven the same as anyone else. They'd approached him about being their leader back then, too, but he'd declined when he decided that he no longer wanted to preach. Now, though, their charter pastor had left and taken a position at a church in D.C., and they needed to replace him.

For two weeks Curtis had debated whether he should accept their more than appealing offer, but in all honesty, he really didn't know how he could pass on it. They were offering him five thousand per week, his choice of any luxury vehicle, and a very respectable housing allowance—something he hadn't been able to negotiate at his previous church because they'd wanted him to live in some modest church parsonage. They were even willing to overlook the fact that he wasn't married as long as he found a wife within the first two years of his contract. But Curtis didn't see a reason to wait that long and was sure that Mariah Johnson, the woman he'd been seeing for the past six months, would jump at the chance to marry him. As a matter of fact, she'd be perfect, because, unlike his ex-wife, Tanya, she knew her place. She was meek, mild, a bit naïve, and completely submissive. She was beautiful but didn't know it, and the fact that she honored God and always tried to do the right thing wasn't going to hurt.

Curtis thought about all the rewards he was going to reap and wondered why he was still somewhat hesitant. But deep down he knew what it was. It was his mother and the scripture she had quoted him over and over, whenever he spoke about his desire to be filthy rich. She quoted Mark 8:36: "For what shall it profit a man, if he shall gain the whole world, and lose his own soul?"

But the more Curtis thought about it, the more he realized that Mark 8:36 really didn't apply to him. It didn't apply because he had no desire to gain the whole world.

He only wanted a very small part of it.

The part that rightfully belonged to him.

Thanksgiving, he'd discovered what he'd dreamed, that he no longer wanted a woman. Sure, though then other pursuits had left ... [illegible] ... a [illegible] ... At a camp [illegible] ... [illegible] place, time.

For two weeks Curtis had debated whether he should accept the marriage [illegible] offer, [illegible]. He really didn't know how he could pass it up. They were offering him two thousand per week, his choice of cities [illegible] ... [illegible] ... [illegible] ... even as [illegible] ... a previous choice because they'd [illegible] to live the [illegible] of rich passengers. That ... [illegible] ... overlook the fact that he wasn't as tired as long as he [illegible] wife within the first two years of his contract. But Curtis [illegible] a reason to wait ... that Mariah [illegible] the woman he'd been seeing for the ... [illegible] ... would [illegible] at the chance to marry him. As a matter of fact, she'd [illegible] perfect, because, unlike his ex-wife, she knew her place. She was [illegible] and [illegible] completely submissive. She was beautiful but didn't know it, and the best thing, she honored God and always tried to do the right thing [illegible].

Curtis thought about all the rewards he was going to reap and wondered why he was still somewhat hesitant. But deep down he knew what it was. It was his mother and the scripture she had quoted over and over whenever he spoke about his dreams to be [illegible] rich. She quoted Mark 8:36, "For what shall it profit a man if he shall gain the whole world, and lose his own soul?"

But the more Curtis thought about it, the more he realized that Mark 8:36 really didn't apply to him. It didn't apply because he had no desire to gain the whole world.

He only wanted a very small portion of it.

The part that rightfully belonged to him.

Chapter 1

A Year Later

Mariah Johnson Black smiled proudly as her husband neared the end of his morning message. It just didn't seem real, him actually being senior pastor of Truth Missionary Baptist Church or that he'd chosen her to be his wife. It didn't seem real that he'd wanted a woman who'd grown up in a run-down two-bedroom apartment on the West Side of Chicago that also housed her single mother and five siblings. But he always reminded her that he'd grown up with nothing himself. Still, every now and then, she had to pinch herself, because she couldn't believe how happy she was. She couldn't believe they'd only been married six short months, and yet Curtis had already bought her a six-thousand-square-foot house in Covington Park, the most expensive Mercedes that Daimler manufactured, and best of all, she didn't have to work for anyone. All she had to do was be the best wife she could be to Curtis and the best first lady to their congregation—two things Curtis said his first wife, Tanya, wasn't capable of. Mariah almost felt sorry for Tanya, because she couldn't imagine how painful it must have been, once Tanya realized what she'd given up. Curtis had told Mariah about Tanya's affair with James, and Mariah couldn't understand how Tanya even considered being with another man. Especially when she had someone as fine-looking and considerate as Curtis. Especially since he had only been with another woman—Adrienne—on two separate occasions. Curtis had told Mariah how he'd apologized and tried to explain everything to Tanya, but that she wasn't willing to forgive him. He'd tried to make Tanya see that this random act of adultery had only occurred because Satan was trying to attack him and their marriage. He'd told Tanya that the only reason God had allowed it to happen was because He wanted to see how strong their faith was and how committed they were to each other as husband and wife.

But thankfully, all of that was behind them now, and while she wasn't happy about Curtis and Tanya's marriage ending in divorce, she knew it was the only reason she was now sitting on the second pew, dressed in a royal blue suit, a matching hat, matching purse, and matching three-inch heels. Mariah also knew that Curtis would never have paid her the least bit of attention if they hadn't worked for the same agency. He'd told her more than once that she was beautiful, but she knew it was only because he felt obligated to do so and not because it was true. She'd been a bit on the heavy side growing up, and her schoolmates had teased her daily. So by the time she was a teenager, she'd lost all confidence in herself and in the way she looked.

But in terms of her feelings for Curtis, she'd actually liked him from the very beginning and had fallen in love with him right after their first date. He was strong, compassionate, tall, dark, and handsome, and from that point she started praying for their relationship to become serious. She prayed that God would give her Curtis even if it meant she had to go without something else in life, whatever that had to be. So when he asked her to marry him, she knew for sure that God answered all prayers.

Mariah watched Curtis twirl his hands, demonstrating what he was saying.

"God will allow you to experience every twist and turn in the road until you are as strong as He needs you to be . . . until you are strong enough to deal with any trial or tribulation thrown your way," Curtis said. "And when it comes to success and prosperity, we have to take the same attitude. Sometimes we find ourselves climbing higher and higher in our chosen careers and all of a sudden a monkey wrench is thrown into the program. And of course, we as human beings don't understand it. We don't understand why God would give us such great success and then, for whatever reason, take us down a notch or two. But the best way I can explain it is to tell you what I heard on the radio last week. I was driving along, listening to 106.3, and it was then that I heard T. D. Jakes make one of the most profound statements. He said, 'A *setback* is a *setup* for a *comeback*.' "

The congregation roared with amens and a good number of people waved their bulletins at Curtis, agreeing with what he was saying.

Curtis thrived on member participation and repeated in song what the crowd wanted to hear him say again. "I *said*, a *setback* is a *setup* for a *comeback*."

"Oh, thank you, Jesus!" one woman stood and yelled out.

"Glory be to God!" another added with her hands lifted toward the ceiling.

"Boy, you know you workin' that Word on us today!" an older gentleman offered.

The organist played a few notes, and Mariah stood with her hands on both hips, waving her head from side to side with quick movements, giving Curtis approval. Then a woman jumped from her seat, shouting her way across three people sitting on the same row. This, of course, was all Curtis needed to see in order to switch into his deep southern preaching mode. He'd told Mariah that he thought it was totally ridiculous to sing the ending of every sermon, but that he'd learned during his days at Faith that his older members didn't feel like a pastor could preach if he didn't do a little whooping and singing with it. And since his older members were the major tithe and offering contributors, he gave them what they wanted.

"I saiddd, that Godd, will allow a setback, which is a setup for a great comeback. I hearddd the Bible say, we may endure for a night, but joyyy, I saiddd, joyyy, will come in the morning," Curtis sang, and then broke out of the pulpit, sobbing and running around the full length of the church, hugging himself tightly. Mariah did the holy dance back and forth across the front of the church, and ten other people did the same thing up and down the center aisle. The spirit was moving frantically throughout the entire church, and continued for almost twenty minutes. Finally, everyone began settling down, and Curtis stood up from where he'd been kneeling and walked back into the pulpit.

"Oh, I tell you, the Holy Spirit is in here today, church," he announced while wiping sweat from his forehead and neck with a white Ralph Lauren bath towel. One of the women in the health unit had brought it over to him, and Mariah was glad they'd remembered to purchase a stack of them. Curtis had mentioned that the generic ones they'd been bringing him each Sunday were much too rough, and that he would much rather have something made by one of the top designers. That way, he wouldn't have to worry about the quality after they'd been washed a few times.

"There is nothing like a visit from the Lord," Curtis continued. "There is nothing in this world that can compare to being in His presence."

"Amen," the congregation spoke in agreement.

Mariah was filled with so much joy that she wanted to burst wide open. She was sure that life could never be better than it was today.

Immediately after church, Curtis and Mariah had gone over to Deacon Taylor's house to have dinner with him and his family. Deacon Taylor was one of the deacons Curtis had appointed just before he lost his position at Faith. The deacon was very loyal to Curtis and dedicated to the church, and he was the primary reason Curtis was now pastor at Truth. He, along with hundreds of Curtis's former members, had requested that Curtis be considered for the job.

Curtis and Mariah had spent three hours visiting with them and were now walking through the kitchen doorway of their own home. Usually they had afternoon or evening services to attend on Sundays, and Mariah was thankful that this was one of those rare instances when they didn't.

"Come here, you," Curtis said, grabbing Mariah playfully yet passionately.

Mariah always felt like melting whenever he pulled her into his arms. She felt so loved and so secure.

"Have I told you how much I love you?" she asked, gazing at him.

"No. Not today, anyway," he said, smiling.

"Well, I do, Curtis. I love you from the bottom of my soul, and all I want is to make you happy."

"Baby, you do make me happy. You've done that since the first day we started seeing each other."

"I really hope so, because I've heard so many women talking about how easy it is for a man to become bored with his wife. And I don't ever want you to feel that way. I want you to tell me if there is something wrong or if there is something I can do differently."

"Look, Mariah, I love you just the way you are. Believe me, I have no complaints."

Mariah sighed with relief.

Curtis removed her blazer and pecked her on the lips. Then he kissed her neck and her chest. Mariah moaned with every show of affection. Curtis unbuttoned her silk blouse, reached under it, and unsnapped her bra. He caressed her breasts roughly, kissing her at the same time.

"Do you want it here or upstairs?" he teased.

"Upstairs," she answered.

"No, I think we'd better take care of each other right here. Don't you?"

"No, sweetheart. Let's just go upstairs so we can be more comfortable," she said, pulling him close and kissing him.

"Okay, but first let me watch you undress the rest of the way."

Mariah always felt fat and uneasy whenever Curtis asked her to do this, but she went ahead and slipped off her blouse, bra, and skirt. Then she removed her nylon hose and panties and took a step toward him.

"No. Don't move. Just let me look at you. Let me look at what God created," he said, relaxing on the sofa and locking his hands behind his head.

"Curtis," she pleaded.

"What? Can I help it if I want to see all of you from head to toe? Because you really are beautiful. Your body is perfect."

"You know this embarrasses me," she told him. Not to mention she didn't think stripping like some nightclub dancer was something a pastor's wife should be doing, anyway.

"But why does it embarrass you?"

"Because it does."

"Well, you might as well get used to it, baby, because the main reason God created Eve was so she could pleasure Adam. So, satisfying your husband is part of your duty."

"I thought Eve was created so that Adam wouldn't be lonely, and so he would have a companion?" Mariah asked.

"Companionship, pleasure. Call it whatever you want, but it all means basically the same thing."

"I guess," she said, losing the mood because of all this conversation and because he was staring at her.

"Come here," he said, reaching his hand out to her. "I hate to say this, but I wasn't truthful with you earlier."

"You weren't truthful about what?" she asked, and sat down next to him. She felt nervous and wondered what he was referring to.

"I wasn't being truthful when I said that I love you just the way you are, and that I have no complaints."

Mariah was speechless, because the last thing she wanted was for him to be dissatisfied with her.

"You still haven't given me oral sex, and that's something I'm used to getting. I know you said you didn't feel comfortable doing it because it seemed lustful and dirty. But the truth is, God doesn't have a problem with anything sexual as long as it's done between a man and his wife."

"I know you keep saying that, but I need more time, Curtis."

"How *much* more time, baby, because I've already given you six months. I mean, how much longer am I going to have to wait for something I've never had to go without?"

"I promise you I'm going to do it very soon."

"You don't seem to have a problem when I do it for you," he said matter-of-factly.

"But it's not like I ask you to do it or like it's required."

"But I can tell that you love it, and not once can I remember you turning it down."

Mariah didn't respond, because she knew he was right. She never, ever turned it down. But even though she enjoyed it, she still felt as though it was somehow unnatural and morally wrong. Especially since Curtis always turned into a ravenous animal whenever they arrived at that point of their lovemaking. He seemed to be obsessed with doing that to her, and it was almost as if he enjoyed it more than she did. But regardless, she just didn't feel comfortable doing it for him.

"Curtis, honey, I know you really want this, but I don't think it's right. I mean, why can't we make love to each other without doing all of that?"

"Because, I want more than just regular intercourse. I *need* so much more than that. And at some point you're going to have to get over this squeamish mentality," he said, turning his head away from her.

"I know, Curtis. And I promise you, I'm going to pray about this every day until God gives me the strength to do it."

"*Pray?*" he said, wrinkling his forehead. "As far as I'm concerned, there's nothing to pray about. Either you're going to do it or you're not. But I'm telling you, if I don't get it soon, I can't be responsible—"

"You can't be responsible for what?" she interrupted.

"Nothing. I didn't mean anything at all. And hey, why don't we just forget about making love altogether," he said, and stood up.

"Okay, Curtis. I'll do it."

"No, that's okay, because I don't want you doing something just for the sake of doing it."

"It won't be like that. I promise. I mean, I've never done anything like this before, but I'm willing to try."

Curtis removed every stitch of clothing he was wearing and stepped in front of her. "It won't be as bad as you think."

Mariah didn't know how she should respond, so she didn't.

"And, baby?" he said.

"Yes," she answered, wondering how she was going to get through this.

"I want you to know that even though I already love you more than anything in this world, I'll love you even more after tonight. I'll love you in a way that you can't even imagine. Our marriage will rise to a whole new level, because we will have finally bonded completely."

"I love you, too, Curtis," Mariah said, and realized that this truly was important to her husband, and that his love for her was all that really mattered. She decided that as his wife, it was her job to keep him happy.

It was her job to keep him faithful.

Chapter 2

Curtis leaned back in his tall black executive-style chair and spun himself toward the window of his church study. It was hard to believe that even after the blackmail fiasco and total scandalizing of his name, he'd still been able to reenter the ministry as pastor of an equally prominent Baptist church. As a matter of fact, Truth Missionary Baptist Church now had over thirty-five hundred members on the rolls, which was five hundred more than they'd had at Faith, and they were now holding two morning services. One at eight and one at ten forty-five. Nine months ago, when he'd first become their pastor, they'd only had maybe thirty-two hundred, and that meant he was the reason they now had three hundred more. The board of deacons was very happy with the work he'd been doing thus far, and so was the congregation. He'd learned a long time ago that most people liked having a great leader and wanted to be told what to do. They didn't seem to mind following a strong, charismatic, intelligent man, and he was glad that God had blessed him with all three qualities. When he was married to Tanya, she'd thought he was full of himself whenever he took charge and told the congregation what to do. She despised when he told them how much money they should give. But he never listened to her because he knew that most people didn't always know what was best and sometimes needed a little direction. Sometimes they needed to have certain requests explained to them in a certain kind of way. Which was why he was now a lot more subtle when he made an appeal to the congregation. Which was why he was going to play Mr. Mild Mannered when he met with the deacons one week from today. He wasn't sure how they were going to feel about some of his new ideas, but he wasn't going to fly off the handle the way he always did with his former board. Sometimes they'd disagreed with him on every point, and Deacon Jackson, Adrienne's husband, had been the ring leader. The man had debated every idea Curtis suggested, but what the deacon didn't know was that Curtis was back. He hadn't seen the deacon in years, and had no idea what church he belonged to, but the joke was still going to be on him. Curtis was going to make sure of it.

When the phone rang, he flinched and returned to reality. Finally, he pressed the speaker button.

"Yes," he said.

"Pastor, if you have some time right now, I'd like to start working on your agenda for the deacon board meeting next week," Whitney said.

"Sure, that'll be fine, just give me a minute to finish writing some notes for you."

"Sounds good," she said, and hung up.

Whitney was Curtis's new executive assistant. She'd been working for the church for two years as a clerk-typist, but when Curtis decided he didn't want the same assistant the former pastor had hired, he told the woman that things weren't working out, and that he would give her a recommendation for any job she applied for outside of the church. Curtis hadn't liked her from the start, because there just hadn't been any chemistry between them. Plus, she reminded him of Monique, his former secretary. She was sorely unattractive, and constantly acted as if she was trying to come on to him. So Curtis spoke to the deacons, and although there was some uncertainty on their part, they allowed him to replace her.

And he was glad he did, because Whitney was every pastor's dream. She was young, beautiful, and extremely organized. She loved her job, and she loved her pastor. The only downfall was that she loved her husband, and hadn't hesitated to make sure Curtis knew it. The very first day she was promoted, she'd marched right into his office, closed his door, and sat down in front of him. She'd caught him completely off guard, and before he could speak, she told him, "I do phones, I do meetings, and I do travel arrangements, but I don't do pastors. And if you agree with all of that, then you and I will get along like best friends." Curtis had laughed almost immediately, but Whitney never cracked a smile. So after a few seconds, Curtis told her that he was fine with all of the above. Just thinking about the whole scenario made him smile, but he had to admit he'd had the highest respect for her ever since.

Curtis heard a knock at the door and told Whitney to come in.

"How's your afternoon going?" she said, walking in. She was dressed in a black microfiber ankle-length dress.

"Actually, my whole day has been going great. Now all I have to do is convince the deacons that it's time for us to use more modern methods and technology when it comes to the way tithes and offerings are paid. Here's some of my ideas," he said, passing Whitney a list he'd been compiling for a while now. She scanned it and shook her head.

"What?" Curtis asked.

"No, don't get me wrong. I understand each and every one of

your points, but I can already tell you right now that you're going to meet opposition from Deacon Thurgood and Deacon Winslow."

"Hmmm," Curtis said, clasping his hands together. "The two oldest deacons on the board, huh?"

"Yep. They're extremely old-school, and they don't like anything that sounds like a scam."

"But I'm not proposing anything like that."

"I totally agree, but I'm just letting you know how they'll see it."

"How did they end up on the board anyway, because most of the deacons that came over from Faith are much younger."

"They came from the church where Pastor Jenkins used to be an associate minister," she said, referring to their former pastor.

"Well, I wish they had stayed where they were, because I'm trying to move this church in an upward direction, and we can't do that if we keep doing things the same as they've always been done. I used to tell my old congregation that we have little because we think little, and I still feel the same way right now."

"Maybe if you can prove in laymen's terms that you're not trying to run a scam and that your ideas will benefit the church as a whole, maybe they'll understand."

"Maybe. But then who's to say? But I guess we'll see soon enough."

"I'll get everything typed up, though, and you can give me any additions as the week goes on."

"Well, now that we have that taken care of, what's going on with my preanniversary committee?" Curtis winked at her. "You know it's only three months away."

"You should be ashamed of yourself," Whitney said, smiling.

"I know, but can you blame me for being curious? I mean, that's going to be a very special day. Especially since the last anniversary celebration I had at Faith was the reason my preaching career ended." He didn't talk about that particular incident to very many people, but he confided just about everything to Whitney.

"I understand. So if you must know, they're planning a monthlong celebration with a different program each Sunday afternoon. They're also planning one full week of evening services right before the actual anniversary weekend."

The services were fine and necessary, but Curtis wanted to know about the gifts—specifically the monetary ones.

"Also," Whitney continued, "each member of the church will be asked to give one hundred dollars and no less than fifty. In addition to that, you'll be receiving all moneys collected at each of the precelebration services."

"What a blessing," Curtis said, but he wished they weren't planning to offer an option where people could pay fifty dollars. Some of them wouldn't even consider paying the maximum once they learned that half of it was acceptable. If only the committee realized that it was better to give the congregation one specific amount with no alternatives, because when they had too many choices, it sometimes confused their way of thinking. Although even if only one thousand of his members gave a hundred dollars, he'd still walk away with six figures.

"Yes, it really is," Whitney agreed.

"Excuse me?" Curtis asked. He'd become so enthralled with what the committee was planning to do, he'd forgotten what he and Whitney were discussing.

"I was just agreeing with you," she explained. "I was saying that all of this really is a blessing."

"That it is," Curtis added.

"Well, unless you have something else, I'd better get back out to my desk."

"No, I think that's it, and I'll let you know if I have anything to add to the agenda."

"Sounds good. Oh, and there is one other thing. I shouldn't be telling you this, but if I don't, you'll probably book your calendar so far in advance you won't be able to take advantage of the trip."

"What trip is that?"

"That's the other anniversary gift. The church is giving you and Mariah an all-expense-paid trip to anywhere you want to go."

"Wow. Now, that's a gift and then some."

"Just thought I'd let you know, but it would be nice if you didn't tell Mariah. That way, at least *someone* will be surprised when it's announced."

"Your secret is safe with me," he said as Whitney walked out and shut the door behind her.

An all-expense-paid trip with Mariah was never going to happen. She was boring him to pieces right here at home, so he couldn't possibly imagine being tied down on some tropical island with her. He'd hoped her giving him oral sex was going to make their sex lives a bit more interesting, but she just didn't know what she was doing. It was only her first time, but Curtis had already decided that she just didn't have what it took to satisfy him. She didn't have any of the sexual skills that any of his former women possessed. She wasn't Adrienne Jackson.

He'd seen Adrienne at a church concert a couple of weeks ago, but he'd made sure not to approach her because he hadn't wanted to stir up any old feelings. The truth: he hadn't wanted to be unfaithful to his new wife after only six months of marriage. He'd decided that he was going to do the right thing this time, no matter what. And he would have, if only Mariah had given him what he needed—if only she'd given him what he had to have in order to survive as a man. He'd stared at Adrienne on and off at the concert for two full hours, but he'd pushed the thought of calling her completely out of his system. He'd tried to forget about how good she'd once made him feel and how willing she was to do whatever he wanted. Anytime, anywhere. But six long months of nothing was long enough. As a matter of fact, it was too long, and it was time for him to do something about it. He wished there was another way, but right now he couldn't think of one.

Curtis dialed Adrienne's work number from memory, as if he'd just phoned her yesterday. There were some things a person simply didn't forget.

"This is Adrienne Jackson speaking," she answered.

"Adrienne. It's me."

There was a pause.

"Are you there?" Curtis asked.

"I'm here. Just a little surprised to hear your voice."

"I know. But to be honest, I haven't been able to get you off of my mind ever since I saw you."

"But you're married again, right?"

"Yes, but—"

"But nothing, Curtis. I mean, there is no but if you're married."

"Okay, okay. You're right. I am remarried, but I'm not happy. We've been together for six months, but I'm starting to realize it was a mistake."

Adrienne laughed at him.

"What's funny?"

"You."

"Why am I funny?"

"You're funny, Curtis, because after all this time you still haven't changed one bit."

"You're right. Because I certainly haven't changed when it comes to the way I feel about you."

"You know, I don't even want to hear it. And if that's what

you called to talk about, then we should end this conversation right now."

"I'm just being honest. I know I made a lot of mistakes in the past, and that I didn't do right by you, but I've been sorry for that ever since."

"Well, I'm sorry, too. I'm sorry that I ever met you, and that I allowed you to make such a fool of me. Do you know how humiliating it was for me to have Thomas find out about that abortion, the condo that you and I were renting, and then have him tell the entire congregation everything he knew about you and me? I mean everything, Curtis. He didn't leave out one thing."

"I know, I know, I know. I was just as humiliated as you were. Even more, if you want to know the truth."

"Well, you got what you deserved."

"So did you and the deacon end up getting divorced?" Curtis said, changing the subject.

"First of all, he's not a deacon anymore, and he hasn't stepped foot inside a church ever since that terrible day five years ago. And to answer your question, no, we didn't get divorced. He did put me out because of you, but after I begged him for almost a year, he finally took me back, and we've been doing great ever since."

"Come on now, Adrienne. This is me you're talking to. You can't be doing that great, because you know you don't love him."

"How in the hell would you know?" she said, and Curtis heard a door shut, probably the one to her office.

"I know because you *never* loved him. You never even loved him before you met me."

"You don't know what you're talking about, and I really don't have time for this."

"I'm just calling things the way I see them, but I'm not trying to offend you."

"Well, I have to go."

"Can I see you?"

"Didn't you hear me say that Thomas and I are still married?"

"Yes, but, Adrienne, all I want to do is talk to you. We can even meet at a restaurant downtown if you want."

"No."

"Adrienne, baby. Don't you remember how good we were together? Don't you remember all the good times we had and how unbelievable our lovemaking was? And can you honestly tell me that the deacon is giving you half of what I gave you in bed? I know Mariah hasn't even come close to satisfying me the way you always did, and I can't take it anymore. I miss being with you, Adrienne. I miss everything about you."

"Curtis, I can't do this again. I can't."

"Just meet me this one time, and if you decide you don't ever want to see me again, I'll back off completely."

"You used me all those months, and then you just dropped me. I mean, how could you be so cruel if you loved me the way you kept claiming?"

"I was totally messed up in the head back then. I was so overwhelmed with my responsibilities at the church, I was miserable with Tanya, and the deacons and I were at each other's throats constantly. And I'll admit I shouldn't have gotten myself involved with those other women when you were all I ever needed."

"Women like who? That girl Charlotte, who had your baby? Or was it the two women you were caught on videotape with?"

Curtis wondered how she knew about the tape, since he'd been told that the deacons hadn't received it until after Deacon Jackson was suspended from the board. But he was sure the news had still traveled pretty quickly by word of mouth. He still remembered all the gossipy women who attended Faith and how they were constantly in his business. But the strangest part of all was that Mariah lived right here in Chicago, too, but hadn't heard one word about his past indiscretions. What she didn't know, though, couldn't hurt her, and her ignorance was for the best.

"Look," he finally said. "Let's not talk about anyone except you and me. Okay?"

"Do you realize how much I loved you and how much I hurt my husband because of it? Do you know how hurt I was when you told me our relationship was over and that I needed to move on? Do you?"

"I know, and I'm willing to try and make that up to you. If only you would meet me for dinner, I'd be able to explain things so much better. I know you're angry because of how things turned out, but if you'll just give me a chance to talk to you."

Adrienne was silent.

"Baby, please. I promise you I'll make it worth your while. If nothing else, our meeting will give us some much needed closure."

"It's not right. And the last thing I want to do is hurt Thomas all over again. You and I did a serious job of that five years ago, and I'll never forgive myself for that."

"He doesn't have to know about one little dinner, does he?"

"I don't even want to take the chance of having him find out."

"I don't just want to see you, Adrienne, I need to see you. I need to see you face-to-face."

"Curtis, why are you doing this?"

Her feathers were finally beginning to ruffle.

"I'm doing it because I'm still in love with you. I've tried hard to forget about you, but I can't. Just one innocent meeting. That's all I'm asking."

"Where?"

"What about the place I took you to when you got that promotion?"

"When?"

"Tonight at six."

"I'll meet you for dinner, but that's it."

"Fine."

"I'm serious, Curtis. That's as far as I'm going."

"I hear you loud and clear."

"Bye," she said, and hung up.

Curtis called the Hyatt to see if they had any last-minute vacancies. He told the 800 operator that any Chicago suburb would do.

Chapter 3

Look, sweetheart," Curtis said to Mariah from his cell phone while pulling his black Escalade into a parking ramp on Wacker Street. "How was I supposed to know that you were cooking me a surprise dinner? I mean if I'd known before now, I wouldn't have committed to this regional ministers' meeting."

Mariah's silence confirmed her disappointment, but Curtis wasn't about to change his plans with Adrienne. He felt sorry for Mariah, but there was nothing he could do about it now.

"Why don't you invite your mother and sisters over? It's not like you ever spend that much time with them, anyway," he said. Although, truthfully, he couldn't have cared less whether they ever visited, because they were much too classless and ghetto.

"I only cooked enough for two," she said.

"Then maybe you could just invite your mother."

"We'll see."

"I'm really sorry, baby, but I promise I'll be home as soon as the meeting is over."

"Fine, Curtis."

"Mariah, I really am sorry about this."

"I said I was fine, didn't I?"

"Whoa. Am I sensing a little bit of irritation here?"

"No. But I'm really disappointed, because I spent all day preparing this meal for you. Macaroni and cheese, baked beans, smothered ribs. I even made you that carrot cake you love so much."

"Well, I said I was sorry, so I'm not sure what else you expect me to do. Unless you want me to ignore my pastoral obligations just so I can come home and be with you."

"No, no, no. That's not what I mean. It's just that I wanted so much for us to spend the evening together."

"I understand that, baby, and we will as soon as I get home."

"I'll be waiting for you."

"See you in a few hours."

"And Curtis?"

"Yeah?"

"I love you."

"I love you, too, baby."

Curtis pressed the On-Star button inside the rearview mirror and ended his call to Mariah. He blew a sigh of frustration and relief. He was happy that Mariah never nagged him the way Tanya always had, but irritated because she always wanted him to spend so much time with her. With the exception of Bible study, other church-related events, and shopping, she didn't like doing much else without him. But starting tonight, she was going to have to end this clinginess and find other interests. She would have to find other ways to occupy her time, because if things went the way he was expecting, he would soon be spending a whole lot more time with Adrienne.

Curtis tossed Mariah out of his mind and maneuvered into a parking stall. Adrienne pulled up next to him in a white Mercedes. Her hair hung freely just past her shoulder blades, just the way he liked it.

He smiled at her, stepped outside of his car, and set the alarm system.

"I see you're still looking as gorgeous as ever," he complimented her.

"Really? Well, you're not."

Curtis laughed. "Okay, I guess I deserve that," he said as they walked toward the restaurant.

"Yes, Curtis, you do deserve that . . . and so much more. Which is why I never should have come down here in the first place."

"You came because you knew it was the right thing to do, and because deep down you know you still care about me."

Adrienne looked around to see if anyone was walking behind them, listening to their conversation.

"This just isn't right," she said matter-of-factly.

When they arrived in front of the restaurant, Curtis opened the door and waited for Adrienne to walk through it. Once inside, Curtis told the maître d' that they had a reservation.

"Right this way, Mr. Black," the slender forty-something man said, and then escorted them to a candlelit circular booth. "Your waitress will be with you momentarily."

"Thank you," Curtis offered.

"So what is it that you wanted to talk to me about?" Adrienne asked almost immediately.

"Us. And I wanted to tell you how sorry I am for causing you so much pain. I must have been completely out of my mind to end our relationship the way I did."

"Hmmph. Well, that's all in the past now, isn't it? So I ask you again, what did you want to talk to me about?"

"You're not going to make this easy, are you?" he said, smiling.

"No, I'm not. Because you treated me like I was nothing—like what we had never mattered to you in the least."

"Now, baby, you know that's not true. What you and I had was special, and I've never been more comfortable with any woman than I was with you. It's just that I got myself caught up in that terrible marriage to Tanya and couldn't see my way out of it without losing the church."

"But you lost it anyway, so what difference did it make?"

"I know, and I've regretted not staying with you ever since. You can't imagine how much."

A very thin woman in her late twenties sat two glasses of water down on the table. "What can I get you to drink?"

"I'll have some brandy," Adrienne answered.

Curtis looked at her in shock, but her eyes dared him to comment.

"I'll have a Perrier with lime," he said.

"Can I bring either of you an appetizer?"

"I'll have a small Caesar salad," Adrienne said.

"I'll have the field greens with vinaigrette," Curtis added.

"Sounds good. I'll bring them right out."

"So when did you start drinking hard liquor?" Curtis wanted to know.

"When? I'll tell you when. It was right around the time your little lying ass decided to dump me," Adrienne spat out.

Curtis stared at her.

"Was that a good enough answer for you, Reverend Curtis Black?"

"Not really, because I still can't believe you're drinking alcohol."

"Why, because it's not Christian-like?"

"Well, now that you bring it up, yes. Because you know very well how sinful it is to drink intoxicating beverages."

Adrienne laughed louder than Curtis would have liked, because people were starting to look in their direction.

"Did I say something funny?" he asked.

"Everything about you is funny. As a matter of fact, you're

the biggest joke I know. Because how in the world can you sit there and judge my drinking when just five years ago you were screwing my brains out every chance you got. And this was all while you were married to Tanya. Not to mention the fact that you have another wife at home right now, but still you're sitting here with me."

"None of us falls short of sin, Adrienne. We all make mistakes."

"Whatever."

It was time to change the subject. "So you say you and the deacon are happily married, huh?"

"Didn't I tell you that he's no longer a deacon?"

Curtis smiled at Adrienne. He'd heard what she said, but *Thomas,* as she referred to him, would always be *the deacon* in Curtis's book, because Curtis liked the way it sounded. He loved the sarcasm of it.

"He'll always be the deacon to me," Curtis said.

"Whatever."

"So?"

"So what?" Adrienne was irritated.

"Are you and the deacon happily married?"

"Yes. *Very* happy."

"If you say so."

"I do," she said, and looked the other way.

Curtis was finally starting to realize that Adrienne wasn't coming back to him without a fight. It was time to do and say whatever it would take to win her over, so he leaned against the leather backrest and clasped his hands together on top of the table. "You know, baby, it would be so much easier if you would at least *try* to forgive me. I know I was wrong for all the pain I caused you, but I'm willing to spend the rest of my life making things up to you. I don't love Mariah, and it's only going to be a matter of time before I ask her for a divorce. She can't do for me what you can. She can't make me feel the way you can. And now that I'm sitting here with you, I realize how much I'm still in love with you. I knew my feelings for you were still strong, but I didn't know that being this close to you would trigger my heart the way it has. I know you don't believe me, but I don't just *want* you back in my life, I desperately need you," he said, gently grabbing her hand.

Adrienne's face softened, but not enough for him to tell what she was thinking.

"Do you hear what I'm saying, baby? I need you to come back to me, because I don't think I can live without you any longer."

"Then why did you marry someone else, Curtis? Why did you do that?"

The waitress returned with their drinks, salads, and a basket of rolls. Then she jotted down their lobster and shrimp orders and left again.

"I don't know why. I guess I didn't think you would ever take me back, and to be honest, I thought it would be better if I left my past exactly where it was. I really wanted to start things right at this new church. And everything might've worked fine, except Mariah doesn't satisfy me. We've only been married for a short while, but I don't love her nearly the way a husband should love his wife. I don't love her nearly as much as I love you."

"I can't do this, Curtis. I can't do this to Thomas, and I won't allow you to hurt me all over again. What we did back then was wrong, and God won't forget that," she said, picking up her brandy.

Curtis reached for her glass. "Adrienne, please don't."

"Why? It's just one drink."

"Because you don't need it and because it's so ungodly. And you know how much that sort of thing turns me off. I can't stand to see any woman drink, smoke, or do drugs."

"Why are you trying to control me, Curtis?" she said, lifting a forkful of salad.

"Baby, I'm not. Our bodies are sacred, and you know as well as I do that it's a sin to harm what God has created," he said, chewing some of his mixed greens.

"Whatever you say."

"So, are you going to forgive me?"

"I don't know. I just don't think I'll ever be able to do that."

"Well, you know what the scripture says. 'Forgive us our trespasses as we forgive those who trespass against us.' And you can't get into heaven if you don't learn to forgive people."

"We won't get into heaven by committing adultery either. I knew it when I first started sleeping with you, and I still know it now. Because it's not like some sins are okay to commit and some aren't. A sin is a sin is a sin, and there's no denying that."

"That's true, but God knows that we are not perfect, and that we are sometimes too weak to ignore certain temptations. It's different for everybody. Some people like to steal, some people like using the Lord's name in vain, and some people use vulgarity and excessive anger on a regular basis. For you and me, it's adultery. I keep telling you that none of us falls short and we have to pray constantly, asking for forgiveness."

"And I've always told you that God doesn't look favorably on people who knowingly commit sins just because they know they can ask for forgiveness later."

"You're making all this much more complicated than it needs to be. Because the bottom line is that I'm in love with you and, right or wrong, I can't do anything to change that."

"But you're married to someone else, Curtis. You could have easily looked me up after you and Tanya were divorced, but you never even tried."

"I know. And I'll regret that for the rest of my life. But it won't always be this way, because I'm not going to stay married to Mariah."

"Really now? And when exactly are you planning to divorce this particular wife?"

"Soon. But I at least have to stay married to her for a year so it doesn't look bad to the deacons or the congregation."

"Oh no, here we go. Have you forgotten the fact that you told me that same lie when you were married to Tanya?"

"I know, but this is different. I promise you that it will only be six more months, tops."

"Two lobster and shrimp specials," the waitress said, sitting the plates down on the table. "Can I get you anything else?"

"No, I think we're fine for now," Curtis said.

"Yes, everything is fine," Adrienne added.

"Enjoy your meals."

Curtis and Adrienne managed to make conversation while finishing dinner and then left the restaurant. When they arrived in the parking garage, Curtis opened Adrienne's car door for her.

"Well, it was good to see—" she began, but Curtis kissed her mid-sentence.

"Curtis, don't," she said, pulling away from him.

He gently stroked her face. "Adrienne. Baby, please. Just give me this one last chance, and I promise I'll do right by you."

"No, Curtis. Please just go," she said.

He pulled her toward him and kissed her again. This time her resistance was less physical, and Curtis could tell that there was still a great deal of fire and passion between them. It felt as though they'd never been apart.

But she jerked away from him.

"Curtis, I told you that I won't do this again, and I want you to leave me alone for good."

"But, baby," he said, pleading.

"No," she said flatly. "I mean it, Curtis. Don't call me and don't try to see me."

"I can't believe you're doing this. Not after all we've been through together. Not after seeing me again and realizing that we still love each other."

Adrienne shook her head, frustrated by his persistence.

"Please, just let me go, Curtis. Please."

Curtis hesitated but then stepped away. Adrienne sat in her car, shut the door, and backed the car away from him. She never looked back, and Curtis wondered what he was going to have to do to change her mind. He wondered how many more phone calls he'd have to make and how many dozens of flowers he'd have to send. Maybe jewelry would do the trick. He wasn't sure what it was going to take, but the one thing he did know was that he needed her in his life again. He needed her more than ever before.

"I don't know, Vivian," Mariah said to her best friend after phoning her a half hour ago. "I guess I'm just feeling a bit uneasy because tonight is the first time he called at the last minute to say he wouldn't be home for dinner. It was so unlike him not to have told me that earlier in the day."

"I hear what you're saying, girl, but he is a very well-known pastor. So I'm sure there are going to be many days when he'll forget to tell you about certain meetings."

"You're right, but it still bothered me. Not to mention it's almost nine and he's still not home yet."

"Maybe they sat around laughing and talking once the meeting was over. Because I'm sure they don't spend all their time discussing just the Bible and what's going on at their churches. I would think they have to socialize at least sometimes."

"Maybe."

"Girl, you have a wonderful man who loves and takes care of you, so stop your worrying. As a matter of fact, I remember you praying that Curtis would eventually be your husband, so I think you need to keep an open mind and just be thankful for what God has given you."

"I am thankful, and I do know that he's a good man, but . . . you know what, I think that's him coming in right now."

"See, I told you. Now get off this phone and go greet that man like a good wife ought to."

"Talk to you later."

"Have fun."

Mariah walked downstairs and saw Curtis removing his blazer.

"So how was the meeting?" she asked, kissing him.

"It was lengthy as usual, but productive. We met until around eight and then I stopped at a deli to get a sandwich. So that's why I'm just now getting home."

"Oh. Well then, I guess you're not hungry."

"No, I'm not. And I'm sorry I didn't make it home for dinner. But what you can do is warm everything up tomorrow when Alicia gets here," he said, referring to his daughter.

"Fine," Mariah said, dreading her stepdaughter's visit. Not because she didn't like Alicia, but because Alicia always made Mariah feel like an intrusion. Curtis kept insisting that things would get better, but they hadn't. It was the same routine every other weekend. Alicia would walk into the house, speak to Mariah with no enthusiasm, and then head up to her bedroom. Mariah was trying to be patient with her, since she'd only been her stepmother for a few months, but she was beginning to run out of ways to get on her good side. She hoped this weekend would be different.

"I'm beat," Curtis said, stretching. "Let's head up to bed."

"And do what?" Mariah teased him.

"Fall into a very deep sleep."

"What about before that?" she said, walking up the winding staircase in front of him.

"Not tonight, baby. I'm really tired, and I have to get up pretty early in the morning."

Mariah felt her stomach stirring. This was definitely a first. Curtis coming home on any day of the week and not wanting to make love to her? She wanted to ask him what was wrong, but decided against it because she didn't want to sound suspicious. Maybe he didn't want her because he was tired of begging for oral sex. He'd said he couldn't be responsible for what might happen if he didn't get what he needed, and that's why she'd done the best she could yesterday afternoon. But she knew with everything inside her that she hadn't satisfied him. He'd told her it was good, but his facial expression screamed another story. She wanted to get better at it and was willing to practice until she was perfect.

When they entered the master bedroom suite, Mariah pulled him toward her and kissed him. They kissed until Curtis pulled away and began removing his clothing. But Mariah wasn't giving up so easily. She wasn't about to let him drop off to sleep before giving him what he swore he needed.

"Sweetheart, let me do something special for you."

"Mariah, honey. I'm really, really tired. But I promise you we'll make love tomorrow."

She heard every word he said, but ignored his wishes. She slid his underwear down to the floor and rested her weight on her knees. Curtis watched her but didn't move. Mariah massaged him and then took him inside her mouth. She tried to pleasure him the exact same way she'd seen some woman pleasure her husband on one of the pay channels. She'd been flipping through them just before calling Vivian and decided to see how this was supposed to be done. She still thought it was unnatural and deplored it, but believed it was her duty to keep Curtis happy.

Mariah hoped she was doing it right this time, and when she saw Curtis's eyes roll toward the back of his head, she knew she was on track. She would only get better as time went on, and then he wouldn't have a single thing to complain about. There would be no reason at all why he'd ever consider going astray. She realized that Vivian was right. There wasn't anything at all she should be worrying about when it came to Curtis.

Chapter 4

Alicia packed her overnight bag and wished she could spend the weekend with her father without his new wife. Mariah was a nice enough woman, but Alicia longed for the time she and her father used to spend alone. Even more, she wanted her father and mother to tell their current spouses that things just weren't working out, and that they'd decided to remarry. Then maybe Alicia and her parents could finally get back to the happily-ever-after they once lived. But she knew it was all wishful thinking because her mother couldn't have been happier with James and her father seemed to be fairly happy with Mariah.

"Alicia, are you ready?" she heard her mother ask.

"Yes, Mom, I'm coming."

"We need to get going because I told Mariah that I'd have you over there in time for dinner."

Alicia showed no concern but gathered up her bag and portable CD player. When she went downstairs, she saw her stepfather smiling at her.

"Have a good time, pumpkin," James said.

"I'll try," she said, forcing a positive attitude.

As Tanya and Alicia drove out of the subdivision, Alicia noticed her best friend getting in the car with her parents and waved at them.

"How come you and Daddy couldn't be as happy as Danielle's parents?"

"Every marriage doesn't work out that way."

"Well, why did you and Daddy get married if you weren't going to stay together?"

"Now, Alicia, we've been through this over and over again for the last five years," Tanya explained. "You know the reason why your father and I ended up getting a divorce."

"Oh yeah, I forgot. Daddy slept with practically every woman at the church."

"Alicia! You know that's not true."

"It might as well be, because what difference does it make if he slept with three women or three hundred. Either way, he was wrong and he broke up our family."

"But he's still your father, and it's time for you to try and forgive him. We've both moved on with our lives, and while I know it's been very difficult for you, you're going to have to accept it."

"I have forgiven him. And everything was just fine until he had to go and marry Mariah. It's just not fair."

"I understand how you feel, but Mariah is his wife. And I want you to start giving her much more respect than you have been."

Alicia turned to look at her mother. "Who said I don't give her respect?"

"Your father told me that you never hold a decent conversation with her and that most of the time you only answer questions."

Alicia wished her father would spend more time being a better father and less time reporting what she was or wasn't doing.

He made her so sick sometimes. It was bad enough that he'd ruined her life when she was nine and now he was trying to do the same thing at fourteen. She was practically grown, and she wondered when he was going to stop treating her like a baby. She wondered when both he and her mother were going to realize that she had her own life to live and that they should simply worry about themselves.

"Why should I talk to her when I really don't know who she is?"

Tanya turned onto Curtis's street. "But that's how you could get to know her. If you don't talk to people, how do you ever expect to build a relationship with them?"

Hmmph, Alicia thought. What her mother didn't know was that she didn't want a relationship with her father's wife. What she wanted was for Mariah to move out of the way or, better yet, go back to wherever she came from.

Alicia didn't respond to her mother's latest comment, and before long Tanya pulled up the circle driveway and stopped in front of her ex-husband's new living quarters. The off-white stucco was gorgeous and the landscaping was immaculate.

Alicia noticed her mother admiring the house. "Don't you wish this was your home instead of Mariah's? I mean, look at it, Mom. It's even bigger than the one we used to live in."

"No, Alicia. I don't wish this was my house. I'm very happy with the house that James and I have, and I'm very happy for your father and Mariah."

"But why? I mean, how can you be happy for a man who treated you like Daddy did?"

"Look, Alicia. That's enough. And instead of discussing grown folks' business, I think you need to spend your time worrying about that failing progress report you brought home yesterday."

Alicia sighed strongly. "Bye," she said, stepping onto the pavement.

"You'd better get rid of that little attitude, Alicia," Tanya yelled.

Alicia glanced back at her mother and then slammed the door behind her.

Tanya got out of the vehicle and followed Alicia. "Girl, have you lost your natural mind? You must think I'm a kid or somethin'."

Mariah opened the door. "Hi, Alicia. Hi, Tanya."

"How are you, Mariah?" Tanya asked.

"I'm fine. Do you want to come in for a few minutes?"

"No, I really have to get going. And, Alicia, you'd better straighten up that face of yours."

Alicia kept pouting.

"What's going on?" Curtis asked, walking toward them.

"Nothing," Alicia answered nonchalantly.

"Curtis, you had better have a long talk with your daughter, otherwise she's going to see a side of me she's never seen before," Tanya said. "This attitude of hers has got to go, because I'm not about to keep putting up with her smart little mouth. And before I forget, I think you should know that she brought home a failing progress report from world history yesterday."

"Alicia? Failing a class?" Curtis commented.

"Yes, and something has got to be done about it," Tanya said, turning to walk back to her car. "Oh, and, Mariah, it was good seeing you again."

"You too, Tanya."

Mariah closed the door, and Tanya drove off.

"Alicia, what is this all about?" Curtis asked.

"Nothing," she repeated.

"Well, it must be *something*, because gifted students who have always gotten straight A's don't bring home failing progress reports."

Alicia gazed into thin air and wished they would all drop

dead. Or maybe it would be better if she died herself. She was so tired of them telling her what she needed to do and sick of them harassing her.

"Girl, do you hear me talking to you?" Curtis said.

"Yes."

"Then you'd better act like it. Now I'm going to ask you again. What is this all about?"

"It's about you and the way you broke up our family. It's about you and how you slept with Deacon Jackson's wife behind Mom's back. It's about that girl Charlotte that you got pregnant. And it's also about you getting married and not spending any real time with me. That's what this is all about, Daddy. It's all about you," she screamed, with tears flooding her face.

Mariah was speechless.

Curtis had no sympathy.

"Alicia, what I want you to do is go up to your room and stay there until I tell you to come out."

Alicia stormed upstairs and slammed her bedroom door. She heard her father and Mariah conversing and wished she hadn't even come for this visit. She hated all of them. Her father, Mariah, and even her mother at this particular moment. This was her first year in high school, and they were doing everything they could to ruin it. So what if she *had* brought home a less than average progress report? It was the first time ever, and it certainly didn't compare to all the horrible things her father had done. That was for sure. So why couldn't they just mind their own business and leave her alone? It wasn't like they really cared about her, anyway. She didn't have one person she could turn to, and she was starting to wonder more and more why she even hung around. Maybe they would all be happier if she disappeared. Maybe then they'd realize what terrible parents they were and that her unhappiness was all their fault.

She lay across her bed, crying silently. She wished she could be nine again. That way, she would stop her father from ever cheating on her mother. That way, the three of them would be together again and she could continue being the happiest little girl in the world.

"Curtis, who is Charlotte?" Mariah asked.

"Baby, sit down," he said, barely looking at her.

"And what's this about you getting her pregnant?"

"She was a girl who attended Faith when I was pastor over there, and as wrong as it was, I had an affair with her."

"You what! How old was she?"

"She was seventeen when I started seeing her."

"Why didn't you tell me you had another child, Curtis?"

"Because I just didn't know how. I was afraid that you wouldn't marry me if you knew. But now I know that I had no right keeping this from you."

"Have you seen her since she had the baby?"

"No. I haven't."

"Is it a boy or girl?"

"It's a boy."

"Well, why haven't you seen him?"

"Because her parents said that if I ever came near her or the baby, they would press statutory rape charges against me."

"Dear God," Mariah said.

"Baby, I'm sorry. I know I should have told you. But it's not like my son will ever be a part of our lives."

"What else haven't you told me, Curtis? I feel so stupid."

"That's everything. I swear on my life. There are no more secrets."

Mariah's head started to pound, and she wanted to go lie down. She was having a hard time digesting any of what she'd just learned and was ashamed of what she was thinking. She almost despised the fact that two other women had given her husband something she hadn't. Tanya and Charlotte had given him his own flesh and blood, and there was only one way she could compete with that. But Curtis had made it clear from the start that he wanted to wait a while before they tried to have a baby.

"Mariah, I am truly, truly sorry for not telling you," Curtis said, holding her. "I was wrong, and I hope you can forgive me. I won't ever keep anything else from you for as long as I live."

She didn't know what to say. She wanted to respond to him, but she couldn't find the words. Her heart ached heavily, and regardless of what Curtis claimed, she wondered what other skeletons he might have dangling elsewhere. She wanted to believe in him, but this newfound information that Alicia had boldly disclosed was a major blow. It had shaken her entire thinking and caused her to wonder if Curtis really was the man he claimed to be.

"Baby, say something," Curtis pleaded.

"The thing is . . . I don't know what to say about any of this."

"You do know why this is happening, don't you?" he asked.

"No. I don't."

"Because Satan doesn't want to see us happy. He's been trying to tear me down ever since I answered my call to preach, and now he's at it again. But this time he's trying to attack you and me through my little girl. He knows how happy I am with you and how much I love my daughter, so that's why he's doing this. So, baby, please don't let him win. Please don't give him what he wants."

He released Mariah from his hold.

"Satan, you are a liar!" he yelled. "You've been trying to get me for years, but today I rebuke you in the name of Jesus. I want you out of my house and out of my life for good. You hear me? Get out of here and find someone else to mess with. I mean it. I want you out of here."

Curtis broke into tears and spoke in tongues.

He seemed so distraught and Mariah felt sorry for him. Alicia walked down the staircase to see what was going on, and Curtis grabbed her tightly.

"Oh Lord, I am so sorry for all the sins I've committed and for hurting so many innocent people. But, Father, I ask you, please protect my daughter and make Satan stop influencing her. Force him to leave us alone so that we can do Your will instead."

Alicia stepped away from her father. Then she walked back up to her room, totally unimpressed. Curtis kneeled down in front of Mariah.

"Baby, I'm sorry. Do you hear me? I'm so sorry I don't know what to do. I was wrong for committing adultery against Tanya and I was wrong for not telling you about my other child. But if I have to, I'll spend the rest of my life making everything up to you."

Mariah didn't bother responding, but deep down she knew she would never see her husband in the same light.

She knew their six-month honeymoon was officially over.

Alicia gazed around her weekend boudoir and wondered why her father was downstairs clowning like that. He always resorted to praising God and rebuking Satan whenever someone cornered him, and he always blamed the devil for every sin he committed. She loved her father, but she was at the point where she just didn't like him very much anymore. She'd been so disappointed in him that day Deacon Jackson stood in front of the congregation and told everyone what her father and Deacon Jackson's wife had been doing. She remembered how he'd said her father had paid for Mrs. Jackson to have an abortion. Alicia hadn't even known what an abortion was until one of her cousins explained it to her a year later. That whole pastor's anniversary fiasco was the reason she now refused to attend any of his church services. She'd only been to his new church once, and that was only because he begged her to come to his installation ceremony.

She was so tired of spending every other weekend with them, but the only reason she continued doing it was that she wanted Mariah to know she had a stepdaughter who would always be in the picture. She wanted her to know that she'd never have her husband strictly to herself if Alicia could help it.

Alicia rose from her bed and sat down in front of the flat-screen monitor on her desk. As of late, the Internet was her only outlet, and she hoped Julian was on-line to chat with her. She loved communicating with him, because he never judged her and always listened to whatever she had to say. He always understood what she was going through and knew exactly what to say to make her feel better. She'd never met him face-to-face, but it was if she'd known him for years and years. They'd only been chatting for two weeks, after meeting in a chat room for young, single Chicagoans, but he'd already said that he couldn't wait to meet her. He'd said that he wanted to spend some time with her because he could tell how wonderful she was. So maybe the time was finally right for them to get together.

She clicked the sign-on button and within two seconds the DSL took her to the AOL Welcome screen. The first thing she saw was a weight-loss promotion. Alicia wondered why there were always so many of them. Not just on-line but also on television. She especially didn't understand why it was so hard for people to lose weight, since she ate anything she wanted and never gained a pound. Although her mother insisted it was only because she was well under thirty.

Alicia checked her e-mail messages and answered the one from Nikki, one of her classmates. She'd told Julian that it was best he didn't e-mail her just in case her mother decided to snoop around her computer. So what they did was add each other to their buddy list. That way, they could see when the other signed on and could chat through the Instant Message feature.

She surfed a few web sites and was just about to sign off when she saw the letters "JMoney1" appear in the upper right-hand corner.

ALICIABLK: Hey, Julian.

JMONEY1: Hey, Alicia. What's up?

ALICIABLK: I was just about to sign off, but I'm glad I didn't.

JMONEY1: So where are you?

ALICIABLK: I'm at my dad's, but I'm sorry I came over here.

JMONEY1: Why is that?

ALICIABLK: Because my mother told him about this progress report I got and he started tripping out about it. But I also told him exactly what I thought of him and how he broke up our family.

JMONEY1: Uh-oh. I'm sorry to hear that.

ALICIABLK: It's not your fault, and I'm just glad you came on-line tonight.

JMONEY1: I've been thinking about you all day. I do that a lot lately.

ALICIABLK: I think about you a lot, too.

JMONEY1: So when am I going to finally get a chance to meet Ms. Alicia Black?

ALICIABLK: I don't know. When do you want to?

Alicia felt somewhat nervous after sending her last response, because even though she really wanted to see Julian, she couldn't dismiss the fact that he was nineteen, and five whole years older than her. She didn't even want to imagine what her parents would say if they ever found out about him. Worse, she wondered how angry Julian would be if he knew she wasn't seventeen like she'd told him. She hadn't meant to deceive him, but she hadn't wanted him thinking she was some pathetic little kid.

JMONEY1: It's on you. I'm available whenever you say you're ready.
ALICIABLK: I'll let you know, but I promise it will be very soon.
JMONEY1: You know I can't wait.
ALICIABLK: Neither can I.
JMONEY1: So what are you doing this weekend with your dad?
ALICIABLK: Who knows? I might ask my mom to come and get me in the morning, because I really don't want to be here with him or Mariah.

There was a longer than usual pause with Julian's response.

JMONEY1: Can I ask you something?
ALICIABLK: Yes.
JMONEY1: What is it that you don't like about your stepmoms?
ALICIABLK: I don't like her because my father and I were so close before she came into the picture, and I can't stand how she caters to him. She's so stupid, and she goes along with whatever he says. My mother never did that.
JMONEY1: But is she nice to you?
ALICIABLK: Yeah. I guess.
JMONEY1: But you still don't like her, though?
ALICIABLK: I don't hate her if that's what you mean.
JMONEY1: You seem to like your stepdad, so why is that?
ALICIABLK: Because he loves me like a daughter and he

doesn't take away my time with my mom. And if it's okay, I don't want to talk about this any longer.

JMONEY1: Okay. I'm sorry. I didn't mean to upset you. I was only trying to help you adjust to your new stepmoms. My stepmoms treated me so much better than my own mother did, so that's why I wondered if yours was nice to you. My mother was an abusive drug addict and she never cared about my brother or me. My father wasn't the best person either, so my stepmoms was all we had to depend on.

ALICIABLK: She's okay, but right now I'm not feeling her. Maybe if she had a backbone and let me spend some time alone with my father, it would be different.

JMONEY1: Hey, can you sit tight for a minute?

ALICIABLK: Sure.

Alicia visited a few more web sites until she heard the Instant Message chime ten minutes later.

JMONEY1: Okay, I'm back. Sorry about that.

ALICIABLK: Julian, can I ask you something?

JMONEY1: Shoot.

ALICIABLK: Do you have a girlfriend?

JMONEY1: No. Why do you ask? Do you want to be that person?

ALICIABLK: ☺Actually, I was just wondering.

JMONEY1: Well, since we're on the subject, do you have a boyfriend?

ALICIABLK: No.

JMONEY1: Good. Because I wouldn't want to have to kick some dude's behind over you.

ALICIABLK: LOL. You are so crazy.

JMONEY1: So tell me, girl. When are we gonna get together?

ALICIABLK: I told you it'll be very soon . . . Maybe in a couple of weeks.

JMONEY1: If you say so.

ALICIABLK: I promise.

JMONEY1: Well, hey, I'm about to roll with one of my boys, but I'll be on again tomorrow night around the same time.

ALICIABLK: Talk to you then.

JMONEY1: Cya.

Alicia signed off the computer and heard Mariah calling her downstairs to dinner. Right now she wasn't even hungry and didn't have one word to say to her father. She certainly didn't want to sit at the table watching him pretend like he was the holiest man alive or listen to him beg Mariah for her forgiveness. Alicia had watched him manipulate people even before she knew what the word meant, and she was sick of it. She'd thought the world of him when she was much younger, but now she knew he was an impostor. She was only fourteen, but even she was old enough to know that her father was going to burn in hell if he didn't stop playing with God.

She decided that she wasn't going to spend another weekend with him for a very long time. Somehow it just didn't make sense to.

Chapter 5

Curtis switched the phone from one ear to the other. "Baby, I'm sorry to tell you this, but as soon as I finish meeting with the deacons and trustees, I have to go visit the Wilsons. I just found out this afternoon that they had a death in their family," he said to Mariah as carefully as he could. She wasn't going to stop him from doing whatever he wanted, but he could tell she hadn't been quite the same ever since Alicia blabbed about Charlotte and his son four days ago, and he didn't want her getting any crazy ideas. Ideas like leaving him and filing for a divorce. He didn't think she had it in her, but he couldn't take any chances. The last thing he wanted was to have to explain to the deacon board why another wife had left him.

"Curtis, what is going on? Last week you called me at the last minute saying you had a meeting, and last night you didn't make it home until after nine."

"But I already told you, Mariah. I was at the church working on next week's sermon."

"But you hardly ever work on Mondays."

"No, but yesterday I felt like working, so I did. I worked so I wouldn't have to work so hard on Thursday and Friday trying to prepare for Sunday."

"Curtis, I'm really getting worried."

"Worried about what?" He frowned.

"Us. Because I'm starting to feel like you don't want to spend time with me anymore."

He was trying to be patient and cordial, but she was starting to get on his nerves. She was starting to sound like Tanya all over again, and he wasn't going to tolerate it.

"Look, Mariah. I don't have the liberty of sitting at home with you all day or coming home every single evening right on schedule. I wish I could, but I can't. I have a church to run, and you're just going to have to understand that."

"I do understand, but ever since last week you've been different."

"Different how?" he asked, raising his voice.

"You seem distant and like you really don't want to touch me."

"Oh Lord. Not all these accusations again."

"What is that supposed to mean?"

"It means that you're fabricating stuff in your head for no reason."

"Well, it used to be that you wanted me every night, but now all of a sudden you don't. And I've been doing everything you said you wanted me to do."

But not the right way, Curtis thought. But that was beside the point, because regardless of how well she tried to make love to him now, she'd never be able to compare to Adrienne in a million years. She'd never be able to give him what Adrienne gave so naturally. Adrienne had always satisfied him without having to work at it, and he liked that. The chemistry they'd shared was unexplainable. It was the reason he was going to call her as soon as he hung up with Mariah.

"This is all in your head," he continued. "You're my wife, I love you, and I certainly don't want anyone else, if that's what you're thinking."

"Well, after finding out about that girl Charlotte, I don't know what to think."

"How many more times do I have to apologize for that?"

"You don't. But I just don't understand why our marriage seems to be changing."

"Look. I really don't have any more time for this, so unless you have something else to discuss, I need to prepare for my meeting. And you need to find something to do on your own."

"Honey, why are you treating me like this?" she said, starting to cry.

"Treating you like what, damn it?"

He regretted his words immediately. He hated using vulgarity, especially in the Lord's house, but Mariah was truly getting under his skin.

"I didn't mean to curse at you, and I'm sorry. But, baby, I really have to go."

"Fine."

"We'll talk more when I get home."

"How long do you think you'll be at the Wilsons'?"

"I don't know, but I'll call you when I leave there."

"I'll be waiting," she said.

"I love you, and I'll see you then."

"I love you, too."

Curtis felt like screaming. He'd wanted a wife who knew her place and one who would love him exclusively, but this was ridiculous. She was smothering him in a way he couldn't handle. He didn't want to lose her right now, because he needed a proper first lady, but she was going to have to stop expecting him to spend all of his free time with her. He'd never been confined in that way before and he wasn't going to allow it now. What he needed to do was have a long talk with her, so she understood how their marriage was going to work. But he would also make love to her at least every couple of days to prevent any further suspicions.

However, tonight wouldn't be one of those nights. He wasn't sure how his evening was going to play out, but earlier he'd sent Adrienne two dozen roses and called to see if she received them, and he was just about to call her again. She'd sounded sort of irritated and hadn't been able to talk for more than thirty seconds, but maybe if he prayed about it and spoke to her in just the right way, she'd finally agree to see him again. Hopefully, it would be tonight, since his schedule was wide open. It was true that he'd been asked to go visit the Wilsons, but he'd quickly fixed that situation as soon as the call came through. He had ten associate ministers and had already assigned one of them to do the honors. His associates were like faithful deputies and they stood in for him on a great number of occasions. Some of the deacons and quite a few of his members thought he should personally visit every family who'd lost a loved one, but he'd made it very clear that he wasn't going to do it. At least not all the time. Yes, he had done it quite often when he pastored at Faith, but when he'd signed on at Truth, he'd told the deacons that it was up to them and his associate ministers to handle those responsibilities. And the only reason he'd remotely considered visiting the Wilsons was that their son had recently signed a lucrative sports contract and had already mailed ten percent of his signing bonus to the church. But right now Adrienne was his priority and the Wilsons would just have to understand.

He picked up the sleek-looking silver cordless phone and then laid it back on its base. When he'd invited Adrienne to dinner a week ago and then called her this morning about the flowers, he'd made both calls from his office phone. But he was starting to think it might be better to use his cellular phone from here on out. He wasn't worried about anyone monitoring his phone calls, but after the way Monique, his former secretary at Faith, had spied on and betrayed him, he didn't want to take any chances. So instead he slid the earpiece into his ear, dialed Adrienne's office, and folded his arms across his stomach.

"So how are you?" he said when she answered.

She sighed but didn't speak.

"So are you still enjoying the flowers?"

"No, Curtis, I'm not. And do you want to know why? Because every single person in my department has been raving over how beautiful they are and how nice it was for my *husband* to send them. So, no, I'm not enjoying them one bit."

"I guess I don't know what to say."

"How about nothing?"

"Baby, look. I didn't mean to upset you, and I only sent them because I wanted you to know how much I've been thinking about you. I haven't been able to do much else since we had dinner."

"Well, I'd appreciate it if you wouldn't send me anything else."

"Okay. If that's how you feel, then I won't."

"Good. And if that's all, I have to go."

"Just like that?"

"What else do you expect me to do?"

"Talk to me."

"Look, Curtis. I don't know if you haven't been listening to me or if it's that you're just plain desperate when it comes to women. But either way, I want you to hear me once and for all: Please leave me the hell alone."

Desperate? Was she kidding? Yes, he wanted her back, but he certainly wasn't desperate, not by a long shot. He could have just about any woman he wanted. Inside the church or outside of it, for that matter. He wondered where she'd gotten such a lame idea and where all this sudden courage was coming from.

Five years ago she'd thought the sun rose and set on him, and she sometimes broke into tears just because he was angry at her.

But he knew this new attitude had everything to do with the fact that he'd been begging her like a sweet little puppy. He'd decided that the nice and polite route was the best way to go, but now he could see that it wasn't working. He also knew that deep down she wanted him back and was only trying to play hard to get. He'd seen it in her eyes when he'd kissed her in the parking ramp.

He knew what he had to do, though. He had to drop this nice-guy act and remind her of who she was dealing with.

"You know, Adrienne, I've poured my heart out to you, I've apologized, and still you're acting as if you hate my guts. As a matter of fact, I've been more patient with you than I have with any woman, but this is where it ends. And just for the record, I think you and I both know that I'm not anywhere near *desperate* when it comes to females."

"I have to go, Curtis."

"Fine. But just let me say one last thing. For the life of me, I can't believe you just ruined a chance at marrying a man who loves you as much as I do and who can give you everything you ever wanted. Not to mention the fact that you've blown a chance at being the next first lady at Truth. And this is all so you can stay married to that boring husband of yours—a man who probably couldn't satisfy a virgin when it comes to making love."

He waited for Adrienne to respond.

But she didn't.

"What a waste," Curtis said, and pressed the end button on his cell phone.

He'd finally rolled the dice and the only thing he could do now was wait for the outcome. There was no sure way to tell how Adrienne was going to react, but he was betting that she'd realize what a fool she'd been and would quickly come to her senses. He was counting on the fact that she'd soon realize she couldn't go on without him.

Curtis walked into the conference room and sat down at the highly shined mahogany table. The deacons and trustees filed in one and two at a time over the next ten minutes until they were all in attendance. They picked up meeting agendas from the table prior to sitting down.

"Before we call this meeting to order, let's first have a word of prayer," Deacon Gulley said. He was a husky middle-aged man, a former deacon at Faith and chairman of the board.

When he finished praying, he said, "Pastor Black has some new business to discuss, so I think we should start with that. Pastor?"

"Thank you, Deacon," Curtis said, leaning forward and resting his arms on the table. "As all of you know, I'm a pastor who believes in keeping up with the times and one who believes that even though this is a church, it has to be run in a businesslike manner. But before I get to what I'm proposing, let me tell you what's been happening the last four weeks. I asked six of my associate ministers to monitor the congregation to see if there was anything we could do to make things more convenient. And what they noticed was that there were a few cash-paying members who had fifty- and hundred-dollar bills but weren't able to get change for them. Which meant they couldn't pay their tithes and offerings. In addition to that, we've been receiving back far too many bad checks from the bank. So what I'm proposing is that we lease and install one or two ATMs in the front vestibule. That way, every member will have access to it, and it will even come in handy when we have unannounced offerings that they didn't bring enough cash for—"

"ATM?" Deacon Thurgood interrupted. "I know you don't

mean one of those money machines that I see at the grocery store and in certain parking lots?"

"Yes, Deacon, those are the machines I'm speaking about."

Deacon Thurgood looked at Deacon Winslow and shook his head in amazement. As Whitney had predicted, both men clearly disagreed with what Curtis was saying. But even though they were his elders and well into their seventies, he wasn't about to let them intimidate him.

"The other item I'm proposing is that we set up an electronic pay plan for members who pay the same tithe amount every pay period. That way, they'd be able to pay their tithes automatically. The benefit would be that they'd no longer have to write a check, carry cash, and when they aren't able to attend service for whatever reason, their tithes will still be deposited on a regular basis. This could also work for people who don't tithe but do give the same amount in offerings every Sunday. Then my final proposal is that we hire two financial planners who would meet with every member who isn't tithing. Some members don't tithe because they simply refuse to do what God has told them. Others can't afford it. But the reason they can't afford it is that they're not managing their money well enough. However, if we hire two qualified professionals, they could help members create budgets that will allow them to pay their ten percent and they'd also be able to pay off unnecessary debt and have more disposable income for themselves."

"I ain't never heard so much foolishness in all my life," Deacon Thurgood chimed in.

"Me neither, Fred," Deacon Winslow agreed. "And all these new ideas is what's sendin' folks straight to hell."

"You got that right, JC," Deacon Thurgood said. "Because that ATM and electronic payment stuff don't sound like nothin' but a scam to me."

Curtis prayed for someone else to comment. Anyone. But

everyone kept their mouths shut. Half the board members were in their thirties, so he couldn't understand why none of them had the balls to speak up. Spineless is what they were. But he wasn't going to show his frustration or anger and instead was going to talk this over with them "nicely."

"Okay, Deacons. I respect both of your opinions, but I'd also like to hear from the rest of the board. And let me just say right now that I'm not trying to propose any schemes here and that all moneys collected will still be deposited directly into the church account the same as always. I'm only proposing these ideas as a way to make giving more convenient for the members. And let's be honest, we can't run this church without the support of our tithes and offerings, so this will ultimately benefit the church as a whole."

"Well, I will say this," Deacon Taylor finally said. He was Curtis's favorite deacon and friend. "An ATM would definitely be convenient for me, because I'm always short on cash and then don't think about it until I really need it. And there probably are some members who just might appreciate having access to one inside the church. Especially on those days when they just don't have quite enough time to stop at another location."

"Well, I guess the next thang we'll be doin' is tellin' people they can pay by Visa, MasterCard, or Discover," Deacon Thurgood said.

"Mmm-mmm-mmm," Deacon Winslow said, laughing. "Paying the Lord with a credit card. Now ain't that a notion."

Deacon Thurgood joined him. "Ain't that somethin'? So, unh-unh, there ain't no way I can 'gree to nothin' like that."

"Naw, me neither, Fred."

Curtis wondered if Deacon Winslow always agreed with everything that *Fred* had to say. These two were running the entire meeting and he wondered when Deacon Gulley, the so-called chairman, was going to speak up.

"Mr. Chairman, how do you feel about my ideas?" Curtis asked.

"To be honest, Reverend, I really don't know. I do hear what you're saying, but I don't think the congregation is ready for ATMs and direct deposit. Or even financial planners for that matter. I know there are a few other churches out there that are already doing some of the things you're talking about, but I think we have to take things slow with our congregation. Because the one thing we don't want is for people to feel pressured into giving or like the ATM is an electronic guilt trip."

"I don't think they'd see it like that at all," Curtis said.

"It's really hard to say whether they would or wouldn't, but that's just how I feel," Deacon Gulley said.

"Well, what about everyone else? Deacon Jamison, Deacon Pryor, Deacon Evans?" Curtis polled the three youngest deacons in the room.

"I think you have some pretty good ideas, Pastor, but I just don't know if they're appropriate for this church," Deacon Evans stated.

"I second that. I don't totally disagree with what you want to do, but I'm not sure the timing is right," Deacon Jamison answered.

"And for me," Deacon Pryor said, "well, I guess, I'm just old-fashioned, so I don't see anything wrong with leaving our system of giving the way it is."

Cowards. Pure, unadulterated cowards. And what could Deacon Pryor possibly know about being old-fashioned? He couldn't have been more than thirty-three. Curtis didn't even want to think about the rest of the members sitting in the room and what they thought, let alone the ones who weren't able to attend the meeting. He was starting to feel like this was Faith Missionary all over again. Back then, the opposing ring leader was Deacon Jackson, but now he had Andy Taylor and Barney

Fife to contend with. He wanted to tell all of them how backwoods their way of thinking was and how they were never going to get anywhere by being so complacent. Didn't they know that change should be seen as something positive? Or that taking risks was very necessary in order to succeed?

"Well, if that's all you have, Pastor, then I think we should move on to the next order of business," Deacon Gulley suggested.

Curtis felt like a defeated heavyweight champion. He'd had so much more control and influence at Faith, but these deacons here at Truth seemed to be a little more on the stubborn side. He wasn't giving up, though. It was just going to take a little longer than he'd thought in terms of making them see the light.

And he had all the time in the world to wait.

Chapter 6

Mariah sliced two pieces of German chocolate cake, slid them on two separate plates, and walked back into the family room. She'd invited her mother over for a visit shortly after Curtis informed her that he wouldn't be home for dinner.

"Baby girl, this cake is too good," Jean told her.

"Isn't it, though. And it's not even homemade."

"Stop it. Are you serious?"

"Yes. I get it from the bakery down the street, and pretty much everything they make tastes wonderful."

"Well, it's a good thing my big ole self don't live anywhere near it, because I'd gain at least a pound or two every single day if I did," Jean said, chuckling.

"Mama, please. You're not nearly as heavy as you claim to be."

"Oh yes I am. Two hundred thirty pounds and only five six? That's way too heavy for any woman. But that's okay, because I'm about to try me another fad diet in a minute."

"When exactly is a minute, Mother?" Mariah asked.

"Just as soon as Easter, Memorial Day, and the Fourth of July are over with."

They both laughed.

"You are too, too much," Mariah added.

"I know. But tell me this. How is that fine-ass husband of yours doing?"

"I can't believe you."

"Girl, you know your mama calls everything the way she sees it. So it's not my fault that Curtis has that beautiful smooth chocolate skin and a body that screams sex every time I see him."

"Mama, you know you're embarrassing me."

"I don't know why. He's your husband and you should be proud of it. You did well for yourself, young lady, and your mama couldn't be more happy for you." Jean scanned the elegant cherry-wood china cabinet and eight-seat dining room table.

"Yeah, I guess I'm pretty happy, or at least I thought I was," Mariah said.

"Now what is that supposed to mean?" Jean set down her empty plate.

"I don't know, Mama. He's just not being as attentive as he was in the beginning, and he's always coming home well after dinner."

"Now, Mariah, you know that man is a big-time preacher with a lot of responsibilities, so you can't expect him to be at home with you all the time. If he was, you wouldn't have this house and everything in it."

"Maybe, but still something isn't right with us. And sometimes he speaks to me so harshly."

"Well, baby girl, I hope you're not nagging that man to death when you know all the pressure he must be under, trying to run that church."

"I don't nag him, Mama. I just want him to spend more time with me. And actually he was until maybe a couple of weeks ago."

"What you need to do is get out of this house more often. You were never a housewife before you married Curtis, so why are you hanging around here now waiting for him to get home? Because I'm telling you, baby girl, you're going to push him away if you keep doing all that complaining."

"What? Are you saying that I should go back to work?"

"No, I'm not saying that at all. I'm just saying you need to find some other interests. Get yourself a hobby of some kind or join some women's organization. You like helping people, so you could even volunteer for some charities. Anything that would get you out of here a few hours a day."

"I head up a young women's organization one day a week at the church, and I also teach a women's Bible study group every other Saturday morning."

"That's all fine and whatnot, but I'm talking about doing something outside of the church. You need to do something that's just for you and you only. Because even though you know I believe a man should take care of a woman, I also think she should have her own identity and do some things on her own."

"I guess."

"You've got yourself a real good man, but you've got to let him have a certain amount of freedom. You can't start making him feel all caught up. If you do, you'll end up forcing him into another woman's bed."

"But Curtis isn't perfect, Mama."

"Well, nobody is, baby girl. You know that."

"No, I mean, Curtis has some serious issues from his past that I just found out about."

"Like what?"

"Like an illegitimate five-year-old son that he never told me about. And the worst part of all is that the mother was only seventeen when he first started sleeping with her and this was all while he was married to his first wife."

"I know that probably hurt you, Mariah, but the past is exactly that. Everybody makes mistakes, but people do change."

"Well then, why didn't he tell me on his own instead of letting me find out from someone else?"

"Who told you?"

"Nobody really. I heard Alicia say it when she was yelling and screaming at him about how he'd ruined their family."

"I know this is a little off the subject, but is she starting to warm up to you any?" Jean asked.

"No, and now she's totally disrespecting Curtis, too."

"She's just hurt because her parents aren't together anymore. And as wonderful as you are to her, she sees you as someone who's in her way."

"I know, but I wish she would just realize that I only want to love her like my own child."

"She will eventually. You'll see."

"I'm just starting to wonder what I got myself into when I married Curtis. Sometimes I think we can pray for the wrong things."

"Now look. I don't ever want to hear you talk like that again. Because I know you haven't forgotten that run-down, roach-infested shack we used to live in. It saddens me every time I think about it, but what makes me so happy now is that one of my babies got an education, married a wealthy man, and made it all the way to the top. Both your sisters are almost forty and still living at home with me, one of your brothers is serving a life sentence for being a drug dealer, one is barely two steps from joining him, and the other is living with a woman and using her. So I'm telling you, baby girl, you might be the youngest, but of all my children, you have the best head on your shoulders and the biggest heart. I know I may not have been the best mother in the world, but I loved you and tried to take care of you the best I could. So that's why I don't want to see you give up what you have. I don't want you to be unhappy, and I don't ever wanna see any man walking all over you, but please try to make your marriage work if you can."

"I am trying, but Curtis has to meet me halfway."

"I'm sure everything will be fine," Jean said, reaching out for her daughter. "And no matter what, I'll always be here for you."

Mariah hugged her mother and wished she never had to let her go.

"I know that, Mama, and I love you so much."

"I love you, too, baby girl. And don't you ever forget that. Not for as long as you live."

At that moment Mariah realized how strong a mother's love could be and decided that maybe it was time she became one herself. Yes, Curtis had said he wanted to wait, but starting a family would bring them so much closer. And she wouldn't have to spend so much time alone when he had business to attend to. She'd finally have another human being that she could love unconditionally and spend all of her time with. She'd have a baby that would love and appreciate her until the end.

She'd finally have everything.

Curtis drove into the subdivision and saw his mother-in-law's car parked in his driveway. But just as he did, his phone rang. He figured it was Mariah, until he saw the word "unknown" displayed on the screen.

"Hello?"

"All I can say is that I must be completely insane to be calling you back," Adrienne said. "And I know that I'm going to regret this for the rest of my life."

"Is that so?" Curtis said rather coolly, and pulled his car to the side of the street. He wanted Adrienne to think he was still angry about their earlier conversation.

"Yes. But while I hate admitting it, you were right about

everything you said. I am still in love with you, and I'm completely miserable with Thomas. He'd make the perfect husband for someone else, but he's just not for me. I've really tried to be happy with him, but it's just not working."

"I've told you before that not every married couple is compatible or meant to be together. And no matter how hard you try to make it work, it won't get any better. Because even though I've tried to be happy with Mariah, she's just not enough for me. She's not the woman I'm supposed to be married to, and it's like I told you before, she's not you."

There was a pause and then Curtis heard Adrienne sniffle.

"Baby, what are you crying about?"

"The fact that I'm so confused and I'm so afraid that if we start seeing each other again, it's going to end up a total disaster. I'm scared to death that things will turn out worse than they did five years ago."

"But I promise you they won't. This isn't like before, and as soon as I divorce Mariah, you and I can finally be married."

"I want to believe you, Curtis. I really do. But you know that's hard for me after all that has happened."

"I understand that, but if you just give me this one last chance, I'll prove everything to you."

"But what if Thomas finds out? Or Mariah for that matter?"

"Nobody's going to find out anything. We'll be even more careful than we were in the past, and it will only be for a short time."

"I just don't know."

"Why don't we talk about this face-to-face," he said, rolling the dice again.

"When?"

"Tonight?"

"I don't know. It's already after eight."

"Where are you now?"

"Still at my office."

"Why don't we get together for maybe an hour or so?"

"But Thomas knows that even when I work late, I'm usually home by eight-thirty."

"Tell him you're going out with some coworkers. Tell him anything, because, baby, I really need to see you."

"Curtis, what are we doing?"

"We're about to stop being miserable."

"Where do you want to meet?" she said.

"The usual place?"

"Fine. I'll see you in about forty-five minutes."

"See you then."

Curtis gazed at his house again, did a U-turn in the middle of the street, and drove back out of the subdivision. To his surprise, he felt a tad bit guilty and somewhat sorry for Mariah. He'd honestly tried to be faithful to her. He'd tried to do what he knew God wanted him to, but it wasn't his fault that Mariah couldn't satisfy him or make him happy. In actuality, it wasn't her fault either, because she couldn't help being the person she was.

He picked up speed after entering the interstate and said out loud, "Lord forgive me for what I'm about to do."

When they arrived at the hotel, Adrienne went in, checked into a room, phoned Curtis on his cell phone, and gave him the room number. They'd agreed that it was best to walk in separately just in case they saw someone they knew. Curtis had been somewhat nervous when they'd gone to the restaurant last week, but he'd decided it was well worth the risk. Rarely had they eaten together out in the open during their first affair, so he figured taking her to a public establishment would be impressive. And impressive it was, because he was sure it had helped convince her that she needed him more than ever.

Curtis took the elevator up to the eighth floor and walked

down the corridor to 803. Adrienne opened the door, and he grabbed her in his arms instantly. They kissed madly and Curtis unzipped the fitted gray dress she was wearing. He slid it off each shoulder and pushed it down toward the floor. She stepped out of it, and Curtis unsnapped her bra and laid her on the bed. They kissed again and he removed everything else she was wearing. Then he removed his own blazer, all the while admiring her body and shaking his head in amazement. She hadn't aged one day, and her body was still just as beautiful as he remembered.

He loosened his tie and began shedding the rest of his clothing. He continued staring at her, barely able to contain himself, and Adrienne lay there watching him with tears streaming down her face. They hadn't said one word to each other, and they both agreed silently that there were no more words to speak. At least not now, anyway, because they'd come here solely to express their feelings and desire for each other.

Curtis made love to her like he never had before. He moved his tongue between her legs like an artist twirling a paintbrush. She moaned and groaned and wept, and Curtis turned up the intensity a whole other notch. He could tell he was driving her wild, and loved all the juice her body was producing. He buried his head deeper and deeper until she screamed at the top of her lungs.

He lifted his body away from her and she sat up and reached her hand toward his crotch. She pulled him into her mouth and Curtis thought he had died and gone to heaven.

"Oh dear God," he declared, closing his eyes. "That's what I'm talking about."

Adrienne was still a master when it came to oral sex, and now he knew he had to say and do whatever it took to keep her in his life.

She moved her lips upward and downward, slowly and then more rapidly, tightening her grasp.

Curtis felt himself preparing to come and pulled away from her.

Then he laid her down and slid inside her.

"Baby, I want you to promise me that you won't ever give yourself to another man for as long as you live," he said.

Adrienne groaned with much satisfaction as he eased in and out of her.

"Baby, did you hear me?" Curtis asked, entering her a bit harder than before.

"Yes, Curtis, I heard you."

"Then tell me that you're all mine, and that you will never give yourself to another man from this day forward. Not even the deacon."

"Curtis, please."

"No," he said, pulling out of her and then in with more force. "I want you to promise me."

"Okay, Curtis. I promise. I'm all yours."

"I mean it, baby," he said. "I wouldn't be able to stand it if you gave this to someone else."

"I promise, baby. I won't."

"Not even the deacon," he said, increasing his speed, and then suddenly he pulled out of her again.

"Curtis, please don't keep torturing me like this. Please just give it to me."

"Not even the deacon," he repeated.

In. And out.

"No, Curtis. I won't even give it to him."

"You know I love you, don't you?"

In. And out.

"Yes. And I love you. I've always loved you."

"And you'd do anything for me, wouldn't you?" he said, forcing her knees toward her chest, pushing himself in and out of her, repeatedly, with all the power and strength he could muster. She moaned repeatedly, and Curtis continued in a lyrical yet forceful rhythm until his body exploded.

They held each other, savoring the excitement. At least that's how Curtis was feeling, anyway, and he hoped Adrienne was satisfied. He wasn't sure what had come over him, but all he knew was that he'd never made love so aggressively until tonight. In a matter of minutes he'd felt this great need to be in control and, as much as he hated to admit it, like he needed Adrienne to know who was in charge. Like he needed to fulfill some burning desire he'd never had before.

"You must have really missed me," she said.

"That's an understatement, but why do you ask?"

"Because I've never seen you act this way before. It was almost like you hadn't had sex in years."

"To be honest, it feels like I haven't. No one has ever come close to giving me the pleasure you do. And Mariah has got to be the worst I've ever had."

"Yeah, right," she said, catching her breath.

"I'm serious. With her, it's missionary style all the way, and you know that bores the crap out of me."

"Well, I hope you just released every one of those pent-up desires, because you were a little rough toward the end."

"I didn't hurt you, did I?" He turned toward her, genuinely concerned.

"No, but it was different and you sort of caught me off guard."

"I'll try not to do that again, because I don't ever want to hurt you," he said, kissing her forehead.

They lay speechless again with Curtis stroking Adrienne's hair.

"Thank you," he said.

"For what?"

"For meeting me at the restaurant the other night and for allowing me a chance to make things right with you."

"That's fine and well, but as soon as we walk out of here, it's back to reality. I have to go home to Thomas and you have to go home to Mariah."

"But this isn't about them. This is about us. And I was serious when I said I don't want you having sex with the deacon anymore."

"And what about you and Mariah?" she asked. "Are you prepared to stop having sex with her, too?"

Curtis was somewhat surprised, because in the old days he'd made all sorts of demands but Adrienne never questioned him about anything. She never had the nerve. But now she was definitely a woman with a new attitude. She was definitely someone he was going to have to handle very carefully now that they were seeing each other again. He'd *try* to be faithful to her for as long as he could, but that's all he could promise. And he wouldn't even tell her that out loud because he knew what he was capable of.

"I won't sleep with Mariah either," he agreed.

"Curtis, I ask you again, what are we doing? What am I doing to myself?"

"You're spending time with the man you love, I'm spending time with the woman I love, and that's all that matters."

"I hate this. I hate that we're about to start all this sneaking around again. I almost lost everything last time, so you have to be very sure about this. You have to be positive that you're going to divorce Mariah in six months, and that I'm going to be your wife."

"Baby, all you have to do is trust me, because I'm really serious this time. I'm really going to marry you," he said, and wondered what lie he'd have to come up with once the six-month deadline began approaching. He wished there was a way he could marry Adrienne, because if he were ever going to love any woman exclusively, it would have been her. But there was no way he could leave Mariah. She was perfect. She was naïve, and she obeyed him. What more could a man ask for? What more could a pastor of a prominent church want? If he married Adrienne, she'd end up being the same as Tanya, ranting and raving about everything he did and then whining about all the hours he spent away from home. He couldn't be harassed like that ever again, so Adrienne would just have to understand. He wasn't sure how, but he had to make her see that the two of them weren't marriage material, and that a lifetime affair was so much more becoming. It was so much more interesting.

He had to make her see that his love for her was sincere, and that if she stayed with him, he would take care of all her financial and emotional needs forever. She'd have the best of everything. She would never want for anything.

He had to make her see that she was being offered a much better way of life than she was currently living. A much happier life than she had with the deacon.

Chapter 7

Alicia pressed the entry code on the keypad near the garage and waited for it to open. It was Friday, so right after school she'd gone shopping with Danielle and her mother and was just now arriving home.

Once inside the house, she strolled toward the kitchen and saw her mother and James standing at the island. They looked as if the world had come to an end. Now what?

"What's wrong?" she asked them.

"Apparently a whole lot," Tanya answered. "Because only minutes ago, your counselor just informed me that you've been skipping your math class all week."

Alicia gazed at them, but decided it was probably best not to respond. Especially since her mother looked like she wanted to kill her.

"So why haven't you been going?" Tanya asked.

"I don't know."

"You don't know? What do you mean you don't know?" Tanya asked with fire in her eyes, moving closer to Alicia. "Last week we found out you were failing world history, now this."

"Sweetheart," James said to Tanya. "Why don't we all go

into the family room so we can sit down and discuss this more calmly."

"No, what I want is for Miss Alicia to explain herself right here and right now."

Alicia's stomach churned, but she was also starting to despise her mother's crazy attitude.

"Girl, don't you hear me talking to you?" Tanya continued.

"Yes."

"Then why aren't you answering my question?"

"Because, Mom. I don't know why I skipped math."

"James, are you listening to this?" Tanya said.

James raised his eyebrows in silence. He'd learned early on that it was better not to interfere in his wife and stepdaughter's confrontations.

"Alicia, I'm really to the point where I don't know what to do with you," Tanya continued. "And I'm completely fed up with all of these reports we keep getting from your school."

"Maybe I should just go live with Daddy," Alicia threatened.

"You know, Alicia, maybe you should. Maybe it's time that you moved out of here and in with your father and Mariah. Maybe I've done all I can do."

Alicia was stunned. Usually her mother became highly upset whenever she spoke about going to live with her father, so she hadn't expected this response at all. She didn't know what to say next, but the one thing she did know was that she'd rather die than go live with her father and his wife.

"What do you think, James?" Tanya asked. "Because maybe it really is time Alicia went to live with Curtis. Maybe he can get her to go to class and do her schoolwork the way she's supposed to."

"Sweetheart," James said. "I don't think that's necessarily the solution."

"Well, is this what you really want to do, Alicia?" Tanya asked.

"I don't know."

Tanya laughed sarcastically. "Well, is there anything that you *do* know?"

"Yes," Alicia spoke boldly, yet in tears. "I know that you and Daddy are divorced and that we're never going to be a family again."

"Alicia, I realize you've had a tough time with all of this, and yes, you're right. Things are never going to be the way they once were. I wish, for your sake, that they could be, but they can't. I know you're still feeling a tremendous amount of pain, but I just don't know how to help you anymore. When we were in counseling a couple of years ago, you seemed to come to terms with everything, so why is this all of a sudden becoming a major issue again? You seemed fine until a few months ago."

Alicia wanted to tell her how right she was. Because until her father married Mariah, she'd still held on to the possibility of her mother and him getting back together. She'd known her mother was married to James, but as long as her father was still available, she'd kept high hopes. She'd even prayed about it every chance she got. She'd even figured out a way for it to happen where no one would get hurt. James would accidentally meet another woman, fall in love, and then tell her mother that he couldn't be with her any longer. But her mother would be fine with it because deep down she'd really want to be back with Alicia's father, anyway. Alicia had played that scene in her head at least a thousand times, but the curtain had been yanked shut the day her father married Mariah. That stupid fairy-tale wedding of theirs had ruined everything.

"Pumpkin, do you think it would help for you to go to counseling again?" James asked Alicia.

"I don't know . . . I mean, maybe."

"Why don't we do that then?" James said, turning his attention to Tanya.

"That's fine," Tanya said. "Because I'm willing to do whatever it takes."

"Can I be excused?" Alicia asked.

"Yes, but until you get your grades back up to where they should be, you won't be going anywhere except school, church, and back home."

"But, Mom, I have Camille's birthday party this weekend."

"Not anymore you don't. Because starting today, you're grounded until further notice."

"Why are you doing this?" Alicia said, sobbing. "Why are you and Daddy always trying to make my life so miserable?"

"Look, Alicia. I've said what I have to say, and I don't want to hear any more back talk from you."

Alicia left the kitchen and went fuming up to her bedroom. She hated her mother almost as much as she hated her father. As a matter of fact, James was the only adult in her life who had any sense. He never harassed her about silly stuff, he never yelled at her, and he always went out of his way to do nice things for her. She was starting to wish that he was her biological father, and that she had a different mother to go along with him. And she was never going to forgive her mother for making her miss Camille's birthday bash. Camille's parents owned a top black magazine and were filthy rich. They were even sending a limo to pick up Camille's closest friends. Not to mention the actual party they were having downtown at the Four Seasons. They were expecting two hundred guests and had rented a suite for Camille and five of her friends. Alicia, of course, was one of them. Her mother had said that it was ridiculous for any parent to spend thousands on any child who was just turning fifteen, but what did she know? Maybe Camille's parents were doing it because *they* truly loved their daughter. Maybe they actually knew how to treat a child that they'd voluntarily brought into this world.

Alicia lay across her bed, still weeping. When she finally calmed herself, she glanced over at her computer. Julian always made her feel better and she was starting to realize that he was the only person she could turn to. Yes, she had her best friend, Danielle, but it wasn't the same as when she shared her feelings with Julian. As a matter of fact, she hadn't even told Danielle about her chats with him, because she wasn't sure how Danielle would take it. Sometimes she blew the tiniest things out of proportion, so Alicia had decided not to mention her new on-line buddy. At least not yet, anyway.

She kicked off her tan platform shoes that mimicked those designed in the seventies and sat down at her desk. Usually when her mother said she was grounded, that also included telephone and Internet privileges, but what her mother didn't know wouldn't hurt her.

She signed on to AOL and waited. As soon as she heard the words "You've Got Mail," she turned down the volume on her computer. She would keep it at mute status until she was no longer on punishment.

She checked her e-mail messages and broke into tears again when she read the one from Camille. It was a note informing everyone that her parents had called in a favor and now a surprise hip-hop music artist was going to be singing at her birthday party. If it was someone Alicia was a big fan of, she would never speak to her mother again.

She read a message from Danielle about homework, and smiled when she saw that Julian had just signed on to his account. She quickly sent him an instant message.

ALICIABLK: Hey, Julian.
JMONEY1: Alicia! What's up with you this evening?
ALICIABLK: You don't even want to know. ☹
JMONEY1: Hey, now what's with the sad face?

AliciaBlk: My mother is acting just as crazy as my father was last week.

JMoney1: I'm sorry to hear that. You've really been having it out with your parents a lot lately, haven't you?

AliciaBlk: Yes, and I'm really getting sick of it. Sometimes I feel like I don't have anyone, and if I didn't have you to talk to, I don't know what I would do.

JMoney1: You know I'm always here for you. I just wish I could talk to you by phone or see you in person.

And why couldn't they speak by phone? Every time he mentioned talking to her or getting together, she sort of shied away from it, but maybe if she could hear his voice, she'd actually feel better.

AliciaBlk: What's your phone number?

JMoney1: (312) 555-2823.

AliciaBlk: Do you want me to call right now?

JMoney1: I've got the phone sitting right here. So all you have to do is dial the number. ☺

AliciaBlk: Okay.

Alicia lifted the receiver and thanked God she'd convinced her mother to install a separate phone line for her. The only extension was in her bedroom, so at least there was no way her mother could eavesdrop or suddenly pick up the phone, yelling at her to get off it. The worst that could happen was her storming into the bedroom, but she still wouldn't be able to find out who Alicia was talking to. And if that happened, Alicia would lie and say it was Danielle, because she and Danielle maintained a permanent pact. They'd promised each other two years ago that if one of their parents ever questioned them about anything, they'd lie for each other until the end. To this day,

Danielle had never let her down. Although sometimes she tended to be a little fearful, and that was the real reason Alicia hadn't told her about Julian.

She dialed the number displayed on her monitor and waited for Julian to answer.

"So what's up?" he said.

"Not much." She was more nervous than she'd imagined, but she loved the sound of his voice. It was so deep, and he sounded so cool!

"You sound like you're uncomfortable with this."

"No . . . not really."

"I like your voice."

"I like yours, too."

"So. Tell me what's going on with your moms."

"I missed my math class a couple of times this week, and she went crazy."

"Well, you know how most parents are when it comes to the school thing."

"Was your mother like that when you were in school?"

"No, she couldn't have cared less whether I went or not. But my stepmoms made sure I got to school and did my homework. And for the most part, I didn't have to do a lot of studying. I used to study for tests the night before and still get an A on them," he said.

"I'm sort of like that, too, but lately I don't feel like doing any of my assignments. Sometimes I don't even bother to answer all the questions on my tests. It just depends on how I feel."

"Why is that?"

"Because I'm just not motivated and because me getting good grades is all they seem to care about."

"You do need good grades if you're planning to get a good job or go to college."

"You didn't go college, and you already have your own place."

"Yeah, but it's only because I have my own business, and I make a shitload of money doing what I do."

"I can't believe so many people buy CDs from you and that you have so many regular customers." Alicia was amazed.

"People love music, and that's one thing in this world that won't ever change."

"I guess not."

"So tell me. When am I going to get a chance to see you?"

Alicia was hoping he wouldn't bring this subject up so quickly. She was hoping the phone call would suffice for a while.

"I don't know," she said. "But soon."

"Soon was fine until I heard your voice. Because, girl, you sound so sweet, and now I can't wait to kick it with you. I can't wait to take you out to dinner or wherever you wanna go."

"I can't wait either," was all she could think to say.

"Well, can I ask you something else?"

"What?"

"Are you sexually active?"

"Why do you ask?"

"I'm just wondering, because your voice is so sexy, and you sound much older than seventeen. You sound more mature than some twenty-year-old women I know."

"Yeah, right," Alicia said, beaming.

"I'm serious. You do."

"Whatever, Julian."

"And to tell you the truth, I'm starting to wish you hadn't called me."

"Why?"

"Because hearing your voice is bringing out some feelings I didn't know I had. Especially for a woman I haven't even seen before."

"What kind of feelings?" She was a little bit confused by what he was saying and needed him to explain. But she loved that he saw her as a woman and not some childish little girl.

"I'd better not say."

"Why?"

"I don't want to embarrass myself," he said, laughing.

"Come on, Julian. Tell me."

"Girl, don't start somethin' you won't be able to finish."

"Like what?"

"Okay, look. I don't usually fall for women just from chatting with them on-line or by talking to them on the phone, but, girl, you're makin' me crazy."

"Are you saying you like me like a girlfriend?"

"That's exactly what I'm saying."

Alicia was afraid to ask any further questions, because she didn't know where the rest of the conversation was headed. But the truth of the matter was she could tell she had feelings for him, too. She had to remind herself that Julian wasn't one of those little boys at her school and that she had to act as grown as she knew how to.

"But we haven't even seen each other before," she said.

"I know, but I'm tellin' you, girl, I've got some straight-up real feelings for you, and if I knew you better, I'd show you just how serious they are, right here on the phone. I'd make you feel the way every woman is supposed to feel."

"And how would you do that?"

"You don't even want to know."

"Yes I do," she said, and wondered how in the world he could show her anything through the phone. He was so silly.

"I know you've heard of phone sex, haven't you?"

"Yeah . . . I guess so."

"Well?"

"I don't know, Julian."

"Why? Are you afraid?"

"No." She spoke quickly.

"Then why? It can't hurt anything and it's the safest sex you can have."

"What if my mother walks in and catches me on the phone with you?"

"If you think she might come into your room, then we won't do it."

"I just don't know, Julian, because I've never done anything like this before."

"All you have to do is listen."

"And then what?"

"You do the things I ask you to do. Okay?"

She was terrified that her mother might burst into her room at any moment, but a part of her wanted to hear what Julian had to say.

"Okay," she agreed.

"What do you have on?"

"A knit top with a chiffon blouse over it."

"Pants or a skirt?"

"Jeans."

"Well, I need you to take all of that off."

"Everything?"

"Yes."

Alicia hesitated, but then told him, "Hold on for a minute."

When she'd removed everything except her bra and panties, she picked up the phone.

"Okay, I did it," she said.

"You took off everything?"

"Yes."

"Even your underwear?"

"No . . . I mean, you didn't say that you wanted me to."

"Well, it's up to you, but this will work so much better if you take off everything."

Alicia removed her bra but simply couldn't will herself to remove her panties. That was going too far and she just didn't feel comfortable doing it.

"Okay, now what?" she asked.

"You took everything off, right?"

"Yes. Everything."

"Do you have a headset for your phone?"

"Yes." Although the only reason she had one was that she and Danielle loved talking to each other and surfing the Internet simultaneously for hours at a time. Sometimes they did research for papers they had to write and sometimes they did it just for fun.

Alicia put on the headset.

"You ready?"

"Yes."

"Okay, now close your eyes."

Alicia followed his instructions and waited nervously.

"Take both your hands and massage both your nipples until you feel them getting hard."

Alicia bugged her eyes open and covered her mouth with both hands.

"And I mean massage them until it feels so good that you don't ever want to stop."

Alicia didn't move.

"Are you doing it?" he asked.

"Yes," she said, and covered her mouth again.

"I bet it feels real good, doesn't it? And if I was there with you, I'd suck both those titties like a baby suckin' his bottle."

Alicia burst into laughter.

"What's so funny?"

He sounded irritated, and now she was sorry she'd laughed at him.

"Nothing," she finally answered. She was still sniggering.

"Well, somethin' must be real funny or you wouldn't be crackin' up like that."

"I'm sorry, Julian. I didn't mean to."

"No, I'm the one who's sorry, because I had no idea you were so immature. You sound a lot older than seventeen, but now I'm wondering if you're even in high school yet."

"I am seventeen," she insisted.

"Whatever. But hey, I'm gettin' ready to bounce, okay?"

"But, Julian?"

"But, Julian, what?"

"Please don't be mad at me."

"I'm not mad, just disappointed."

"I'm so sorry, and I promise I'll make this up to you."

"And how do you plan on doing that?"

"I don't know, but I will."

"Well, like I said, I have to go."

"Are you going to be on-line again tomorrow?"

"Maybe. Who knows?"

"You're really, really mad at me, aren't you?"

"I told you I wasn't. Now I have to go."

He hung up and Alicia felt so stupid. How could she have been so childish when all he'd done was try to make her feel like a woman? She had to make him realize how sorry she was and that she was more than willing to try that phone sex thing again. This time she would do everything he told her and she wouldn't do one thing to upset him.

She grabbed her bra, hooked it back on, and heard a knock at her door.

"Yes," Alicia said.

Her mother walked in. "What are you doing?"

"Nothing. I'm just changing out of my school clothes."

"Do you have homework?"

"Yes."

"Then as soon as you finish dinner, that's what I want you to work on for the rest of the evening. Oh, and by the way, being grounded also means no personal phone calls and no Internet."

"But, Mom—"

"I mean it, Alicia," Tanya said, and closed her daughter's door.

Alicia fell across her bed and wished she lived in another household.

Chapter 8

Mariah fastened the last button on the crème-colored silk blouse and tucked it inside her black linen skirt. Now she wished she'd bought the skirt in at least two other colors, because the wide waistband slimmed her down more than usual. She'd found it at Saks several months ago, and since she and her friend Vivian were planning to go shopping in a couple of days, it wouldn't hurt to see if they still had them.

She did a once-over in the mirror to confirm that her makeup was intact and to see if her hair was still in place. She glanced at her watch and saw that she had ninety minutes to get to the church. Every Wednesday she oversaw and advised a teenage group called YGM, an acronym for Young Girls Ministry. In any given week there were usually twenty to thirty attendees, and Mariah loved working with them. They came from all walks of life and not all of them were actual members of the church. Wanting to make a difference in the community, she'd started the ministry right after marrying Curtis. She'd told him that there were so many underprivileged children with problems in the city of Chicago, but that she wanted to concentrate on teenage girls, ages seventeen through nineteen.

Specifically those who came from broken homes, those who had already had a baby or had had an abortion, and those who had lost all interest in going to school. She was proud of what she was doing, because the ministry had only started out with five or six girls.

Mariah lifted her Louis Vuitton tote from the dresser, slid her Bible inside, and grabbed her car keys. After setting the alarm system, she left the house and drove out of the driveway. Even with traffic, she would arrive at the church almost an hour early, but that was how she'd planned it. The YGM gathering always ended about a half hour before weekly Bible study, and she could easily speak to Curtis in between, but she wanted to have a short talk with him beforehand. He hadn't come home until well after nine again last night, and she was really starting to get worried.

Last Monday it was the writing of his sermon that had kept him out late. Last Tuesday he'd had a meeting with the deacons and trustees and then had to go sit and pray with the Wilsons because of a death in their family. It seemed like there was one excuse right after another, and with the exception of four days ago, when he'd taken her to a Saturday matinee and then dinner on Sunday, she hadn't seen very much of him. Yes, he'd made love to her on each of those days, but he hadn't touched her on Monday or last night. She'd questioned him about his whereabouts, but when she'd noticed how irritated he was becoming, she'd stopped. She'd decided that it was best to sleep on everything she was thinking and then discuss it with him this morning. But by the time she woke up, he was already showered, dressed, and on his way out. She'd made another attempt at questioning him, but he insisted he had an early morning meeting, and that they would have to speak later.

She drove into the church parking lot, parked her car, and then headed straight up to Curtis's study.

"Hi, Whitney," Mariah said to Curtis's secretary.

"Hi, Sister Black. How are you?" She stood and hugged Mariah.

"I'm well."

"Same here. Are you here to see Pastor?"

"As a matter of fact I am. Is he in there?"

"Yes."

Mariah knocked once and entered Curtis's study.

"Do you have a few minutes?" she asked.

"What kind of question is that? Because you know I have all the time in the world for my beautiful wife."

He stood, walked toward her, and kissed her on the lips.

Mariah pushed his door shut and wondered why his tone was much more pleasant than it had been over the last couple of weeks. She wondered if he was just putting on airs for Whitney, wanting her to think their marriage was perfect.

"Well, Curtis, it really doesn't seem like that lately," she said, sitting down in front of him.

He leaned against his desk. "I know, baby, but it's truly been a very rough month for me. I'm preparing sermons every week, trying to get the officers to agree with some of the things I'm proposing, and you know all the other responsibilities I have with the members. I know I haven't been spending as much time with you, but, baby, duty calls."

"I understand all of that, but still something seems different. You're different."

"Different, how?"

"You're staying out much later than normal and you act like you don't even have the same desire for me."

"Only because I'm tired all the time. And it's not like I'm twenty years old anymore. I'm thirty-eight."

"You were also thirty-eight just a few weeks ago, but it didn't seem to be a problem."

"But I just told you, I've been very tired."

"I know that, but I'm still worried about our marriage."

"Well, I don't know what to tell you, baby, except that I love you and that you and Alicia are the two most important people in this world to me."

"But, Curtis, I'm sure she's feeling neglected, too, because you really don't spend much time with her either. And I'm sure she thinks I'm the reason you don't, and that's why she doesn't have much to say to me."

"Alicia knows that I love her and that being a pastor means I can't spend as much time with her as I'd like to. Even when I was pastor at Faith, she always understood that. She was only a little girl, but she even understood it better than her mother."

"Look, I know you have a lot of responsibilities here at the church, but I just didn't know it was going to take you away from me day and night. It wasn't like that in the beginning, so that's why I'm trying to figure out what's going on now."

"Look, I'm sorry that you're unhappy, but this is pretty much how it's going to be. I won't always be as busy as I was this past month, but being a pastor is a twenty-four-hour job. You never know what's going to happen or when you're going to be called."

"Then I guess I don't have a choice but to get used to it. Is that what you're saying?"

Curtis pulled Mariah up from the chair and held her hands. "It's not that you don't have a choice, baby, but I need you to stand by me. I need you to support what I'm trying to do as a minister. And more than anything, I need you to keep loving me."

"I do love you, Curtis. You know that. But I still feel like something is missing. I mean maybe it's time we started thinking about a baby. I know you said you wanted to wait awhile so we could have some time alone, but I think it's time for us to start right now."

"Yeah, but the thing is, you still really haven't bonded with Alicia, and now with the way she's acting, she'll really be upset if we brought a new baby into the picture."

"But how am I supposed to bond with her when she's only around every other weekend? And even then she doesn't say any more than what I ask her."

"I don't know. But I still think having a baby will push her away even further. So it's just not the right time," he said, walking away from her and back around his desk.

"Well, when will it be?"

"I don't know. Maybe next year. Maybe sooner."

"What difference is a few months going to make?"

He was really starting to anger her and she couldn't help wondering if Alicia was the real reason he wanted them to hold off on having a baby.

"A few months can make a world of difference when you're talking about the emotional well-being of a child. You know Alicia hasn't been herself, and now she's all of a sudden having problems at school. So the last thing I want is to make her even more rebellious."

"So that's your final decision? We have to wait until next year?"

"I'm sorry, but yes."

"Fine, Curtis."

Mariah grabbed her tote and turned toward the door. It was all she could do to keep from crying.

"Baby, wait," he said, walking toward her. "I know you're upset, but I really need you to understand why we have to take our time with this."

She turned and faced him, tears flowing down her cheeks. She couldn't remember the last time she'd felt so unhappy.

Curtis pulled her into his arms. "Baby, why are you crying? I mean, is having a baby right away that important to you?"

"Yes. It is."

Curtis sighed deeply. "Okay, I'll tell you what. Give me a few months to see if I can help Alicia with whatever it is she's going through, and then we'll start trying."

Mariah still didn't see why they had to wait. Especially since she knew he wasn't going to make any real attempt at rebuilding his relationship with Alicia. These days he seemed to have an excuse for everything, and Mariah wondered when the man she married was going to show up again. She wondered because this certainly wasn't the same man she'd fallen in love with and made a commitment to.

"Is that okay with you?" he asked. "Can you at least wait that long?"

"Fine. Whatever you want, Curtis."

"It's not just about me, because I want us both to agree on this."

"If we have to wait, then we have to wait."

"Thank you, baby, for being so understanding. And I promise you, it won't take as long as you think."

If that were true, then why was her intuition telling her something different?

Why was she feeling like things were only going to get worse between them?

"The only thing my mother ever cared about was smoking her crack pipe," Ebony said to Mariah and the other twenty YGM members in attendance. They were sitting in one of the classrooms located on the educational wing of the church and had been for thirty minutes.

"She never kept food in the house and she never did anything for me or my brother and sister," Ebony continued. "And because I'm the oldest, I had to make sure they had something to eat and clothes to put on their backs. I had to do whatever I could, and that's why I ended up dropping out of school."

"You shouldn't have had to take on your mother's responsibilities, but you will definitely be blessed for taking care of your siblings," Mariah said.

"But, see, that's what I don't understand, Sister Black. I don't understand why I had to be born into this situation to begin with. I mean, why couldn't I have had a mother like you or some other woman who cares about people? Why couldn't I have been given two parents who are married to each other and who are working hard to take care of their children?"

These were the types of questions that always bothered Mariah because there were never any real answers. It especially bothered her when the questions came from someone like Ebony, a highly intelligent eighteen-year-old who was currently enrolled in a GED program but clearly belonged at a top university. It was hard to explain that everything happened for a reason, and that joy really did come in the morning the way the Bible promised.

But Mariah tried to answer as best as she could. "I don't know why you ended up with the life you have or even why I grew up the way I did, but I do know that if you stay prayerful and keep your faith in God, everything will work out the way it's supposed to. I'm a living witness to all that I'm saying. I grew up on the West Side of Chicago with five brothers and sisters and we barely had food to eat. And it wasn't because my mother didn't care about us or because she did drugs. It was simply because she had six children and never got help from either of the two men she conceived us with. But she's the first one to admit that she never should have kept having children, knowing that the men in her life were no good and that she wasn't married to either of them. My life back then was hard, but it still didn't stop me from doing the best I could in school or from going to college. And even though we were poor, that ended up being a blessing, because that's how I qualified for all the financial aid I received. I majored in accounting and eventually became the director of grants and funding at the largest social service agency here in Chicago. And of course, that's where I met my husband."

"And now you're livin' as large as you wanna be," Rayshonna said. "And married to that fine ole Pastor Black."

All the girls laughed at Rayshonna. She was the comedian of the group and the liveliest.

"You're terrible," Mariah said teasingly.

"I'm just callin' it the way I see it, Sister Black. You got it like that, and you know I'm tellin' the truth."

"Well, I appreciate your observation, Miss Rayshonna," Mariah said. "But I will say this, it's not just about money and material possessions, it's about being happy. I always dreamed of having nice things, because I went without so many necessities when I was a child. But being happy and content is what's truly important."

Mariah wanted to make sure they understood that having a beautiful home, nice clothing, and a luxury vehicle didn't mean a thing if you weren't happy. She'd known that for years, but now she was learning it firsthand, in her marriage to Curtis. Although she hoped they were just going through a phase and that it would pass pretty quickly.

"I just hope I'll be able to go to college, too, once I get my GED," Ebony said. "I only have one more test to take next month, and then I'll have it."

"Good for you," Mariah said, and everyone applauded.

"Way to go, girlfriend," Rayshonna said, giving Ebony a high-five.

"I heard that," Shamira, a seventeen-year-old mother of two, said.

"We're going to celebrate big-time when you get it," Carmen insisted.

"That we will," Mariah guaranteed. "I'm not sure what we're going to do exactly, but we'll make sure it's something special."

"Now I can't wait until I get mine," Carmen said, smiling.

"You will," Mariah said. "You'll be finished with it before you know it."

Mariah's heart went out to all of the girls, but she had a very special place in it for Carmen. She was such a sweetheart and an amazing survivor. Her father had shot and killed her mother right in front of her when she was only five, and she'd lived with an aunt who physically abused her until she was twelve. Carmen had even shown everyone the print of an iron on her back, which was a result of her aunt chasing her. But eventually her aunt was reported by a neighbor and the authorities removed Carmen from the home. Then, as fate would have it, she was assigned to Sister Fletcher, a foster mother who was a member of the church. Sister Fletcher's husband was deceased and her biological children lived out of state, so she gave Carmen all the love and attention she needed. But when Carmen turned seventeen, she still dropped out of school. Sister Fletcher had told Mariah about it three months ago, and Mariah had suggested that Carmen attend the ministry meetings. Now she was doing a lot better emotionally and was attending an alternative school, working to complete her GED.

The girls spoke among themselves and Mariah noticed that it was almost time for them to end their session.

"I have something that I want all of you to read before our meeting next week," Mariah said, passing out booklets to each of them. "It's a book that specifically discusses how to find success in all areas of your life. It talks about the fact that you have to first believe in God, then believe in yourself, and then believe in whatever you're trying to accomplish. Because if your ability to believe manifests in that order, you'll quickly start to see positive changes in your life."

Everyone flipped curiously through the material and Mariah was glad they seemed interested.

"I think you'll enjoy reading this, and the other thing I want to keep encouraging all of you to do is stay prayerful. Prayer is very powerful when it comes from the heart, and I think you'll see God making a major difference in your life as you continue to communicate with Him. Prayer can give you so much peace, and regardless of what you are going through, God does hear all that you ask for."

"Then why doesn't He answer all the time?" Ebony wanted to know.

"Actually, He does, but it's just that He doesn't always answer when or in the way *we* want Him to. But He does always answer when the time is right. Sometimes we want what we want when we want it, but certain things aren't right for us. And then sometimes we want things to happen instantly, when it would be so much better if they happened at a later date. But that's just human nature, and it's perfectly normal to feel that way."

"I hear what you're saying, but it's still hard to understand sometimes," Ebony said.

"I know, but as you continue building your relationship with God, your understanding of Him and how He works will improve more and more."

"I agree," Carmen said matter-of-factly.

"Well, girls, unless you have something else you'd like to share this evening, I think it's time we dismissed."

Everyone agreed, the girls hugged Mariah and each other and then left the room.

Mariah couldn't help thinking about the advice she'd just given Ebony. Especially since she hadn't taken it herself when she met Curtis. She'd prayed over and over, asking God to make Curtis her husband, and it had happened. But now she wondered if God had actually blessed her with Curtis or simply allowed the marriage to happen because she wanted Curtis so badly. At the time, she hadn't cared about any possible consequences or even considered the fact that some people weren't nearly who they claimed to be, and she hoped she wasn't going to be sorry for it. She was such an optimist and had been told many times that she was much too trusting of people in general, but she couldn't help who she was. She'd always tried to do the right thing, and she always treated people the way she wanted to be treated. She couldn't understand why Curtis or anyone else would want to take advantage of that.

But maybe she was blowing her problems with Curtis way out of proportion. Maybe she was being too hard on him about all the time he was spending away from home, too. Because it wasn't like he had a normal nine-to-five. It wasn't like he could leave his work at the office when he was senior pastor of a church like Truth Missionary. The man had weekly sermons to write and preach, prayer service and Bible study to teach, the sick and shut-in to see, and sometimes he did revivals for out-of-town churches when they requested him. Of course, sometimes he received help from his associate ministers and deacons, but he really did have a whole lot of responsibilities. Maybe Curtis really was as busy as he claimed. Maybe she was expecting far too much from him and needed to find other things to do with her time, just as her mother had suggested. Her mother had also told her not to keep nagging Curtis, but that's exactly what she'd been doing. And it wasn't like he was staying out till the wee hours of the morning, anyway.

She decided that she wasn't giving up on him or their marriage. She was going to have faith in the love they shared and trust that everything would work out in the long run.

She decided it was best to stay positive and give her husband the total benefit of the doubt.

Chapter 9

Curtis drove through the intersection of Golf and Roselle over in Schaumburg. He was headed west toward Barrington and was on his way to visit some of his minister friends. He was also talking to Adrienne.

"You miss me?" he asked.

"You know I do," she said. "We've been together almost every other night, but I guess I just can't get enough of you. I haven't felt this good in a long time."

"Baby, neither have I, and if I hadn't promised the boys that I'd get together with them, I'd spend this evening with you, too. We only meet once a month, though, so I didn't want to renege on them."

"It's not a problem. But we are still on for Saturday, right?"

"Absolutely. Mariah is going shopping downtown with one of her girlfriends, so I'm all yours for the entire day."

"And you're sure your friend is okay with us using his condo?"

"Positive. I've already cleared it with him, and I'll be getting the key when I see him tonight."

"I can't believe it's in the same suburb where we used to rent ours."

"It's practically déjà vu."

"We were so happy back then."

"I know, baby, and I promise you we're going to be even happier this time around."

"That's what I keep hoping, Curtis, but I'm so afraid. I mean, I hear what you're saying, and I want to believe you, but I don't think I'll be completely comfortable with any of this until I see your divorce papers. And I think it's only fair for you to know that there is no way I can even consider leaving Thomas until then."

Curtis didn't like the sound of that. He didn't like it because more than anything, he wanted the deacon out of the picture. He needed him out of the way so that he could gain better control of Adrienne's emotions. He wasn't sure what he would have to do to convince her to get rid of the man, but he had to come up with something.

"I know I didn't do right by you before, but I'm telling you, baby, I'm totally committed to you for the rest of my life. Right now I'm in this situation with Mariah and you know it has to be handled very carefully, but I will divorce her."

"That's fine, but all I'm saying is that I won't leave Thomas until you show me proof in black and white."

"But don't you think it would look a lot better if you went ahead and divorced the deacon at least a few months before I divorce Mariah? Otherwise everyone will know we were planning this whole thing, and that we've been seeing each other all along."

"Maybe, but I can't do that. So as much as I love you, Curtis, and as much as I want to spend the rest of my life with you, these are the conditions."

"If that's how it has to be, then that's how it has to be."

"It does. And just so we're on the same page, we agreed last

Tuesday on the six-month time frame, so that means you have until the beginning of October to file for your divorce."

Curtis wanted to laugh out loud. He couldn't believe what he was hearing or that she was giving him an ultimatum so early in the relationship. She was acting as if they had a written contract, and Curtis could tell she was dead serious.

But he knew what he had to do. He had to keep seeing her three to four times a week like he used to. He'd make love to her in every way imaginable. So much so that she would no longer be able to think straight. She was trying very hard to stay in control, but when he finished with her on Saturday, she wouldn't know what hit her. She would beg to be with him under any circumstances.

But he decided to go along with what she was saying just to halt any confusion.

"The beginning of October it is. Or before if I can make it happen."

"I hate to be so technical about this, but it's the only way I can protect myself."

"I understand. But hey, I'm just pulling up to the condo, so I'd better go," he said, parking in the driveway behind a blue Jaguar and right next to a burgundy Escalade. There was also a black Lexus 430 parked closer to the garage.

"So I'll speak to you tomorrow?" she asked.

"I'll call you first thing in the morning when I get to the church. And don't you work too late."

"I'll try not to, but I'm working on this special marketing report that has to be finished by Monday morning. And it's not like I can come in on Saturday to do it."

"No, you definitely can't do it then, because you'll be with me until sundown."

"You know I'm looking forward to it. But I'll let you go, and you have a good time tonight."

"I love you, baby."

"I love you, too."

Curtis stepped out of the car, strolled up to the front door, and knocked.

"Hey, Rev, glad you could make it," Tyler said, opening the door of his four-bedroom condo. He was Curtis's closest minister friend and confidant.

"Me, too, man," Curtis said, hugging him.

Curtis shed his blazer, loosened his tie, and joined the three men at the glass table.

"You want anything to drink?" Tyler asked.

"Whatcha got?"

"Alize, Zinfandel, and I think there's some sort of Merlot in the fridge, too."

"Now, you Negroes know I don't drink intoxicating beverages," Curtis said.

"Oh yeah, that's right," Malcolm said, turning up a bottle of Miller Genuine Draft. "We forgot. You don't *drink*, you just sleep with as many women as you can."

They all roared with laughter.

"Well, I never said I was perfect, and y'all know from experience that some things are just too hard to give up," Curtis told them.

"I know that's right," Cletus said. "Because if I didn't have all those fine women at my church, I don't know what I would do. And that's the truth."

"God *is* good," Tyler added. "I mean, just look at this beautiful condo the church is paying for, and all I had to do was tell them I needed a retreat away from home. I told them that I needed somewhere I could go meditate, relax, and clear my head from time to time, and they totally went for it. They even agreed to purchase one this large because I told them we could also use it for out-of-town ministers and their families who were visiting our church. That way, they wouldn't have to stay at some hotel."

"Man, you got it made, because I would love to ask for something like this from Truth," Curtis said, admiring his surroundings. "But since I've only been there nine months, I figure I'd better take it slow when it comes to asking for more perks."

"You doin' the right thing, because you don't want them gettin' antsy about anything," Malcolm agreed. "If you ask for too much too fast, they'll start gettin' all suspicious on you."

"I second that motion," Cletus said. "Because the name of the game is trust. And once you have them trusting you one hundred percent, you can ask for practically anything you want. They'll be loving you and eating out of the palm of your hand without you even asking them to."

"And the women will do more than that," Tyler said. "They'll do any and everything you ask just because you're *the pastor*."

"I've got the four of mine so caught up that they all know about each other," Cletus said. "They pretend like they don't, but they all know exactly what's going on. And now I've gotten them so under control they're on a schedule."

"Man, you are too crazy," Malcolm said, cracking up.

"What kinda schedule?" Curtis asked, reaching inside a bowl of beer nuts.

"All four of them have a certain week of every month. I usually see them on Mondays, since that's my day off, and they each know which Monday is theirs."

"You have got to be kidding!" Tyler exclaimed, lifting a piece of pizza.

"I'm serious, man. Just like the mass choir sings on the first Sunday, the male chorus sings on the second, the young adults on the third, and the children on the fourth, I've got my women lined up the same way. If I didn't, how would I keep all of 'em straight?"

"You're a trip," Tyler said. "And if I were you I'd watch out before I ended up gettin' busted."

"No, see the difference between the three of y'all and me is that I stick with the young, dumb, and naïve ones," Cletus boasted. "That way, all you have to do is take 'em to a decent hotel and throw 'em a few dollars every now and then. After that, you have total control."

"You know, man, you might have something there," Curtis said. "Because now that I'm back with Adrienne—"

"What do you mean, now that you're back with Adrienne?" Tyler interrupted. "Last we heard, you'd seen her at some church concert but weren't planning to call her."

"Yeah," Malcolm teased. "You were going to be Mr. Nice and Faithful to your new wife, if I remember correctly."

"That's right," Cletus joked. "You were going to walk the straight and narrow until death do you part."

"Lord knows I tried, but it didn't work," Curtis admitted. "Anyway, we got together for dinner and then this past week I took her to a hotel a few times. But now she's ridin' me about divorcing Mariah."

"Already?" Tyler asked.

"Well, I sort of told her that I would do it in six months."

"You what?" Tyler exclaimed.

"Are you serious?" Cletus chimed in. "You really want to divorce that fine-ass Mariah?"

"No, I'm not divorcing anybody, but if I hadn't promised Adrienne that I would, she never would have started seeing me again. So I did what I had to do, but now she's issuing all these ultimatums."

"Man, you couldn't pay me to be in your shoes six months from now. That's for doggoned sure," Malcolm said.

"Me neither," Cletus said. "And I'd like to know exactly what you plan on doing about it."

"I don't know, but I'll think of something by then. Have to."

"You'd better," Tyler said. "Because somehow I don't think a woman like Adrienne will accept rejection all over again. I mean, you just don't keep playing with a woman who loves you the way Adrienne loved you before and obviously still loves you now."

"If I were you, I'd watch my back," Cletus said.

"Man, I don't think it's that serious," Curtis said confidently, but deep down he knew he had to craft something suitable before October. For the life of him he didn't know what excuse he could come up with, but he knew it had to be good. It had to be something that Adrienne would be pleased with.

"Alright, don't say we didn't try to warn you," Cletus said. "And it's because of mess like this that I don't deal with real women. They require way too much work, and it's so much easier when you stick with twenty-year-olds. As a matter of fact, once they turn twenty-five or so, I don't have much use for 'em."

"Well, as far as I'm concerned, I think you would all feel a whole lot safer if you stuck with one mistress," Tyler said. "I might dabble every now and then, but for the most part I stick with my wife and my main girl."

"I agree," Malcolm said. "One good mistress is more than adequate when you have a wife at home. And the only time I tend to stray is when I just can't help it. Because everyone here knows what it's like when certain out-of-town churches come to visit or you visit some out-of-town church and there's that certain woman who you just can't take your eyes off of."

"Yeah, I hear what you're saying, because even though I've dealt with multiple women in the past, I'm going to try to stick with just one from now on," Curtis said. "And I've definitely learned my lesson about dealing with women inside my own church. So that's totally off-limits."

"Well, I'm sticking with my four," Cletus argued.

"We don't doubt that," Tyler teased. "But hey, on a different note, Curtis, man, did you talk to your officers about installing those ATM machines and offering direct deposit to your members?"

"Man, yeah. But they weren't too receptive. And two of the older deacons practically lost it. They acted like I was planning to commit a felony or somethin'."

"I'm sorry to hear that, because when I spoke with mine, they wanted to know more. They also didn't see a problem with us hiring financial planners," Tyler said.

"But, see, that's the thing with your officers, they hired you to lead the church, and they're allowing you to do it," Curtis acknowledged. "And even though I have a lot of young officers and a few from the old church, they're too afraid to stand up for what they believe in. Some of them are a little on the conservative side, too."

"Then what you have to do is find some skeletons," Cletus said.

"Meaning what?"

"Meaning you need to talk to some of those gossip columnists at your church. Every congregation has 'em, and I'm sure they'll be more than happy to tell you what they know about your little deacon board. Because you can bet your last dollar that every one of 'em has something in his past or something he's doing right now that would give you grounds to make him step down from the board. And push come to shove, I would hire a private investigator if I had to."

"I really hadn't considered anything like that, but you might have a point," Curtis agreed, and wished he'd thought of that himself. If he could get rid of Deacon Thurgood and Deacon Winslow, he'd be halfway to the finish line.

"You've got to do what you have to do when you're dealing with some of these fools. Otherwise you'll be fighting a losing battle for all eternity," Cletus said matter-of-factly.

"Yeah, you do have to get rid of the ones who won't go along with the program," Malcolm said. "I did that five years ago, and I haven't had any problems ever since."

"It's a shame, but they're right, Curtis," Tyler said. "You have to get a group of men who will let you do what you think is best when it comes to running *your* church. You need to make sure that at least ninety-five percent of your officers are pro-Curtis Black before you try to approach them with that ATM and direct deposit proposal again. But you do need to take care of it at some point, because if you can get the direct deposit thing going, Cletus and Malcolm can show you how to funnel some of it into your own account."

"And in the future, you need to make sure that every deacon and trustee you appoint is a very able lieutenant. You have to make sure they have the balls to back you up in front of anybody," Cletus said.

Curtis nodded. "I should have done that when I was at Faith, because if I had, I might still be pastor over there."

"You probably would be," Tyler said. "Because it sounds like your main rival was Deacon Jackson, and it's not that hard to get rid of one man."

Curtis was glad he had three true friends in his age range who were successful senior pastors. Each of them was the man he wanted to be when he grew up. They were the men he was on his way to being before he was kicked out of the pulpit. Curtis had always taken great pride in knowing that he was on top of things and that he had a good head on his shoulders, but Tyler, Malcolm, and Cletus were on a different level. They'd all been in their positions for eight or more years and each had his entire church under command. They also had a ton more members than Curtis. Tyler, Curtis's knight in shining armor, had over ten thousand members. Malcolm had around eight, and Cletus had just over six. They were the true definition of success, and Curtis had learned a long time ago that if a person truly wanted to be successful they needed to network with those who were doing much better than them. They needed to watch and learn from people who were already what and where they aspired to be.

"So which flick are we going to indulge tonight?" Cletus asked, walking over to Tyler's brand-spanking-new forty-two-inch plasma TV.

"Man, I hadn't even noticed your new screen," Curtis said, turning around. "How much did that set you back?"

"It set *New Hope* back about seven grand, and the thing is, I didn't even ask for it," Tyler said. "One of my trustees is manager at some electronics store, and he suggested to the entire board that it would be nice for me to have the latest technology. So after discussing it, they decided it would make the perfect birthday gift from the church."

"That's how it's supposed to be," Cletus said. "Every church should take care of its pastor before it does anything else."

"I do have to admit, they *are* very generous to my family and me," Tyler said. "Tina thinks the world of just about everyone at the church, and my two daughters feel the same way."

"I can see why," Curtis said. "My congregation feels the same way about Mariah and me, too, and it does give you a good feeling."

"So which one will it be, boys?" Cletus reiterated, flipping through a stack of DVDs. "Or maybe we should order pay-per-view through the satellite."

"Man, you must be crazy," Tyler said. "You know the title of the movie will show up on the bill and the bill goes straight to the church."

"Oh, that's right. My bad, brother."

"Wouldn't that be somethin'," Malcolm said, laughing.

"So I think you'd better pick one of those in that stack," Tyler said.

Cletus flipped through them again and said, "*Beautiful Black Bunnies* it is."

Chapter 10

"Mom, do you think James will take me to the father-daughter dance in a couple of weeks?" Alicia asked, leaning against the island. At first she'd decided not to go, but after Danielle practically begged her to change her mind, she did. And she had another motive, too.

"I'm sure he would be honored, but are you sure you don't want to ask your father?" Tanya said, tossing a bowl of lettuce. They were just preparing to sit down for dinner as soon as James came back downstairs.

"No, because, like always, he's probably too busy."

Alicia didn't want her father to escort her anyway, and she was going to make sure to brag to him about her night out with James just so it would piss him off. She wanted him to know, for a change, what it felt like to be disappointed.

"You won't know unless you ask him," Tanya said.

"But, Mom, I don't want Daddy to take me. And if that's who has to do it, I won't go at all. James is the one who spends time with me and who takes my friends and me anywhere we want to go. He even takes us with him to see the Bears and the Bulls when they play at home."

"I understand that, Alicia, and I'm glad you appreciate James as much as you do, but I still don't want you to overlook your father. I know he's made some mistakes, but this might be a good opportunity for you to spend some time with him alone. Especially since that's what you've been saying you want."

"I did, but now I'm through with him. I don't care if I ever see him again, and even when I get married one day, I'm having James walk me down the aisle," Alicia said, and felt like bawling. She hated her father for neglecting her the way he was, and she was going to make him pay for it. She didn't want to use James to punish her father, because she did genuinely love James, but she just didn't know what else to do to get her father's attention.

"I think you should talk to James about it to see what he thinks."

Alicia took the salad bowl and sat it on the table near the patio doors. Then she brought over a pan filled with warm garlic bread. Her mother had fixed her famous lasagna and Alicia couldn't wait to eat some of it.

"By the way, I called your counselor today, and he said you haven't missed one class this week, and that you've turned in all of your history assignments," Tanya said. "So that's why, even though you're still grounded, I'm okay with you going to the dance."

Alicia didn't know what to say. She was a little perturbed that her mother saw a need to keep checking up on her, but she wasn't going to make a big deal out of it. Maybe last week she would have, but not after chatting with Julian on-line a couple of days ago. He'd told her that life would be a lot easier if she simply went to class and did her homework. That way, her parents wouldn't have anything to complain about, and they wouldn't have a reason to keep punishing her. She hadn't agreed at first, but there were two things he'd said that had made her rethink her position. He'd told her that even though she was angry, she needed to remember everything her mother had gone through with her father and be thankful that James was the sort of stepfather that treated her like his own. He told her that, to him, it seemed like her mother and James were always there for her and that she should work very hard at trying to appreciate that.

She still didn't like the fact that her mother was trying to control her life, but she had to agree with what Julian said. Her mother *had* been a good wife to her father, and she'd always gone out of her way to be a good mother. When she was married to her father and even now that she was married to James. So Alicia decided she was going to do the right thing when it came to school, but she wasn't going to let her father off so easily.

"Boy, that smells even better than before I went upstairs," James said, playfully yanking Alicia's ponytail as he walked by her.

"Stop it," Alicia said, laughing.

Tanya smiled at both of them and sat down at the table. Alicia and James did the same.

"Do you want to say grace, Alicia?" Tanya asked.

They all held hands and closed their eyes. "Dear Lord, thank You for my mom, thank You for James, and thank You for the food we're about to receive. Amen."

Tanya and James spoke in unison. "Amen."

"This is still sort of hot," Tanya said, scooping out a square of lasagna and placing it on James's plate. Then she put a piece on Alicia's and then hers.

"So how was school today?" James said, picking up the tongs inside the salad bowl.

"Didn't Mom tell you?"

"Tell me what?"

"That I haven't missed any more classes, and I've turned in all of my history homework."

"No, she didn't, but I'm really glad to hear that, because I was starting to worry about you."

"I think we were all worried," Tanya said.

Alicia knew her mother was including her father when she said "all," but Alicia knew he didn't care one way or the other. The only thing he cared about were his precious little Mariah, that new church of his, and how much more money he could get.

"I still scheduled a counseling session for us next week, though," Tanya said.

"Not with Daddy, too, I hope."

"Yes, with Daddy, too."

Alicia pursed her lips.

"It's for you, him, and me," Tanya continued. "And in the future, we can include James and Mariah if you want."

Mariah? For what? She wasn't Alicia's mother, and she was never going to get a chance to be. So why would she possibly need to come to counseling with them? If Alicia had anything to say about it, it would never happen. Mariah was an outsider, and it was best for her to stay where she belonged: outside.

But Alicia wasn't going to share her thoughts out loud.

"James, can you take me to the father-daughter dance in a couple of weeks?"

"Well, pumpkin, you know I'd be happy to, but I don't want to disrespect your father either."

"You won't, because I'm sure he already has other plans."

"Have you asked him?"

"No. He always has other plans."

"But I still think you should ask him. You know? Just out of respect."

"Why? Don't you want to take me?"

"Yes. You know I do, but it's just that I think you should at least acknowledge your father."

"But I don't want him to take me."

"I think you do, and you're only saying that because you want to hurt him."

Alicia didn't know how he knew what she was thinking, but he had her pegged to a tee.

Tanya looked on in silence.

"Look, Alicia," James said, tearing a piece of garlic bread. "I know you haven't been too happy with your father lately, but I think you need to give him another chance. I'm not trying to make excuses for him, but we all make mistakes from time to time."

"Daddy makes mistakes *all* the time, and ever since he married Mariah, he hasn't cared one thing about me." Alicia swallowed hard, trying to stop tears from rolling down her face.

"That's not true, Alicia," Tanya said. "Your father may have a strange way of showing it, but he does love you. It's the one thing I can say about him."

"Then why doesn't he act like it?" Alicia said, wiping her face, her chest elevating.

"We can't answer that, sweetheart, but don't ever think that he doesn't love you," Tanya said, holding Alicia's hand. "Because he truly, truly does."

"So why don't you give him a call when we finish dinner," James said. "If he says he can't take you, then two Saturdays from now, it'll be you and me out on the town. But I at least want you to ask him."

None of this had turned out the way Alicia had wanted. She'd planned on having James escort her, and then she was planning to parade tons of photos of them in front of her father. She wanted him to know how it felt to be left out and replaced. But now James and her mother had made her realize that she did want her father to take her. He probably already had some previous church engagement, but she would call him like James suggested.

They continued eating and discussed the fact that Easter was this weekend, that there were only six more weeks of school, and that they were taking a family vacation to Disney World at the end of June. Alicia was even more excited when they told her Danielle could go with them to Orlando.

After Alicia finished loading the dishes in the dishwasher, she went up to her room to call her father.

"Hello," Mariah answered.

Alicia rolled her eyes toward the ceiling.

"Hi, Mariah. Is my daddy there?"

"No, honey, he's not. He got together with some other ministers for a meeting, but you can call him on his cell phone if you need him right away."

"Okay, then, thanks."

"Alicia?" Mariah said.

"Yes."

"Can I talk to you for a minute?"

About what? was all Alicia could think to say.

"What did you wanna talk about?"

"Well, basically I just wanted to tell you that I'm here for you if you ever need me, and that I'm hoping you can start spending more time over here with your father and me."

What Alicia wanted was to spend more time with her father. Not with Mariah.

"Okay," Alicia said just to hurry her off the phone.

"And while I know I haven't been your stepmother for very long, I'm really hoping that we can start building a relationship with each other. Maybe we could go shopping together. Summer will be here pretty soon, so maybe we could get you a whole new summer wardrobe."

"Actually, my mom is taking me shopping for summer stuff next week."

"Well, I know it's a little late, but have you already gotten an Easter outfit?"

Duh. Easter was only three days from now, so what did she think?

"My mom bought my Easter dress sometime last month, but thanks for asking."

"Well, maybe we can do something else. I remember you saying that you weren't coming to stay with us this weekend since it's Easter, so can we expect you next weekend?"

"Actually, I have a father-daughter dance to go to, and I want my mom to help me get ready for it," Alicia bragged, but felt like kicking herself because she hadn't wanted Mariah to know about the dance until after she'd told her father.

"Oh, is that why you're calling your father? He'll be so excited. I never got to do things like that with my father when I was growing up, because he never came around."

Then, that means you know exactly how I feel, don't you? Alicia thought.

"Well, it was good talking to you, Mariah, but I'd better go so I can call my daddy."

"It was good talking to you, Alicia, and remember what I said, you can call me anytime."

"Okay, bye."

Alicia pressed the flash button and dialed her father's cell number.

"Hi, baby girl," he answered.

"How'd you know it was me?"

"Caller ID of course."

"Oh."

"So how are you?"

"I'm fine, but who's making all that noise in the background?"

"Those are just some other ministers having a few laughs. But hold on a minute while I go into another room."

They sounded like wild animals instead of ministers, but she wasn't going to tell her father what she was thinking.

"Okay, so to what do I owe this precious phone call?" he said.

"My school is having a ninth-grade father-daughter dance on the twenty-sixth, and I wanted to see if you could take me."

"Of course I can, baby girl. You know I wouldn't have it any other way. What time is it?"

"Six o'clock, and you have to wear a tux."

"Well, you know I already have one of those, so I'm all set. But what about you? Do you already have a dress for it?"

"No, but I'm sure Mom will take me out this weekend to get one."

"Well, if she can't, you know Mariah would be happy to take you, too."

"No, that's okay, I'll just have Mom do it."

"Well, I'm glad you called me, baby girl, because I haven't heard from you since you spent the weekend with us. I'm sorry for yelling at you, but the last thing I want to see is you failing one of your classes. You're too smart for that, and I won't be content until you've graduated from high school and gone on to college. I've been saving for your college education since the day you were born, and even though I had a setback when I left Faith, I never took any money from that account. So you getting the right education is very, very important to me."

Alicia was a little shocked at what she was hearing. She'd heard him mention a college fund when she was younger, but she hadn't heard him talk much about it in the last few years. At least he cared about something that had to do with her, and while she still wasn't happy with him, she was elated to know that he was saving money for her education. Most of her friends couldn't care less about their parents saving for college, but Alicia knew just how expensive it actually was.

"I know it is, Daddy, and that's why I've turned in all of my history assignments." She wasn't sure if he knew about her skipping an entire week of math classes or not, so there was no sense in bringing it up.

"I'm glad to hear it. So tell me, how's your mom doing?"

"She's fine."

"Tell her I said hello, and that if she needs money to get your dress, she can call me."

"I will."

"And, Alicia?"

"Yes."

"You do know that I love you, right?"

"Yes."

"I know I haven't always done the right things, but next to God, you really are the most important person in my life."

"Then why don't we spend time together the way we used to before you married Mariah?" she asked, though she hadn't meant to.

"Is that what you think? That Mariah is the reason I haven't been able to see you as much?"

"Yes, because we did a lot of stuff together before you met her."

"Well, let Daddy tell you a little secret. Mariah complains almost every day because she says I'm not spending any time with her either. So, baby girl, it has absolutely nothing to do with her and everything to do with the fact that I'm trying to get situated at my new church. I have the same responsibilities that I had when I was pastor at Faith and a whole new set of duties to go along with them."

"Well, I still wish you'd make more time for me, because I miss seeing you," Alicia said, and wondered if her father was telling the truth. If he was, she was glad to know that he hadn't placed Mariah higher than her on his list of priorities.

"I miss you too, and I'm going to try to do better, starting with your dance next week."

"Okay, well, I'd better let you go, Daddy. But don't forget, it's at six o'clock on Saturday. Not this Saturday, but the next one."

"I won't forget. I'll have Whitney put it on my schedule, and I'll also put it in my Palm Pilot. And, baby girl, you know you should come hear your daddy preach this Sunday for Easter."

"I already told Mom and James that I was going with them to our church," she said, knowing full well her mother and stepfather wouldn't have minded one way or the other.

"Oh well, I just thought I'd ask. Maybe another time then. Also, I guess I'll see you next week, because your mom left me a voice message a few days ago saying we have a counseling session scheduled."

"Yeah, we do."

"Okay, well, I'll see you then, baby girl."

"Okay. Good-bye, Daddy."

"I love you."

"I love you, too."

Alicia hung up the phone feeling happier than she had in a long time. She couldn't wait to tell Julian how good his advice had been and how she was finally working things out with her parents. She was still sorry that she'd laughed at him that day he'd tried to have phone sex with her, but now at least he wasn't angry anymore. He wasn't angry because she'd called him back the very next night and two other nights thereafter and did everything he told her to do. She'd experienced sensations she didn't even know existed, and she wished she could feel that good all the time.

But two nights ago when they'd chatted on-line, Julian had told her that phone sex was nothing, and that he could make her feel ten times better than that if she wanted him to.

He told her that all she had to do was come to his house for a visit.

But two nights ago when they'd chatted on line Julian had told her that phone sex was nothing, and that he could make her feel ten times better than that if she wanted him to. He told her that all she had to do was come to his house for a visit.

Chapter 11

Right after Mariah pulled the taupe skirt from the sale rack, she checked to see if it was a size 10 and smiled. She and her best friend, Vivian, were standing in the misses department at Saks, down on Michigan Avenue.

"Girl, the one thing I was hoping to find was another one of these skirts, and now it's even on sale," Mariah said.

"You can't beat that. But then, you could afford it even if it was still regular price."

"Girl, please. I'm always looking for bargains just like everyone else."

"Yeah, right, but not because you have to, Miss Thing," Vivian teased.

Mariah loved Vivian like a sister. She was down-to-earth, very caring, and told everything exactly the way she saw it. In a word, she told the truth whether a person wanted to hear it or not. And she was beautiful, too. She wore a size 8, and at five eleven she looked more like a supermodel than the web site developer that she was. Her skin was smooth, she had crystal white teeth and a smile that would warm the attitude of an enemy. Even her hairstyle, which was barely one inch in length, was becoming of her.

"You know, V, I'm really glad we decided to go shopping today, because now I know that I really needed to see you," Mariah said, still searching through the sale items.

"I'm glad we did, too, because it's been a long time since we've gotten together. Especially since you married that fine-as-wine minister of yours. But as they say, I ain't mad atcha, because if it were me, I'd be spending all of my time with him, too."

Mariah hadn't told her how scarce Curtis had been the last few weeks or about his not wanting them to have a baby. She wanted to pour her heart out right then and there, but there were too many customers surrounding them. Actually, there were more people than usual shopping in all the stores, since it was the day before Easter. So it was better to wait until they went to lunch.

"Look at this." Mariah held up a to-die-for sleeveless turquoise blouse.

"That's absolutely beautiful. You should definitely try that on."

"I would, but it's a size eight and it's got your name written all over it."

Vivian admired it and pulled out the price tag. "I'm loving it, but this is way too rich for my blood."

"But the question is, do you want it?"

"Girl, I'm not paying sixty dollars for this. And on top of that, it has the nerve to be on sale."

"Give me that," Mariah said, laying it across her arm on top of the skirt she was purchasing for herself.

"You know you don't have to do that," Vivian said.

"I know, but I want to. And if it's okay with you, I don't want to discuss it any further, thank you very much."

"Oh, so now you're running things, I guess?"

"You do catch on very quickly," Mariah said, and they both laughed.

"You know I really appreciate it," Vivian said, hugging Mariah.

"I know, and if you see anything else you want, all you have to do is say the word."

They made their purchases, left Saks, and walked over to Water Tower Place. Once inside Lord & Taylor, Mariah found a pair of fuchsia shoes and matching purse to go with the fuchsia hat she'd ordered from a specialty catalog two months ago. All of her accessories would accent the off-white suit she was wearing to church tomorrow, so for the most part her shopping was complete. Vivian ended up finding the perfect deep teal skirt to go with the blouse Mariah had bought her, and Mariah offered to buy that, too. Now they were sitting inside FoodLife, a unique food court, if you will, filled with a variety of restaurants. Vivian was a devout vegetarian, so they'd both purchased huge salads and bottled water.

"So what do you and Curtis have planned for this evening?" Vivian asked, patting the corners of her mouth with a napkin.

"Not one single solitary thing."

"Okay. Is there something you're not telling me?"

"It's the same thing I told you about when we spoke on the phone a couple of weeks ago. But now he's gone even more than ever before. Even right now I don't have the slightest idea where he is. He mentioned something about going to look at some new cars with one of his minister friends and then doing lunch with him. But I don't believe it, because he just saw Tyler the other night."

"Well, why do you think he would lie?"

"Because he has way too much lost time. He comes in around nine or ten on most nights, and the only reason he came home right after Bible study on Wednesday is because I was all upset."

"Why? What happened?"

"I told him that I wanted us to start a family, but he was adamant about having us wait. He says it's because he wants Alicia to get used to the idea of me being in the picture, and that he wants us to spend more time with her. But now I think he just doesn't want to have a baby with me period."

"Well, you've only been married for a few months, so maybe he just wants to have some time with just the two of you."

"But that's just it, we don't see much of each other at all. He gets up bright and early every morning, works out for an hour, and then heads to the church. And then he doesn't get home until nighttime. Sometimes he shows up early evening, but not very often. It's always some ministers' meeting, some meeting with the deacons, some revival at another church. It's always something. And the one thing I haven't told you is that I accidentally found out that he had a son with a teenager five years ago."

"He what?"

"He has a son, and the only reason I know about it is because Alicia mentioned it when she was arguing with him. But if that hadn't happened, I know he never would have told me."

"I don't know what to say," Vivian said.

"Of course you do, you always have something to say, but you don't want to hurt my feelings. But right now, V, I really need to hear what you think, because I'm not sure what I should do about this."

"Well, first of all, any man who has fathered a child with a teenager and didn't bother to tell his wife certainly can't be trusted. I mean, you just don't hide serious information like that. And now that you're saying he's never at home and doesn't want to have a baby with you, I would have to question what he's really doing when you're not with him. And as much as I hate to say it, Mariah, I would have to wonder what whore he's laying up with."

That was the Vivian that Mariah knew all too well. But even though she'd asked her to say what she thought, hearing her words still hurt terribly.

Vivian obviously noticed. "I didn't mean to be so blunt, but, girl, something doesn't seem right with Curtis. Not based on what you're telling me."

"I know, and I feel so stupid. I feel like I'm some naïve little girl, and I don't understand why I've always had to be so trusting of everyone."

"There's nothing wrong with having a big heart, and it only becomes a problem when someone takes advantage of you."

"The sad part is that I love him so much. He has become my whole world, and now when I complain about what's going on, he tells me I need to find other interests and that he can't run a church and be with me at the same time. Even my mother said I should find other things to do and that I should stop nagging him."

"No disrespect to your mother, girl, but if you're telling me that the only time you see your husband is around bedtime, then you have every right to nag the shit out of him. I know you told me that he wasn't at home as much as he used to be, but I had no idea that this had become an every-night thing."

"Like I said, he is home early on some evenings, but it's usually when I've gone on and on about how alone I feel. He only does it to pacify me, and I always allow it."

"Have you thought about following him?"

"No."

"Well, you should. All you have to do is wait for brother to leave the church and then follow him to his final destination. Because I'm telling you, the only way to catch any man dead in his tracks is to see it with your own eyes. It's the only way you can confront him and prevent him from denying it at the same time."

"I don't know. I just hate having to go to such extremes," Mariah said, folding her arms and feeling defeated.

"But if he's messing around, it's the only way you're going to be able to prove it. I've never been married, but you know I *have* busted a couple of boyfriend-wannabe-players in my time."

But that was just it, Mariah thought, Curtis wasn't some boyfriend, he was her husband. He was the man who stood with her before God and his congregation and took everlasting vows. He was the man who'd said he loved her more than anything and that he wanted to spend the rest of his life with her.

"You know, all I ever wanted in life was to fall in love with the right man, be the best wife I could be, and live happily ever after," Mariah confessed.

"And you deserve nothing less than that. So that's why I'm saying you have to see if Curtis's nightly excuses are legitimate or if he's laying up in a hotel somewhere. And don't get me wrong, I pray that he's been telling you the truth, but if he's not, then you have to give him an ultimatum. Either he can stop messing around or he can sign some divorce papers and pay you alimony."

Mariah cringed at the thought of losing him and wished he would just go back to being the man he was when she met him. That way, she wouldn't have to play detective, trying to find out if he was sleeping with another woman. Although if he was but was willing to stop doing it, she would gladly forgive him. She didn't dare share her thoughts with Vivian, though, because she knew Vivian would think she was crazy.

"When I get home, I'm going to talk to him again," Mariah said.

"That's exactly what I would do, except I wouldn't just talk to him, I'd tell him flat out that you're not going to keep spending all of your evenings by yourself and that you want to start going with him to some of these so-called church events he can't seem to miss. And you know what else? I would have a talk with his ex-wife. You said she seems pretty pleasant, so maybe she'll be willing to shed some light on Curtis. I know he told you that he only messed around on her twice and that that's the reason she divorced him and the reason he lost his church, but the one thing you can always count on is that there are definitely two sides to every story."

"This is true."

But Mariah wasn't too keen on calling Tanya, because the last thing she wanted was for his ex-wife to learn that she and Curtis were having problems. No woman wanted her man's ex-wife or ex-anything to know that there was serious trouble in paradise. Maybe she would call Tanya as a last resort, but she was hoping that there wouldn't be any need for something so drastic.

"If I were you, I wouldn't even take the chance of him not being at home when I got there. I would call him right now and tell him to get his behind home."

Mariah didn't want to do that either, but she went ahead and pulled out her cell phone just so Vivian wouldn't think she was a wimp.

She dialed the house but he wasn't there. She dialed his cell phone and heard it ring four times before his voice mail connected.

She didn't bother leaving a message.

Vivian looked on curiously.

Mariah didn't bother explaining.

Why? Because she knew Vivian was right. She knew she had to confront her husband in a way like never before.

"I still can't believe that after all these years, here I am lying in your arms again," Adrienne said, smiling.

"And just think, this is only the beginning," Curtis said.

It was almost 9 P.M. and they'd been lounging around Tyler's condo since ten that morning. They'd ordered lunch from a nearby restaurant, Italian for dinner, and they'd already made love three times.

"I really didn't mean to stay here so late," Adrienne said.

"Well, you know how time flies. And it flies even faster when you're with the person you want to be with."

"I guess I can't argue with that, because this is clearly the best day I've had in a long time. I finally feel like I know what it's like to be with you for a long period of time again. Remember when we used to spend all those hours together?"

"How could I forget? Those were some of the best times in my life. Which is why I can never, ever . . ." he said, raising Adrienne's chin so she could look at him. "I can never be without you. My soul is so at peace when I'm around you, and no one has ever made me feel that way."

"I'm glad you're comfortable with me, because you know I've always felt that way about you, too. I know it sounds crazy, but at one point I used to think I couldn't live without you. I loved you that much, and that's why I was so depressed when our relationship ended like it did."

"Shhhhh. Baby, please. I know you can't help thinking about that, but from this day forward, let's just try to think about today and all the good times ahead of us."

"Okay, you're right. I promise not to talk about the past if you promise not to ever leave me again."

"You have my word on that."

"I do have to tell you something, though."

"What's that?"

"Today was the first time Thomas questioned me about where I was going."

"You told him you were going shopping with a friend and then to dinner, right? So why would he question that?"

"He's questioning it because I haven't had sex with him since you and I were first together again. And even though I keep trying to act the same toward him, my whole persona is different. I can feel myself avoiding him, and I know he's starting to think something is wrong."

"Well, what did he say when you left this morning?"

"He said he hoped we weren't about to have the same problems we had five years ago."

"I wouldn't worry about that. He's just a little suspicious."

"I know, but we still have a few months to go before I tell him I want a divorce, and pretty soon he'll be questioning me every time I leave the house or every time I come home later than usual."

"That's why I think you should tell him you want a legal separation until that time. That way, you won't have to deal with him at all," Curtis said, kissing her forehead. "You know what I'm saying, baby," he said, hugging her tightly.

He was hoping that maybe all of the deacon's questions would cause Adrienne to feel so uneasy that she'd finally move out and get her own place. Curtis would even help pay all her monthly expenses. Especially since he'd be staying there with her on a part-time basis. He hadn't spent the entire night away from home with another woman, not even when he was married to Tanya, but it was just a matter of time before he did. He'd even considered doing it tonight, but he had a feeling Adrienne wasn't going to agree to it. She'd be too worried about the deacon and what he'd have to say about it.

"Curtis, did you hear me?" she asked.

"What? Yes," he said. It was obvious that he'd been daydreaming.

"Then what did I say?"

"You said . . . well, I don't know exactly, but I heard you," he said, stumbling.

Adrienne pulled away from him. "And that's why you're not getting any more of this either." She drew the covers across her body, smiling.

"Is that a fact?" He pulled her back closer to him and slipped under the sheet with her.

"Yes. It is."

"So you're not going to give Daddy one last piece of dessert before the evening is over?"

"No, because you were ignoring me."

"Okay, I'm sorry. Tell Daddy again what you said."

"I said that if you want me to leave Thomas right now, then you're going to have to file for your divorce a lot earlier than you planned."

She was breaking the mood, and Curtis hated when she got serious on him in the middle of foreplay. It was the one thing he honestly didn't like about her. It was almost as if she did it on purpose, because she knew he couldn't stand it.

"You know I can't file for a divorce this soon after marrying Mariah, because of the church. So I guess you'll have to stay with the deacon until I do."

"I guess I will, but don't keep asking me to leave him if you're not planning to leave Mariah," she said, and moved away from him again. This time she sat up on the side of the bed.

"Look, baby, I'm sorry. But let's not fight, okay? If it bothers you that much, then I won't bring it up again. We'll stick to the plan, and in October we'll both file for our divorces."

"Fine," she said, turning to look at him.

"You are so beautiful, you know that?"

He pulled her on top of him.

They kissed and caressed each other and made love one last time before leaving Tyler's condo.

When they were outside, Curtis pressed Adrienne against her car and kissed her again.

"I love you so much," she said.

"But not more than I love you."

Curtis watched her back out of the driveway and wished there was some way he could end his marriage to Mariah and marry Adrienne. Because at this very moment, that was what he really wanted.

But he knew it was only because his heart and loins were doing his thinking for him.

In reality, he knew he had to keep Mariah, because the church would want him to and because he could control her much better than he could Adrienne. Once upon a time, Adrienne had been just as easy as Mariah, but the more he spent time with Adrienne, the more he could tell she now had a mind of her own. Yes, Adrienne loved him, but she wasn't the same pushover she used to be.

Curtis pulled out of the driveway and thought about something less straining. He thought about the fifteen-hundred-dollar suit he'd seen in *GQ*. He thought about his nine-month-old Cadillac SUV and how it was time for something new. He hadn't decided what he was going to buy, but this time it was going to be something that cost near or in the six figures. It was going to be something people noticed whenever they saw him driving it. They would know he was someone to be respected.

Curtis smiled and began reciting portions of the Easter sermon he was going to preach tomorrow morning.

"Where in the world have you been all day, Curtis?" Mariah asked. They were in the family room now, but she'd been standing right in front of the garage door as soon as she heard him pull inside of it.

"I told you before I left. Tyler and I went car shopping and then we had lunch. And after that I went by his house with him and had dinner with his family."

"Do you think I'm stupid, Curtis?"

"No, baby, I'm telling you the God's honest truth. I wouldn't lie to you about something like this."

"So are you saying that if I pick up the phone and call Tyler's wife, she'll tell me that you were over there?"

"What? Call his wife? Have you lost your mind?"

"No, because I want to know if that's really where you were all evening."

"You are not about to embarrass me, Mariah. Do you want them to think we're having problems and that you don't trust your own husband?"

"No, but I'm sick of you coming up with all these reasons why you have to be gone."

"I'm not just coming up with reasons. I spent the day with Tyler because you said that you and Vivian were going shopping most of the day."

"But I've been back home since around five o'clock. But now it's eleven and you're just now waltzing in here," she said. She was surprised by her own tone and she could tell he was, too.

"And how was I supposed to know when you were going to be back here? What did you want me to do, sit around waiting on you all afternoon?"

"Yes, because I spend every single boring day of my life waiting for you."

"Why are you so upset?"

"Because I'm sick of all your excuses and all your lies, Curtis."

"Lies? I know you're not standing there calling your own husband a liar."

Mariah sighed and turned away from him.

"Wait a minute," he said, grabbing her shoulder. "Don't you ever walk away from me. You started all this madness, now stay here and finish it. So answer me."

"Answer what?" she said, shocked that he'd grabbed her the way he had.

"Are you going to stand there and call me a liar to my face?"

Mariah didn't know how to respond because she didn't want him to become any angrier than he already was. It was probably better to back down, but she just couldn't dismiss everything that Vivian had suggested. She had to stand up for herself or Curtis was never going to stop treating her the way he was.

"I'm not calling you a liar, I just want to know why you're never home and why you always find all these other things to do so you won't have to be with me."

"The bottom line is this, Mariah: When I tell you something, you had better start believing it. And while we're on the subject, let me make myself clear about something else. You're my wife, but you don't have the right to question me about anything. I told you that at the beginning, but you seem to have forgotten. A wife has her place and the Bible clearly states that a wife must submit to her husband. And that's all you need to concern yourself with. Not with where I've been or with what I'm doing."

Yes, she'd heard him speak about that, but until now he'd treated her like she was an equal. Like she was his wife. And she couldn't understand at all why now he was speaking to her like she was beneath him. Almost like he couldn't stand the sight of her.

But she wasn't about to back down to him.

"Are you seeing someone else?" she asked.

"What?" he said, laughing. "Woman, now I know you've lost it. And where is all this really coming from, anyway? All this ranting and raving you're doing? Although, come to think of it, I know exactly where it's coming from. That big, tall, man-looking Amazon you call your best friend."

"This has nothing to do with Vivian," was all she could say.

"Of course it does. It has everything to do with her, and the only reason she's pumped you up like this is because she doesn't have a man herself. She's miserable and lonely, and she wants you to be the same way. And you're crazy enough to fall for it."

"But that's just it, Curtis, I am miserable and lonely, and that's the whole point I'm trying to make."

"Well, if you are, it's your own fault, because I told you to find something to do."

"But what about us? I know you're busy with the church, but, Curtis, it's gotten to the point where you only spend maybe one or two evenings with me a week. And now all of a sudden you're claiming you have to do work on Mondays when you promised me that we'd always do something together on your day off."

"That was before I found out how much work I had to do."

"Well, as much as I hate to say it, I can't go on like this."

"Can't go on? I know you're not trying to threaten me, are you?"

"No, I'm just saying that I can't keep being unhappy like this."

"Have you forgotten that you had nobody before you met me? That is, unless you count that low-life family of yours who've never even seen the inside of a church, let alone gone to one."

Mariah burst into tears.

Curtis walked past her, then glanced back. "I wish you would try to walk out on me and my church. If you do, you'll regret it for the rest of your life. Now this conversation is over."

Chapter 12

Every pew inside Truth Missionary Baptist Church was filled. It was Easter Sunday and there were at least a thousand more people than usual in attendance. Mariah tried not to focus on negative remarks, especially when she was at church, but she couldn't help thinking about her favorite aunt and what she used to say. "I go to church every week of the year, but not on Easter. I don't go because it's the one Sunday that every lukewarm, juke-joint, holy-rollin' Christian is guaranteed to be at church. And all they come for is to show off their new outfits. Then you don't see not one of them again until next year."

Mariah didn't know about the lukewarm, juke-joint part, because it wasn't her place to judge people, but it was amazing how full the church always was on Easter Sunday. There were more colossal hats and loud colors than one could find at the circus. But the saddest part of all was that she'd quickly fallen into the same category. Before she'd met Curtis, she attended a church with only five hundred members and wore the same business suits she wore to work. She never wore hats, and it was highly unusual for her to sport a flamboyant suit like the one she was wearing today. It was doubly unusual for her to match a purse to every pair of shoes that she owned.

She'd had no desire toward dressing to impress, but Curtis had told her that if she was going to be the first lady of his church, she was going to have to act like it. He'd told her that it was up to her to set an example for the rest of the women in the church and that under no circumstances was she to ever dress beneath any of the members. He'd even told her that it was time-out for those nondesigner purses she carried on the weekdays, too, and had personally taken her to buy three new ones. One from Louis Vuitton, one from Coach, and one from the Fendi store. She still remembered how shocked she'd been when she realized he'd spent fifteen hundred dollars in total. It had seemed ridiculous to her at the time, but it wasn't long before she'd acquired those same exquisite tastes. Before she met him, she had no problem with shopping at JCPenney, Lerner's, and, for special occasions, Marshall Field's. But now it didn't feel right unless she frequented Saks, Nordstrom, and Neiman Marcus.

Mariah returned her attention to the morning worship and watched her husband stand up and walk across the pulpit. He was preparing to deliver his Easter message, and this was the first time since marrying him that she didn't want to hear him preach. She hadn't ever felt as hurt and as angry as she had last night, and she didn't know what she was going to do about her situation. She wished she had the courage to pack her bags and leave the way Vivian had suggested when she called her this morning, but she wasn't strong enough to do it. She wanted to be, but a part of her was hoping that maybe Curtis was just going through a phase. Maybe he'd been single for so long that he needed some time to regroup and get used to his new life with her. Maybe he was acting so terribly because of all the stress that came with being a pastor. She wanted to believe all of the above, but she knew none of those reasons was the problem. She knew deep within her soul that Curtis was seeing someone else.

Mariah watched Curtis as he began to speak.

"Oh, what a time, what a time," he said, holding either side of the podium. "Choir, you all are truly singing from your hearts today. Singing for the Lord. Singing for that great and wonderful man who died on Calvary for all your sins and mine. But oh, didn't he get up early one Sunday morning just like he said he would? He rose just like he promised. He stayed true to his word, church," Curtis said, pounding the podium with his fist. "Oh, I tell you, I'm happy today. I'm happy because someone loved us so much, He sacrificed His own life so that we might live eternally."

Curtis spun around three times right where he was standing.

"Give the Lord a great big handclap," Curtis said, following his own instructions.

The congregation applauded loudly.

When it quieted down, Curtis continued.

"You know, the fact that we are so blessed doesn't mean that we're any better or any more of a Christian than the next person. We just as easily could have been drunks or drug addicts, living on the street. And the only difference is that God, for whatever reason, decided to favor each and every one of us here."

Hundreds of members yelled amen. Mariah just didn't have it in her this morning, and she saw Curtis looking over at her, probably trying to figure out why she wasn't into what he was saying.

He turned his Bible to where he wanted to read and gazed back across the congregation.

"I'm not going to preach about Easter Sunday this morning, because just about everyone in here knows that Jesus died on the cross and why he did it. No, what I want to talk about today is something else that also might help you in your daily lives. But before I do, I want my beautiful wife to stand up for a minute."

Mariah hated when he did this. She hated how he always put her on the spot like she was the Queen of England. But since all eyes were planted on her, she didn't have much choice but to do what he'd asked.

"Isn't she looking good today?" he said. "I mean, don't get me wrong, she always looks good, but today she looks especially nice in that off-white and fuchsia."

Amens echoed across the entire church.

"There ain't nothing like having a beautiful wife to look at every day."

"*Amen*, Pastor," one gentleman said loud enough for everyone to hear.

Laughter resonated throughout the congregation.

Mariah smiled graciously and took her seat.

"I hope y'all don't think I'm standing up here bragging, because I'm not. It's just that I love my wife, and I want the whole world to know it," he said, looking at Mariah. "Honey, I just want you to know that I thank God for bringing you into my life. He brought us together for a reason, and I'm just glad about it."

He hugged himself, rocked from side to side, and visually fought back tears.

Mariah felt like going home.

Curtis finally settled himself and said, "Today I want to speak on the subjects of adultery, fornication, and lust."

Mariah heard members yelling everything from "All right now" to "Preach today" to "Fix it up." They couldn't wait to hear what he had to say.

"So if you have your Bibles, please turn with me to First

Corinthians, chapter six. After that, we'll be reading in Jeremiah, Proverbs, and Matthew."

Bible pages rustled until everyone arrived at the designated spot.

"Before we begin, though, I just want to clarify the difference between fornication and adultery. *Fornication*, you see, is the illicit sexual relation between unmarried individuals."

"Uh-huh," a woman sang.

"*Adultery* is when someone has sexual relations with someone other than his or her own spouse."

"True, true," an older gentleman said.

"And when we turn to Matthew, we'll find that even looking at someone with a lustful heart is also an act of adultery."

Mariah wondered when he'd decided to preach this particular sermon and wondered why he was doing it. She wondered if he was trying to convince her that he wasn't an adulterer himself. If he was, he'd soon learn that it was going to take a lot more than some sermon to make her believe what he was saying. It would take even longer for her to ever trust him the way she had when she first met him.

She listened for a few minutes longer, but when she couldn't listen anymore, she tuned Curtis out and waited for his sermon to be over.

It was unfortunate, but for the first time since she'd joined Truth Missionary Baptist Church, she didn't want to be there.

Mariah hung her suit in the walk-in closet and slipped on a two-piece lounging outfit. Curtis eased up behind her and grabbed her around the waist.

"Baby, you haven't said more than two words to me since we got home," he said. "So what's wrong?"

"Nothing. I'm tired and I don't feel well."

"But you didn't say much at the restaurant either."

Mariah ignored him and walked into the master bathroom. She turned on the faucet and squeezed a few drops of facial cleanser inside her palm. She massaged the makeup from her face, went over it with toner, and then saturated her face with moisturizer. When she came back out to the bedroom, Curtis was waiting for her.

"Baby, come sit down for a minute," he said. "Please."

She wondered where this pleasant nature of his was coming from, but she took a seat and didn't say anything.

"I'm sorry for the way I spoke to you last night and for being gone all day with Tyler. I was totally out of line, and I won't ever treat you that way again."

"But it's not just about yesterday, Curtis. It's about every day for the past three weeks or so."

"I know. That schedule at the church is killing me, and after we argued last night, I prayed and asked God to deliver me from it. So what I'm going to do is start delegating more of my duties to my associate ministers and start saying no to some of these outside services. I can't give up everything, but you were right when you said I promised to take every Monday off and spend it with you."

Mariah wanted to stay angry at him, but he was making it harder by the minute. Maybe she'd been wrong about Curtis. Maybe she'd jumped the gun when she'd accused him of sleeping around. Maybe Vivian had pushed her to confront him much too quickly.

"The thing is," he continued, "I took on leadership of a huge church and got married three months later. And before I knew it, I started feeling totally stressed out. Then one thing led to another and before long both you and Alicia were on the back burner."

"It's not that I don't understand all the pressure you're under, because to a certain extent, I do. But you really hurt me last night when you said all those terrible things to me."

"I know, baby, and I'm sorry. I don't know what got into me. I guess I felt like you were trying to interrogate me for no reason."

"But I did have a reason, and I also wanted you to tell me why our marriage was all of a sudden falling apart."

"I know, and like I said, I'm sorry."

He hugged her, and she couldn't help yielding to his embrace. As she closed her eyes, warm tears rolled down her face.

"You know it really bothered me last night when you said you couldn't go on with the way things were," he said. "Because, Mariah, baby, I just couldn't stand it if you actually wanted to leave me."

"I only said that because I'm so unhappy. You know that I love you, Curtis, but it's starting to feel like you don't love me anymore."

"But I do. With all my heart. And that's why I felt compelled to tell the whole church during service this morning."

"But you do know that you embarrassed me, right?" she said, smiling.

"Well, I didn't mean to."

"Well, you did."

"Then I'll try not to do that again. But you are as beautiful as I told them."

Curtis gently leaned her back onto the bed and removed all of his clothing. He helped her remove her lounging set and pulled her toward him.

"You know, baby, I was thinking about what you said," he continued.

"What?"

"You know. That you thought it was time we started a family."

"And?"

"Well, I think it's time, too. At first I didn't, because of Alicia, but I had a long talk with her the other night when she called me about the dance, and I think this will be fine with her."

"So what are you saying?"

"I'm saying that I want you to stop taking your pills as soon as your doctor okays it."

"Curtis, I don't want to do this if you're not really ready."

"But I am ready. I've been thinking about it ever since you came to my office to talk about it. But after last night, I agree that we do need something that will be a part of both of us."

"You just don't know how happy that makes me," she said.

"It makes me happy, too."

They held each other and made passionate love and Mariah couldn't remember Curtis ever being so patient with her. She didn't know if he was serious about everything he'd said or if he was simply trying to appease her for the moment. But she was going to assume he was being genuine. She just didn't see how she couldn't. Especially since she'd married him for better or worse. Vivian wouldn't be too happy, and now Mariah wished she hadn't told her all those awful things about Curtis. She wished Vivian could see them now and that she could've heard how well Curtis explained everything.

She lay there in her husband's arms, exhaling deeply. She was glad to have him back and felt completely relieved.

She couldn't wait to have his baby.

Chapter 13

Mom, let a few more curls drop down in the back," Alicia said, sitting in front of her mother's master bedroom dressing mirror. Tanya was helping her get dressed for the big dance Alicia and her father were going to.

"Don't worry. I will. But first I want to make sure we've got the curls loose enough. Otherwise none of them are going to hang the way they should."

Alicia was tickled pink. She was so excited about the new gown her mother had bought her, and she couldn't wait to see her father in his tux. He always looked handsome in any suit, but still she couldn't wait to see him in evening attire. He would definitely be the best-looking man in the whole gymnasium.

"This is going to be the best night that Daddy and I have ever had together."

"I think it will be, too, so aren't you glad James talked you into calling him?"

"Yeah, but I still wish James could have gone, too. I know I couldn't take both of them, but I sort of feel sorry for him, because he doesn't have his own daughter to take to dances."

"There will be other stuff he can take you to, and I don't think he feels bad at all, because he knows how much you love your father."

Alicia heard what her mother was saying, but she still wondered what it felt like to want children and not be able to have them. Her mother and James didn't talk about it to her, but Alicia had overheard her mother on the phone with her own mother down in Georgia. She'd told her that since they'd been trying for two years straight, they were just going to be thankful for everything else that God had given them and accept the possibility that they would never have a child together. Alicia remembered how sad her mother had sounded, but she never really showed it.

"Mom?"

"Yes," Tanya said, pinning strands of Alicia's hair.

"Am I ever going to have a baby brother or sister? I mean besides the one Daddy had with that girl."

"I don't know. Why? Do you want one?"

"I don't know. I guess it really doesn't matter to me one way or the other. Sometimes I think it would be fun, but some of my friends have little brothers and sisters who get on their nerves."

Tanya laughed. "I'll bet."

"So I guess I'm happy with things just the way they are, as long as I can be with Daddy."

"Well, that's good to hear, because you seemed so upset these past few weeks."

"I know, but I won't ever act like that again. I didn't mean to talk to you the way I did either, Mom."

"Apology accepted. And I also think it was a good idea for us to go back to counseling. Even if it's only once a month."

"I really like Dr. Pulliam. She always makes me feel so comfortable, and she always knows what to say."

"Yeah, I like her, too," Tanya said. Then she positioned a few more ringlets and spritzed Alicia's hair with holding spray.

"Now all we have to do is put on your makeup and then you can slip on your dress."

Alicia sat quietly as her mother smoothed on a light layer of Lancôme foundation. After that, she applied barely a touch of eye shadow, drew eyeliner on the lower lids, brushed mascara on her lashes, and gently swept blush on her cheeks. She finished by dusting pressed powder across her entire face.

"What do you think?" Tanya asked.

Alicia turned toward the mirror and grinned from ear to ear. She stood up and hugged her mother.

"Thanks, Mom."

"You're welcome, sweetheart. You look absolutely beautiful."

"Now I have to get my dress." She was so excited she didn't know what to do.

"Wait a minute. We need to put on your jewelry."

"Oh yeah," Alicia said, picking up the rhinestone earrings and placing them in her ears. Her mother clasped together the matching choker.

In her room, Alicia removed her robe, pulled on her panty hose, and slid on her dress, which was satin, periwinkle, and off-the-shoulder. It was striking, if Alicia had to say so herself. She looked so grown-up.

"It's almost five-fifteen, so Daddy should be here any minute," she said, slipping on two-inch off-white heels.

"We'd better get downstairs so we can take some pictures," Tanya said.

Alicia grabbed her purse and they went down to the family room.

"Nobody told me that Miss America was showing up here tonight," James said, and Alicia blushed like she didn't know him.

"She does look stunning, doesn't she?" Tanya said.

James snapped shots of Alicia and Tanya and Tanya did the same for Alicia and James. Then he set the camera and they took a photo with the three of them together.

"It's five-thirty," Alicia said, peeking through the blinds. "Maybe I should call him."

"I'm sure he'll be here," Tanya said. "He's probably just running a little late."

Alicia didn't say anything, but she was starting to get nervous.

"I'm glad we got a dress with a matching shawl, because it seems like it's going to be a little chilly tonight," Tanya continued.

"Sweetheart, why don't you have a seat until your dad gets here," James said, and Alicia knew it was because he sensed her anxiety.

She sat a while longer, but just when she looked at the clock and saw that it was five forty-five, the phone rang. She watched her mother walk into the kitchen to pick it up and felt distressed.

"Hello," Tanya said.

"Tanya. Hi. Where's Alicia?"

"She's right here waiting for you."

"Well, let me speak to her."

"Where are you?"

"I'm running a little late, but I'll be there."

Tanya walked the phone over to Alicia and said, "It's your father."

"Hello," Alicia said, practically holding her breath.

"Baby girl, Daddy is so sorry. He got caught up with some church business, and it threw him a little late. But I'm on my way home now to get dressed."

"To get dressed? The dance starts in less than fifteen minutes, Daddy."

"I know, but we'll just have to be a little late. Okay?"

"Well, what time are you going to pick me up?"

"I'm only maybe twenty minutes from the house, and all I have to do is shower real quick and put on my tux. So I should be there to get you around seven."

"But the school is almost thirty minutes away, and the dance is over at nine o'clock," Alicia said, tears already welling in her eyes.

"I know, baby girl, but at least we'll still have an hour and a half to be there."

"I don't wanna go. So let's just forget it," she said, dropping her purse.

"Why?"

"Because I don't want to."

"Baby girl, please don't cancel the whole evening just because I messed up on my timing."

"No, let's just forget it."

"Okay, maybe I can get there by six forty-five."

"No, Daddy, I *said* I don't wanna go."

"But, baby girl, you and I have been looking forward to this for two weeks."

"I knew you were gonna do this, Daddy. You always say one thing and then you do another. And I'm sick of it," she screamed, crying. "I'm sick of you treating me like this, and you don't ever have to worry about me bothering you again."

She threw the phone down on the circular sofa and ran upstairs. Tanya looked at James and hurried behind her.

"Look, Mariah, don't start this again," Curtis said, stepping out of the shower. "I've really messed up with Alicia, and I'm not in the mood for all this nagging."

She was really starting to irritate him, and he couldn't wait to get away from her for the rest of the evening.

"But I don't understand why you have to go back out this late when you were already gone all afternoon. You did the same thing last Saturday, and since it's already after nine, why can't you just go to the hospital after church tomorrow?"

"Because I'm going tonight, that's why. I already told Brother Fairgate that I would come by and pray for his wife as soon as Alicia's dance was over. So he and his family weren't expecting me until around ten, anyway."

"And who are the Fairgates? Are they new?"

"No, they're not new."

"Well, I've never heard that name before."

"Woman, there're over three thousand members at that church, so I'm not surprised that you haven't. I mean, what do you expect? To know every single person who's a member there?"

"No."

"Well, you sure act like it."

"Is she in critical condition or something?"

"Sweet Jesus." Curtis sighed. "I don't know all of that. All I know is that she's low sick, and they want me to come pray for her."

"Okay, then, I'll just go with you."

"For what?" he said, turning to look at her, frowning.

"Because it won't hurt for me to be there with you. I should go visit the sick with you more often anyway."

Why was she trying to make his life so difficult? Didn't she know that if he'd wanted her to go, he would already have asked her? Why couldn't she just accept what he was telling her and climb off his back?

"Maybe some other time," he finally said. "Because with everything that has happened between me and my baby girl, I need to be alone. I know you mean well, but I need some time to figure out how I'm going to make things up to her."

"Well, where were you earlier?"

"I've already told you that I ran some errands and took care of some church business."

"Then what was so important that you couldn't even get home in time for Alicia's dance?"

He was about to end this useless interrogation.

"For the hundredth time, I told you I got caught up at the church and then I got caught up in traffic. You know how the Dan Ryan can be on a Saturday."

She looked at him and he could tell she hadn't believed a word of what he'd said. But it didn't make any difference, because as soon as he stepped into his other shoe, he would be walking right down those stairs and right out the back door.

"I don't like this, Curtis."

He raised his voice. "You don't like what, Mariah?"

"The way you've been acting today. You seemed like you were really trying all last week, and now it's like you're a different person again. It's almost like you hate being here with me."

"Think what you want to, because I'm through trying to convince you. Jeez. You tell a person the truth, and they still don't believe you," he said, heading down the stairway.

"Curtis, just let me ride over there with you," she pleaded.

"I'll see you when I get back," he said, and walked out of the house.

And he couldn't have been more relieved to be free of Mariah and her relentless cross-examination. More importantly, he was never going to forgive himself for disappointing Alicia. And he was a little upset with Adrienne, since he'd told her that he couldn't see her today because he had to escort Alicia to her dance. But against his better judgment, he'd gone ahead and met with her over at Tyler's. He'd told her he could only stay for two hours, but when they'd both fallen asleep, two hours had turned into four, and they hadn't woken up until five. He still didn't know how he'd allowed himself to get so relaxed and fall off to sleep the way he did. But he knew it partly had to do with how tired he'd been for the last couple of days. He'd been working as hard as always and then spent all day Monday and every single evening with Mariah just the way she wanted. But that meant he hadn't seen Adrienne. And of course, by Thursday she'd started sounding suspicious.

So now, since he'd been trying to satisfy both of them, his life was spinning out of control. They were placing far too much pressure on him, and it was time he put a stop to it. Adrienne was much easier to deal with because he didn't have to see her every day, but Mariah was getting under his skin. She was getting beside herself, and he knew it was because he'd told her they could start a family, and because he'd made love to her six days straight. But by Wednesday he'd become very bored with her again, and had made the decision to call someone else. He'd tried for years not to do it, but now, with all this talk about having a baby, he longed for his only son. As much as he hated to admit it, he longed to spend just one night with his son's mother again. He needed Charlotte to add up the rest of the equation.

Her father had told him he'd have him arrested if he ever tried to see her, but it was a chance Curtis was willing to take. He hadn't known how he was going to contact her, because even though he trusted Whitney, he would never ask her to do his dirty work. So, finally, he asked Denise, one of his clerk-typists, for a mere two-hundred-fifty-dollar bonus, to call her parents' house. He hadn't told Denise any details, and when Charlotte's mother had answered, Denise had asked for Charlotte. Denise had told her to hold and then transferred the call to Curtis's office. He could tell that someone was in the room with Charlotte, so he'd given her his cell number and asked her to call him as soon as possible. Which she did about thirty minutes later, and it was then that they agreed to meet tonight at ten.

Charlotte was just the medicine he needed to calm his nerves.

Chapter 14

Curtis strutted into the room at Embassy Suites over in Lombard, a northwest suburb, hugged Charlotte, and said, "It's really good to see you." She'd trimmed off most of her hair, but she still looked good. That tiny waist of hers was still a lot smaller than her hips, too.

"It's good to see you as well," she said. "And I have to tell you, I was really shocked to hear your voice today."

She took a seat on the sofa, and Curtis sat next to her.

"Well, after five years, I felt it was time. I mean, I've thought about you a lot, but I had no choice but to respect your father's wishes."

"Actually, I'm glad you didn't try to contact me, because for the first two years all Dad talked about was how he should have had you arrested. He was so hurt and so angry about me getting pregnant."

"It never should've happened. You weren't even out of high school when we first started seeing each other. And we should have been more careful when it came to birth control."

"Maybe, but all I knew was that I was in love with you, and I would have done anything to be with you."

She was definitely telling the truth about that. Curtis could still remember how infatuated she'd been with him and how she didn't even mind him taking her to cheap motels. Whenever he'd told her to jump, all she wanted to know was how high and for how long. It was almost like she craved everything about him.

"So how have you been?" he asked.

"I've been doing well, considering I'm a single parent."

"Well, I'm glad to hear it."

Curtis couldn't help feeling sorry for her and even a touch of remorse because he knew he hadn't done right by her. He knew he'd taken advantage of a young teenager who didn't know whether she was going or coming.

"And what about my son?"

"Oh, so you know that I had a boy, then?"

"Yeah, I heard it from a member who still attends Faith."

"Well, he's doing fine and growing taller every day. I think he's going to be as tall as you, and as much as my father hates it, he looks just like you, too."

Curtis smiled, but now he regretted losing the first five years of his son's life. He regretted not being there for him and not being able to provide for him, because his son deserved so much better. He tried to imagine what he looked like, but what he wanted was to see him with his own eyes.

"Do you have a photo of him?" he asked.

"Of course," she said, pulling out her wallet and snapping it open. "This is the most recent. We just had it taken a few weeks ago."

Curtis took the picture and stared at it. He couldn't take his eyes off the handsome little boy who was staring right back at him. He couldn't remember ever feeling this proud, not since the day Alicia was born.

"Can I have it?" Curtis asked.

"Sure."

"So what's his name?" Curtis asked, swallowing hard. He hadn't planned on being this emotional, and the last thing he wanted was to break down in front of a woman.

"Matthew."

"Hmmm, he looks like a Matthew, too. He really is a handsome little dude."

"That he is, and his grandparents think he's the greatest thing on this earth. They have him so spoiled, but he really is a good little kid. He's everything to me."

Curtis sighed, still looking at the photo.

"So I heard through the grapevine that you got married again and that you've got another church," she commented.

"Yeah, I do. I didn't think I'd ever get back into the ministry, but the next thing I knew, I was accepting a position at Truth."

"So do you like being a pastor again?"

"Yeah. But it's still just as stressful as always."

"And what about your wife? Are you guys happy?"

Curtis chuckled. "I guess it depends on how you define being happy."

"Meaning?"

"Meaning, I needed a wife in order to keep the position at Truth, and I'm living a pretty decent life in general."

"But are you happy?"

"Sometimes, but sometimes I pretty much just go through the motions."

"Then that's too bad."

"Why do you say that?"

"Because what's the point in being married if you're miserable all the time?"

"Sometimes you do what you have to do."

"I guess. But I'm just saying I don't want that for me."

"So are you seeing anyone?" Curtis said, slipping in the question he'd been wanting to ask for a while now.

"Sort of, but it's nothing real serious."

"Does he spend time with Matthew?"

Curtis knew he didn't have the right to call any shots, but he just didn't want to hear about some other man playing daddy to his son.

"The three of us have gone a few places together, but that's really it."

"Oh."

"So how's Alicia?" she asked.

"She's fine, but she's not too happy with me right now."

"Why is that?"

"It's a long story."

"I'll bet she's as beautiful as ever."

"She is. But she definitely has a mind of her own."

"I can imagine."

"So tell me," Curtis said, turning his body toward her. "Is there a chance I can see my son one day?"

"I don't know. Because even though Dad doesn't mention you that much anymore, I think he would go through the roof if he thought you were anywhere near Matthew. And I don't think he was bluffing when he said he'd press charges against you."

"But maybe you could bring Matthew to see me without him knowing it."

"I just don't know. I mean, I do want you to see Matthew, and I want him to know who his father is, but I don't want to jeopardize my relationship with my parents. They've allowed us to live with them all these years, and they've done everything they could for both of us. It wouldn't be so hard if I was living on my own, but I'm not."

Curtis didn't know what else to say, and Charlotte looked at him sympathetically and said, "I'm sorry."

"If that's how it is, then that's how it is. But can I ask you something else?"

"What's that?"

"What about you and me?"

"I wondered how long it was going to take for you to bring that up," she said, smiling.

"Why? Are you offended?"

"Should I be?"

"Maybe."

"Well, I'm not."

"You know I've missed you."

"No, Curtis, what you missed were the things I used to do to you."

"This is true, but I missed you as a person, too, because we had some great times together."

She had definitely matured over the years, even more so than he expected.

"And you think because we used to have some great times, you can simply call me up, meet me at a hotel, and screw my brains out?" she asked. Curtis didn't say it out loud, but yes, that's exactly what he'd been thinking. Of course, his priority was meeting his son, but from the moment he'd heard her voice on the phone, he hadn't been able to take his mind off her. He didn't know what sort of person she was now, but back in the day, she'd been the freak of the week. He hadn't understood how she'd become so experienced at the age of seventeen, but she knew what she was doing. She knew how to satisfy him in ways that Tanya and even Adrienne couldn't learn.

"Look," he said. "I'm not going to lie to you. I'm married, but I'm not happily married. And this time it's even worse than when I was married to Tanya."

"But I heard you just got married a few months ago."

"I did."

"Well, didn't you know she wasn't the one before then?"

"I knew she was a nice, decent woman and that any church

would love to have her as a first lady. And at the time, that's what was important to me."

Charlotte shook her head in disbelief. "But now you want to start seeing me again?"

"Well, maybe if you hadn't come here looking so fine, I wouldn't be heated up like this."

"Yeah, right."

"I'm serious."

"Well, the thing is, I'm only one semester from finishing my bachelor's degree, and I don't need any more heartaches."

"Really? What are you majoring in?"

"Prelaw."

"Well, congratulations. I'm very proud of you."

"You should be, because it wasn't easy being pregnant and devastated all while trying to finish up high school. But my parents insisted that I do it, and then they encouraged me to go to college."

"Well, all I can say is that I will never hurt you again. You're the mother of my son. And that's why I'm being on the up-and-up about my marriage to Mariah."

"In a perfect world, you would have married me instead of someone else, though."

"I know, and I regret that I didn't," he said, stroking her cheek.

"I think it's time for me to go," she said, moving to the edge of the sofa.

"So soon," he said, rubbing her thigh.

"Curtis, please don't do this."

"Baby, I can't help it. You know how wild and crazy you always made me feel, and that hasn't changed."

"Do you know how long it took me to get over you?"

"And I'm sorry for that, but all I want is a chance to make it up to you. I want a chance to make things right with you and my son."

"But you're married. And that means we can never be a family."

"You never know what the future holds for any of us," he said, touching her chin and turning her face toward him.

"But I don't want to be hurt again. I don't ever want to love any man the way I loved you."

"I think you're still in love with me now, but you're just trying to fight it."

"I've gotta go," she said, and stood up.

When she stepped to the door, Curtis hugged her from behind and kissed the sides and back of her neck. He maneuvered his hands under her shirt and grasped her breasts.

She moaned and dropped her handbag to the floor.

"I promise I'll do right by you this time," he said, still kissing her.

"Curtis, why are you doing this?" She dropped her head back against his chest.

"Because you want me to, and because I wanna make love to my son's mother again."

From that moment, Charlotte didn't ask any further questions, and Curtis led her into the bedroom. He hadn't wanted to betray Mariah with Adrienne and Adrienne with Charlotte, but he couldn't help himself. He'd wanted things to be different, but at least he wasn't seeing anyone new. He still wasn't seeing any women from his own church, either, and to him that was a step up.

He needed Charlotte to help relieve all the stress he was under.

Mariah stared across the parking lot and saw Curtis walking toward his car. When he'd left the house, claiming he was on the way to the hospital, she'd finally taken Vivian's advice and followed him. She'd watched him go into the hotel, and now here he was three hours later, just coming out. She'd cried herself into a frenzy the moment she saw him walk in there, but she'd decided it was better not to confront him. It was better to wait and see just who he was sleeping with.

She started her car, drove down the first aisle and over to the second. She saw Curtis and some woman tightly embraced, so she accelerated toward them with her brights on. She screeched the tires only inches from where they were standing. Curtis yanked the woman away from Mariah's car, but she jerked away from him with her mouth stretched open. And when Mariah stepped out of the car, the woman rushed over to her own, started it, and drove away in a hurry.

"Curtis, why?" Mariah said, yelling. "Why are you doing this?"

"Are you crazy? You could have killed us."

"Is that all you have to say?"

"What else do you want me to say? Because right now I'm trying to figure out why the hell you followed me here."

"Because I'm your wife, Curtis."

"I don't care who you are. And I'm tellin' you right now, don't you ever fix your mind to even think about following me again," he said, stabbing his finger toward her face.

"But we're married," she said, dumbfounded. "And you said you loved me. And you promised me that you weren't seeing anyone else."

"Please," he said, pushing past her.

He got in his car, turned on the ignition, and cracked his window. "You know what? You look like an absolute fool standing out here this late at night."

Mariah felt like the world was coming to an end, and her head pounded. She pleaded to him with her eyes, begging for understanding, but he shook his head in disgust and drove off. He left her standing there looking like the fool he'd said she was.

She dragged herself back over to her car and tried to gather her composure. How could a man she loved so much be so cruel and inconsiderate? How could he have looked her in her face, lied day after day, and then told her he was excited about them starting a family? How could he have changed so drastically in such a short period of time? She still remembered the day she met him, the day he asked her to marry him, and the day she'd become his wife. But now Curtis was a very different person. She didn't know who he was, but he certainly wasn't the man she'd first known. He wasn't the man the deacons and the rest of the congregation had come to depend on. When he'd been gone all day last Saturday, deep down she'd known he was with someone else. But when he'd wooed her so attentively and so genuinely after service on Easter Sunday, she'd succumbed. She'd tried to tell herself that all her suspicions were a result of her imagination. She'd tried to let bygones be bygones, and she told herself that it was normal for all married couples to have occasional problems and disagreements. But finding your husband casually strolling out of a hotel in the wee hours of the morning with a woman who looked young enough to be his daughter wasn't acceptable. She'd never seen the woman before, but she wondered if the woman could be the mother of his child. She wondered if Curtis had been seeing her all along and had lied when he said he'd never seen his son.

As she drove out of the parking lot, she broke into tears again and had to pull to the side of the road. What was she supposed to do now? How was she supposed to stay married to a man who had no problem messing around on her? How was she going to explain to her mother that she couldn't stay married to a man like Curtis, no matter how much money he made?

She tried to settle herself again and started down the street.

She wondered how such a wonderful fairy tale had quickly turned into a nightmare.

* * *

"Curtis, do you think I'm stupid?" Mariah said, following him into the kitchen.

"No, but I'm telling you it wasn't what you think."

"Then why did she run away and why didn't you tell me that before storming out of the parking lot?"

"Because I was so upset with you for following me around like some kid. But I'm telling you, the only reason I was at the hotel was because the young woman you saw me with was threatening to commit suicide."

"I don't believe you're standing there trying to make me believe a lie like that."

"It's not a lie. I hadn't told you because I prefer to keep my counseling sessions confidential. But she's been coming to my study at the church for over a month now. And the last time I saw her, she was so depressed that I gave her my cell phone number and told her to call me if she needed someone to talk to. So right after I left the Fairgates, she called and I drove to the hotel."

"Just stop it, Curtis. Because what you don't know is that I followed you from the house straight to the hotel and you never even went to any hospital. I waited out in that parking lot for three hours, until you finally decided to come back out."

"You must have followed somebody else, because I definitely went to the hospital before going to that hotel."

What was he trying to do? Make her think she was crazy? She'd seen what she'd seen, and she didn't know how he could actually stand there trying to deny it.

"It *was* you," she said. "I saw you park, I saw you get out of the car, and I saw you walk into the hotel."

"Think what you want, but I know what the truth is, and if you don't want to believe it, then I'm sorry."

"You know, the thing is, Curtis, I can't do this anymore. I

can't go on like this. Do you understand what I'm saying?" She was so exhausted and so baffled that she didn't have any more fight in her. She didn't have any more arguments for the testimony he kept trying to give.

"You don't have a choice *but* to go on," he stated. "I've told you that before."

"No, Curtis, listen to me. I won't stay married to a man who is being unfaithful and who is no longer in love with me."

"No, you listen. You married me until death, and if you make one attempt to walk out that door, you'll wish you never met me. Do you hear me?" he said, grabbing her arm.

"Curtis, stop it."

She tried pulling away, but he tightened his grip and jerked her closer to him.

"I can see now that I haven't made myself clear. You are my wife and nothing is going to change that. You keep talking all this craziness about me not being in love with you, but the truth is I've *never* been in love with you. I only married you because the church required me to have a wife within my first two years. And since I was already seeing you and I did care about you, I decided it was a done deal. But I was never in love with you. I could never *be* in love with you. And just so we understand each other, I will never allow you to jeopardize my position at the church, and I will do whatever it takes to make sure of it. Do you understand me?" he said, holding her face in a firm grip so that she was looking straight at him.

She burst into tears again. "Curtis, why are you hurting me like this?"

"Because you're making me," he said, and released her.

She turned to walk away.

"And don't think you're not going to church this morning," he said.

"What? Curtis, I know you don't expect me to go anywhere

looking like this." Her eyes were bloodshot, she'd been up all night, and the eight o'clock service was only six hours away.

"Not only do I expect it, that's what you're going to do. When you married me you married Truth Missionary Baptist Church. And as far as I'm concerned, this house, that car you drive around in, and all the money I give you are more than an even trade. And if you don't like it, you'd better start pretending like you do."

Mariah stared at him as if she didn't know who he was. He was acting like he'd been smoking crack or something. He was acting like some crazed maniac who was completely out of control. And she could tell that he was dead serious. Right now she didn't have a choice except to do what he told her.

But that wasn't going to last forever. All her life she'd gone along with the program, tried to keep the peace, tried not to make any waves, tried to make sure that everyone liked her. But she was tired of it. She was tired of being afraid like the way she was now of Curtis. She was tired of accepting the existing conditions just because someone else wanted her to.

She didn't know how she was going to get out of this marriage and as far away from Curtis as she could, but she knew she couldn't live the rest of her life in fear. The only problem was, he'd proven that he would put his hands on her, and she believed he would do anything to keep his church. She'd seen the very angry, even deranged look on his face when he said it.

So, for now, she would treat their marriage and their life at church business as usual. She would bide her time until God delivered her from this whole mess.

Chapter 15

Mariah stood in front of the living room window enjoying the bright sunshine that shone straight through it. She'd gone to church against her will, and was glad to be home again. Even better, Curtis hadn't been there with her. He'd dropped her off immediately after service, claiming he had some sort of business to tend to and was then going back for evening service. She'd never expected in a million years that she'd be happy to be alone, but that's exactly the way she was feeling.

Over the last half hour she'd debated whether she should call Tanya. Vivian had suggested it when they were shopping and then again when Mariah had spoken to her earlier in the week, but Mariah still didn't know if it was the right thing to do. She didn't know if Tanya would be receptive toward meeting with her or toward answering questions about her ex-husband. She just couldn't be sure, but at the same time, she didn't know anyone else who could help her.

Mariah made a decision, then walked into the kitchen and picked up her purse before she lost her nerve. She pulled out her personal phone book, found Tanya's number, and dialed it.

"Hello?" a male voice answered.

"James?"

"Yes."

"Oh, hi. This is Mariah."

"Hey, how are you?"

His cheerfulness eased Mariah's apprehension.

"I'm good," she said. "And you?"

"I'm fine."

"Well, I was wondering if Tanya was around."

"As a matter of fact, she is. Hold on for a minute."

Mariah felt her stomach quivering.

"Hello?" Tanya said.

"Hi, Tanya. It's Mariah."

"How are you?"

"Not so good, and while this is really awkward for me, I was hoping we could get together."

Tanya paused.

"It's about Curtis," Mariah explained quickly.

"Sure, when do you want to meet?"

"I truly hate to impose, but are you free this afternoon?"

"Actually, yes, and if you want, you can come over here. Alicia is down the street at one of her girlfriend's, and James is on his way out to the golf course."

"Only if you're sure you don't mind."

"Not at all."

"Okay, then, I'll be there in about thirty minutes."

"Sounds good."

Mariah was relieved. She didn't know how their face-to-face conversation was going to go, but she was glad that Tanya sounded so agreeable.

When she pulled into James and Tanya's driveway, she turned off the ignition, took a deep breath, and stepped out of the car. Then she went nervously up to the front door and rang the bell. Tanya invited her in and offered her a seat in the living room.

"Can I get you anything?" Tanya asked.

"No, I'm fine. But thank you."

"So," Tanya said, sitting down on the sofa, but at the opposite end from Mariah. "What's going on?"

"Well, first let me thank you for agreeing to talk to me and for inviting me into your home. Not every ex-wife would treat me as nicely as you have, and I really appreciate that."

"It's no problem at all. Curtis and I are divorced, but there's no reason for you and me to have issues with each other."

"I agree totally. And that's why I took a chance on calling you."

"I'm glad you did."

"What I wanted to talk to you about is Curtis. I wanted to find out if everything he told me about your marriage to him is true."

Tanya laughed. "Girl, I doubt it. Because as much as I hate saying this, if he'd told you everything, you probably wouldn't have married him."

Mariah didn't know what to say, and she feared what she sensed Tanya was going to disclose.

"Curtis and I fell in love during grad school, he told me he was called to preach, and then we got married. And everything was perfect. That is, until we left the church in Atlanta and moved to Chicago. Because that's when everything changed. He started staying out all the time, and he started grafting for money. Then, eventually, I started questioning him every time he came home, and we started arguing like enemies. It even got to the point where Curtis started grabbing me and pushing me. Hmmph," Tanya said sadly. "One time Alicia witnessed what he was doing to me and she fell down the stairs and broke her arm."

"Oh my God," Mariah said, shaking her head.

"Hard to believe, isn't it? Especially since he's supposed to be a man of God."

"Yes, and the thing is, he was so wonderful to me in the beginning. He seemed like he loved me so much."

"Well, the one thing no one can deny is that Curtis is probably one of the most charming men alive. He not only wins over women, but he does the same thing with all his church members."

"So is it true that you divorced him because he was messing around with this woman named Adrienne?"

"That was part of it, but what exactly did he tell you?"

"He said that he was only with her twice, but that you wouldn't forgive him. And then when Deacon Jackson found out, he told the church and they got rid of him."

"And that's all?" Tanya said, frowning.

"Yes, and the only reason I found out about the girl he had a baby with was because Alicia was yelling at him about it."

"She didn't tell me that," Tanya said, resting her elbow on the back of the sofa.

"Yeah, she was pretty upset with him that day. But Curtis claimed he didn't tell me about the baby because he didn't think I would marry him if I found out."

"Curtis, Curtis, Curtis. Well, that might be his side of the story, but let me tell you what the truth is. Curtis messed around with Adrienne the entire time he was at Faith, he messed around with Charlotte when she was a teenager, and he was caught on videotape with two women he couldn't have known very well. Then, on top of all that, I found proof that he'd paid for Adrienne to have an abortion, and he was secretly renting this little hideaway for them over in another suburb."

"What!"

"And that's not everything, but it would take me an eternity to tell you about all the money schemes he tried to rig up. And he even tried to get me to convince the deacons that we needed more money because he wanted this huge raise."

"I feel so stupid."

"Don't. Because Curtis is good at what he does. He's a manipulator, and he's used to getting what he wants whenever he wants it. I'm just sorry I wasn't in a position to tell you about him before you married him."

"Chances are I wouldn't have listened to you anyway, because I was so taken with him. He was so wonderful to me, and I prayed that he would ask me to marry him."

"Well, what is he doing now? Is he staying out late?"

"All the time. And last night I followed him to a hotel and saw him come out with some girl who was maybe in her early twenties. But he swore it wasn't what I thought."

"Girl, Curtis only does that so you'll think you're losing your mind. But I'm telling you from experience, whatever you saw or thought you saw, that's what it was. And don't ever think otherwise, because Curtis is a huge liar."

"I can see that now. But the other thing is that he's grabbed me a couple of times."

"I'm sorry to hear that, but like I told you earlier, Curtis can be very abusive when you question him about his women."

"And when I told him I wasn't going to keep putting up with the way things were, he told me I would regret ever knowing him if I tried to leave."

"He told me the same thing, and that's why I told Deacon Jackson everything I knew about Curtis and his wife. I didn't mean for Deacon Jackson to broadcast what he knew to the congregation or yank Curtis out of the pulpit, but I knew I had to do something to bring Curtis down."

"Well, I don't know what I'm going to do, because I don't even know who he's messing around with."

"Maybe not, but I would do whatever I had to to find out."

"I hate having to follow him again, but it sounds like I don't have any other choice."

"You don't. And if you're saying that woman you saw was in her early twenties, I'm wondering if it was Charlotte. Because it's hard for me to believe that he would never try to see his son."

"I thought about that, too, but he said her father told him to stay away from them."

"I know, but eventually I think Curtis is going to totally disregard that."

Mariah tried to blink back tears.

"I know it's hard because I've been there," Tanya said. "But the quicker you can get out of your marriage to Curtis, the better off you'll be."

Mariah was speechless but she couldn't thank Tanya enough for being so candid with her. Now she knew for sure that Tanya wasn't the monster Curtis had portrayed her to be.

"You know, Mariah, this is on a different subject, but I want to apologize for the way Alicia has been treating you. I've spoken to her about it on several occasions, but she still doesn't seem to be hearing me."

"Thanks, but it's really not your fault. And now that I know the full story on Curtis, I realize Alicia has been through a lot with her father, and that's why she doesn't trust me. I just wish she knew I would never try to come between them."

"She'll be okay eventually, and I'm hoping the counseling sessions will help her more and more with what she's feeling," Tanya said.

"I hope so, too, because she doesn't deserve being neglected the way she is by Curtis. And last night was the absolute worst, because he knew how important that dance was to her."

"Yeah, but Curtis doesn't care about anybody except himself. I do think he loves Alicia, but he's terribly selfish. He was like that when I was married to him, and he hasn't changed."

"After hearing everything you've told me, I don't think he ever will."

Mariah and Tanya spent another half hour talking about Curtis and everything they could think of, like old friends. Finally, Tanya gave Mariah a tour of their house, and then Mariah thanked her again and left.

Once in the car, she phoned Vivian.

"She's nothing like Curtis made her out to be," Mariah said.

"Really?"

"No, and, girl, she told me that Curtis messed around with Adrienne for years, and that he was caught on videotape with two other women."

"Get out."

"I know. Can you believe it?"

"Well, to be honest, I don't put anything past most of these big-time ministers around here. And it's hard for me to believe I hadn't heard about what went on with Curtis. Chicago is a huge city, but usually the word on these ministers travel pretty quickly."

"I hadn't heard anything either, so I guess it was kept pretty quiet for some reason."

"He is such a joke, but he's no different from the rest of these phonies standing in the pulpit every Sunday. Some of them might be on the up-and-up, but most of 'em are straight-up hypocrites. All they wanna do is rob innocent people of their paychecks and then sleep with as many women as they can."

"Gosh, Vivian, how did I let him fool me like this?"

"Because you saw what you wanted to see. Women do that all the time. Me included. But Curtis takes the cake, and I hate to even think about what else he's probably doing."

"How about putting his hands on me?"

"I *know* he didn't."

"He did, and it wasn't the first time."

"Girl, you should've picked up anything you could find and cracked his skull with it. How dare him."

"I wish I had the guts, but you know I don't."

"Well, I do, and if he ever puts his hands on you again, all you have to do is call me . . . and then you can call 911 so they can come get his body."

Mariah couldn't help laughing at Vivian.

Vivian chuckled, too. "I'm laughing, but I meant what I said, Mariah. And anyway, why did he put his hands on you in the first place?"

"Because I followed him and caught him at a hotel with some young girl."

"You what? And you're just now telling me?"

"I didn't know how," Mariah admitted.

"And how old was this girl?"

"Maybe in her early twenties, but it was hard to tell."

"And what happened when you caught them?"

"She ran and got in her car, and Curtis went off like everything was my fault."

"You know, the more I listen to you, the more I realize this Negro needs to be taught a lesson."

"All I want is to get out, get divorced, and get on with my life."

"But someone like Curtis isn't going to let you out that easy. Not someone who has already physically abused you. When someone does that, they think they own you."

Mariah knew she was right, but she couldn't deny that she was too afraid of Curtis to stand up to him. She couldn't deny either that a part of her was still in love with him. She wished she could be as strong as Vivian, but she just didn't have it in her.

"All I can do is have faith that this is going to work out," Mariah finally said.

"Faith is good, but sometimes you have to take matters into your own hands. Especially when you're dealing with a joker like Curtis."

"I hear what you're saying, Vivian, but it's just not that easy."

"Well, why don't you come stay with me until you figure out what to do?"

"Not right now, but if things get worse, I will."

"Okay, it's your call."

"Well, I guess I'd better let you go, because I'm almost home."

"Call me if you need me, no matter what time."

"I will, and, Vivian? Thanks for listening."

"Girl, please. What are friends for?"

"I know, but I still hate bothering you with all this madness."

"Bother me anytime you feel like, because I won't be satisfied until you're out of this."

"I'll call you tomorrow."

"You be careful, okay?"

Mariah ended the call, and as she drove through the last traffic signal, just before their subdivision, she prayed that Curtis still wasn't home yet.

She thanked God her gynecologist had advised her to finish her current pack of birth control pills before stopping them altogether.

Chapter 16

"If I tell you something, you've got to promise on your life that you won't repeat it," Alicia said, swearing Danielle to secrecy. They'd just come back from visiting another neighborhood friend, and now they were lounging on Alicia's bed.

"I won't," Danielle promised eagerly. "I won't tell anybody."

"I don't know," Alicia said. "Because if you do, I'll be in trouble for the rest of my life."

"I told you I won't. Now what is it?"

"I met this guy on-line, and I've been chatting with him almost every day."

"Really?" Danielle was excited.

"Yes, and, girl, he is so nice."

"Man, Alicia. How old is he?"

Alicia smiled proudly. "Nineteen."

"Oh—my—goodness." Danielle giggled. "He's a grown man."

"I know, and he's really liking me, too."

"What does he talk about?"

"Everything. My schoolwork, the way I feel about my parents. Just everything."

"Does he wanna meet you?"

"Yeah, he brings it up all the time."

"And what do you tell him?"

"That we'll meet soon, but I never say when."

"But aren't you sort of scared?"

"Sort of. But he makes me feel so much like a woman. He doesn't treat me like a child the way my parents do."

"Oh man." Danielle giggled again. "He sounds so cool."

"Girl, he is, and on top of that, he taught me how to have phone sex."

"No way! And I can't believe you've been talking to him on the phone, too."

"Yep. And, girl, one night I thought I was going to go crazy."

"Why?"

"Because it felt so good. I had this tingly feeling that I've never had before, and ever since then I've been thinking about Julian every hour of the day."

"Julian? That's his name?"

"Yep."

"I like it."

"I know, and every time I talk to him, I keep trying to picture what he looks like."

"Do you think he's cute?"

"It sounds like it."

"Did he tell you how he looked?"

"Yep, a little."

"Well?"

"He said he was medium height, muscular, and had a slammin' haircut. Then he said every girl he met wanted to get with him."

"Man, he must be really fine, then."

"I know, that's what I was thinking, too."

"I can't believe you're just now telling me after all this time."

Alicia couldn't believe she'd told her at all. Danielle was her best friend, and she told her just about everything, but this Julian situation was different. It was different because if her mother found out, she would kill her. Especially since Alicia was already on punishment because of those missed math classes. Of course, her mother had allowed her to accompany Danielle over to Tiffany's a couple of hours ago, but that was only because she felt sorry about Alicia missing the dance.

"You'd better not tell anybody, Danielle, because if you do I'll never speak to you again," Alicia threatened.

"I told you I won't. I'll die first. But tell me some more about the phone sex thing."

"I can't explain it. You'd have to be on the phone yourself to understand."

"Does he say nasty stuff?"

"Yeah."

"Like what?"

"Danieeellle." Alicia was embarrassed.

"What does he say?"

"All kinds of stuff, but I'm not gonna repeat it."

"You are *so* wrong for not telling me."

"Why? Because it's not like I can remember all of it, anyway."

"You just don't wanna tell me," Danielle said, pouting.

"Okay, okay. He talks a lot about my kitty-kat, but he always uses the P word when he does. Then he talks about sucking on both my—"

"Ewwwww, girl. He is so nasty."

Alicia placed her hand over Danielle's mouth. "Will you be quiet. You're talking too loud."

"Sorry," Danielle said, and they both laughed.

"But you know what else?" Alicia said. "I'm thinking about telling him to pick me up this week."

"Are you serious?"

"Yep."

"But what if your mom finds out? Or even your dad?"

"Skip him. He doesn't care anything about me, and to prove it, he couldn't even get here on time for that dance last night. He never does anything he says, but Julian is always there for me, and he always knows how to make me feel better."

"But maybe you should at least see a picture of Julian first."

"He doesn't have one he can e-mail me. I already asked when I sent mine."

"You didn't tell me that."

"I forgot, but he said I was one of the finest women he'd ever seen."

"He called you a woman?"

"Yep. I told you he doesn't treat me like a child. Plus, I told him I was seventeen."

"You are such a trip. And he believed you?"

"Why wouldn't he? Because when I get my makeup on, I look way older than fourteen."

"I guess. But if it were me, I'd be afraid."

"That's because you've never talked to him. He is so understanding, and I know I can trust him because he's always saying I should do what my parents tell me. And you know most boys wouldn't care one way or the other. He even told me that I needed to try to get along with Mom and James because they're the ones who are here for me. Then he told me how important it was for me to do well in school."

"Oh. Well, maybe it'll be okay then, because only a decent guy would say all that. But do you think he'll try to have real sex with you?"

"I don't know."

"You're not going to let him, are you?"

"No," Alicia said, but deep down she wasn't totally against it. Not when he'd promised her he could make her feel even better in person than he had on the phone.

"Well, what if he gets mad at you?" Danielle said.

"He won't, because he's not like that."

"Well, how are you gonna sneak out of here?"

"I don't know, but I'll figure out something. And I might have to ask you to cover for me."

"Unh-unh, Alicia."

"What do you mean, unh-unh?"

"I mean I can't do that."

"And why not?"

"Because if you end up being gone for too long and your mom calls me, I won't know what to say."

"I'll tell you what to say."

"I don't know, Alicia."

"Whatever, Danielle."

"Come on, Alicia, please don't be mad at me."

"And you're supposed to be my best friend," Alicia said, mumbling to herself as she got up and went over to her desk.

"I am your best friend."

"No you're not, because best friends will do anything for each other. Anything at all."

"But what if something happens to you? What if we both end up getting in trouble?"

"We won't. Because I'm not about to get caught."

Danielle looked at her timidly.

Alicia noticed. "Okay, if you don't want to do it, then fine."

"And you won't be mad?"

"No."

"Yes you will."

"No I won't, so let's just forget it."

Alicia turned on her computer, wishing she hadn't told

Danielle anything. She was angry with her for not wanting to assist with her alibi, but Alicia wasn't going to lose any sleep over it. She wasn't going to hate her for it either, because Danielle couldn't help being a child. She hadn't been dealing with a grown man the way Alicia had, so Alicia sort of understood why she was frightened.

"Are you getting ready to sign on to AOL?"

"Yep."

"When you finish, I wanna sign on to my account to see if I have any messages."

"Okay," Alicia said, and then heard the phone ringing.

"Hello?"

"Hi, baby girl. It's Daddy."

Alicia refused to speak to him.

"Baby girl, are you there?"

"Yeah." She was as nonchalant as possible.

"Look, I know you're angry with me, but I'm really sorry about last night."

Alicia didn't know what he wanted her to say.

"I messed up, and I'm going to do something real special to make it up to you."

Did he want a blue ribbon or something? She hated his voice, she hated him, and she wished she never had to see him again.

"Baby girl, say something. Because you know it kills Daddy when you're upset with him."

"I have to go, because Danielle is here," she said, looking over at her friend.

"But do you forgive me?"

"What difference does it make? You don't care anyway."

"I do care, and I've been worried about you ever since you hung up on me."

"Uh-huh," she muttered, and couldn't care less about what he was saying.

"Look, why don't you spend next weekend with us, and we'll do whatever you want."

Alicia had had about all she could take from her father, and it wasn't going to be long before she said something she might regret.

"I don't think so, Daddy."

"Come on, baby girl, we could have a real nice time. Mariah could pick you up after school, take you home to pick up your clothes, and then the two of you could meet me at a restaurant. And after that we can do anything you want."

Mariah, Mariah, Mariah. Lies, lies, lies. Yeah, yeah, yeah.

"I said *no,* Daddy. I don't want to spend the weekend with you or your precious little Mariah. And I don't want you calling me anymore either."

"Alicia, why are you speaking to me like this?" Curtis asked.

She could tell he was stunned by her words, but he'd be mortified when he heard what she had to say next.

"The thing is, Daddy, why would I need you calling me when I already have a daddy right here in the house with me?"

"Girl, what are you talking about?"

"I'm talking about James. He's more of a father to me than you've ever been, and that's why I'm going to ask him if I can start using his last name."

"Okay, I've had it, Alicia. I told you I was sorry, and I refuse to stay on this phone listening to you talk crazy."

"Bye," she said.

She heard the phone click and threw her cordless onto its base.

"He makes me so sick," she said.

"Man, Alicia, I can't believe you spoke to your father like that."

"Please. I'll talk to him anyway I feel like, because all he does is tell a bunch of lies every time I hear from him. He couldn't even take me to a funky little dance."

Danielle gazed at her in silence.

"But it doesn't matter, because I'm through with him."

"But he's your father."

"I don't care. I'm still not having anything else to do with him."

"Maybe you need to give him one more chance."

"For what? He's missed just about everything that was important to me, and I'm not doing this shit with him anymore."

Danielle raised her eyebrows as if she hadn't heard her best friend correctly.

"What?" Alicia said. "Julian curses all the time, so it's not like it's a big deal."

"My mom would kill me if I said any of those words."

"Well, it's not like my mom is going to hear me either."

"Danielle," Tanya yelled upstairs.

Danielle opened Alicia's bedroom door. "Yes, Mrs. Howard?"

"Your mother called and said it's time for you to come home, sweetie."

"Okay, I'll be right down."

"I wish you could stay longer so you could see me on-line with Julian."

"I know, but I have to get ready for school tomorrow. And I also have some English homework to do."

"Okay, well, I'll see you in the morning then."

"Hey, I'm sorry about your dad."

"Girl, I'm fine. He's the one who's trippin'."

Danielle walked into the hallway and down the staircase.

Alicia signed on to her computer and saw that Julian was on, too. She felt her stomach stirring, her heart fluttering, and she was starting to wonder if she was in love with him. She wasn't sure how love was supposed to feel, but she knew this was different. She'd liked this boy on the football team last fall, but she hadn't felt anything near the way she felt when she communicated with Julian. Plus, that guy on the team was just a boy and not at all the man Julian was.

JMONEY1: What's up, Alicia.
ALICIABLK: Hey, Julian.
JMONEY1: So how was the dance your father took you to?
ALICIABLK: We didn't go. He was late getting home, and when he told me we were going to be an hour and a half late, I told him to forget it.
JMONEY1: Aw, man. I'm sorry to hear that, sweetheart.

Sweetheart? Alicia felt like she couldn't breathe. He'd never called her that before, and now she wondered if he was in love with her, too.

ALICIABLK: I'm over that, though, because it was just some kiddie dance, anyway.
JMONEY1: I thought you said it was for juniors and seniors and their fathers?

Dang. She'd forgotten that she'd told him that. There was no way she could let it slip that she was a freshman.

ALICIABLK: It was, but a lot of juniors and seniors I go to school with are so childish.
JMONEY1: I hear you. So what have you been doing today?
ALICIABLK: I went to visit a friend and another friend of mine came over here afterward. She just left, though.

JMONEY1: So have you decided when you're going to let me see your fine little self?
ALICIABLK: Not yet.
JMONEY1: Well, I don't know how much longer I can wait, because, girl, I'm really starting to think about you all the time. Sometimes I can't even handle my business, and my boys are starting to tease me about being whipped.

Alicia felt her stomach turning flips again.

ALICIABLK: I think about you all the time, too.
JMONEY1: Are you afraid your parents will find out?
ALICIABLK: No. Not really.
JMONEY1: Then what are you afraid of?
ALICIABLK: Nothing.
JMONEY1: Well, I don't want you doing anything you don't want to, but I don't know how much longer I can keep doing this on-line thing either.
ALICIABLK: Do you want me to call you?
JMONEY1: No, because that's almost the same thing. I mean, it's not like I can actually see you or spend any real time with you. And to be honest, it's sort of played out.
ALICIABLK: You sound upset.
JMONEY1: No, I'm not upset, but I don't want to keep this thing going between us if we're never going to see each other. I've got some real strong-ass feelings for you, but if this isn't going to happen, then I need to know. That way, I won't expect anything except a friendship from you, and I can start looking for someone else to get serious with.

Alicia didn't want that. Whether she was ready or not, it was time to stand up and be the woman he expected her to be. It was time to stop putting him off and time to schedule their first date together.

But first she needed to know one thing.

AliciaBlk: Julian, can I ask you something?

JMoney1: Shoot.

AliciaBlk: Have you ever been in love before?

JMoney1: Once.

AliciaBlk: When?

JMoney1: Back in the eleventh grade.

AliciaBlk: And how did you know?

JMoney1: I can't explain it, but you just know. The same way I know . . .

AliciaBlk: The same way you know what?

JMoney1: I don't think I should say, because if we're not going to take our relationship to the next level, I don't want to get hurt.

AliciaBlk: How would you get hurt?

JMoney1: Because if you don't feel the same way I do, then I'll be left looking like a fool.

Alicia paused, not knowing what to say next.

AliciaBlk: Well, how do you feel?

JMoney1: I told you I don't think I should say.

AliciaBlk: Please . . . ☺

JMoney1: Okay, I think I'm in love with you. Are you satisfied?

AliciaBlk: Yes, because I think I'm in love with you, too.

JMoney1: Then what are we waiting for?

AliciaBlk: Nothing. Not anymore.

Alicia had no choice but to meet him. They'd finally confessed their love for each other, and she didn't want to go another day without seeing him. She *wouldn't* go another day without seeing her own man. Her father had lied and disappointed her on so many occasions, but thanks to Julian, she finally had someone she could depend on. She finally had someone who cared about her and didn't see her as an intrusion.

She finally had someone who would never neglect her.

Chapter 17

Alicia stared straight ahead as Julian drove the black Escalade EXT pickup away from her school and turned the first corner. He was more gorgeous than she'd imagined, his muscles were cut in all the right places, and he owned a very expensive vehicle. But what mattered most was that he was nineteen and clearly in love with her.

"I'm really feeling that outfit," he complimented. Alicia was wearing a Tommy Hilfiger blue jean suit and a pair of mule tennis shoes.

"Thanks," she said, only glancing at him for a second. She thought about complimenting him on the black short-sleeve pullover and black jeans he was wearing, but the words wouldn't spill out of her.

"You seem nervous," he said.

"No. I'm fine," she lied.

"You *were* telling me the truth when you said you were seventeen, right?" he asked, smiling.

"Yeah. Why do you ask?"

"I dunno. I guess because you look a little younger."

She couldn't believe he was saying that. Not with all the eye shadow, mascara, lip gloss, and foundation she was wearing. She'd even asked one of the senior girls from her dance class to help her apply it. But maybe Julian wasn't very good at guessing someone's age.

"So I finally get to see you in person, huh?" he said, slowing at a stoplight and looking over at her.

"Yep." She blushed.

"But you know I'm trippin', right?"

"Why?"

"Because you're way finer than that picture you e-mailed me. All that babylike skin and long beautiful hair. Mmm-mmm-mmm. And got a tight-ass little body, too."

Alicia smiled and wanted to burst wide open. She was still a little tense, but not nearly as tense as when she'd first sat in his truck. She couldn't wait to tell Danielle every detail.

"So where did you tell your mother you were going after school?"

"I told her I was staying after for a track meet and that one of my friend's parents was taking us out for pizza when it was over."

"And you think she'll believe it?"

"Yep. But I need to be home around eight."

Julian glanced at the digital clock and said, "That doesn't give us a whole lot of time together."

Alicia wanted to beg him to understand, but she didn't want to sound like a baby.

"But that's cool," he said. "We can work with that."

Alicia was relieved.

They drove a few more miles into a suburb called Hazel Crest and then pulled into the parking lot of Julian's apartment complex. It was three stories tall, structured of light tan brick, and it seemed pretty quiet. But the fact that they were barely ten miles from where she lived made her a bit uncomfortable.

When they entered the building, they climbed three levels

and walked through his front doorway. His apartment was the bomb. Red leather furniture, black and pewter accessories, and a very colorful painting hanging above the sofa. Now she knew Julian's business was doing well. He really had it going on, and she was proud to be with him.

"You can have a seat if you want," he said, dropping down on the sofa and patting the spot next to him.

"I like your apartment," she said, taking a seat.

"Thanks. It's not bad, but I saw this smokin' condo I wanna get before the end of the summer."

"Oh."

"Is there something you wanna watch on TV?" he asked, picking up the selector.

"Anything is fine," she said, hoping she sounded mature.

"What about BET?"

"Okay."

After flipping through channels, Alicia saw J.Lo and LL Cool J singing to each other on a video. Alicia loved this one and bobbed her head to the music.

"So I see you're a J.Ho fan like the rest of America."

"Why do you call her that?" Alicia was offended by his comment.

"Don't get upset," he said. "I'm only kidding. But that is what Jamie Foxx called her on one of his stand-ups. He said that's who she was when she danced on *In Living Color.*"

"Please," she said. "J.Lo is my girl."

Julian laughed and Alicia loved the way he sounded.

"And you probably already spent a ton of money on those boots she's wearing, too."

"Nope. But I'm getting a pair this fall, though."

"Figures."

Julian looked at her for a few seconds, seeming to admire what he saw.

"Why don't you come a little closer," he said.

Alicia froze up.

"Come here," he reiterated.

She hesitated, but finally slid over next to him. Their hips were now touching, and he placed his arm around her. It felt great to be cuddling with him, and her nervousness was now passing, slowly but surely.

Alicia pretended that she was consumed with the video, but Julian lifted her chin and gazed into her eyes. "You . . . are . . . one . . . fine . . . little . . . thing. You know that?"

She smiled again, and he kissed her. With his tongue and everything. She'd only tongue-kissed one other boy, but she hadn't liked it very much because he'd slobbered all over the outside of her mouth. But Julian, on the other hand, definitely knew what he was doing, so she kissed him right back.

When the doorbell rang, he pulled away from her.

"Hey, that's probably somebody coming to buy a CD, so why don't you go into my bedroom and shut the door. That way, I won't look so unprofessional."

"Okay," she said, walking in the direction he was pointing.

When she was inside his bedroom, she sat down on the wooden sleigh bed and turned on the television. Julian was such a businessman, and if she'd been even a couple of years older, her mother probably would have been thrilled about him. Alicia could tell he had a good head on his shoulders, and she wondered what it would feel like to be married to him. She knew she was still too young, but maybe at some point Julian wouldn't care how old she really was.

She heard a door shut but knew it was probably Julian coming out of his office or CD storage area. She would ask him to show it to her before she went home. Although she wondered why his computer was here in his bedroom. But maybe he had two of them.

"Sorry about that," he said, opening the door.

"That's okay," she said.

"Can I see your office?" she asked.

"Yeah, but not today. It's sort of messy, and I need to get it in order before I show it to you."

"Oh. Well, do you wanna go back out to the living room?"

"No, why don't we just stay in here, because if another customer comes by, you'll have to come back in here, anyway."

Alicia didn't see any chairs, so she felt kind of nervous again.

"Now that's what I'm talkin' about," Julian said, motioning his arms to the beat and rap lyrics that 50 Cent was reciting. "That's a bad man," Julian said proudly.

Alicia liked gangsta rap, too, but her mother always had a fit whenever she caught her listening to it. Her mother hated it because of all the profanity and because most of the girls in the videos looked naked. But Alicia kept trying to tell her it was only entertainment.

When the video ended, an auto commercial aired, and Julian walked around the bed and stretched across it. He rested his head on Alicia's lap, but she didn't move.

"So where were we?" he asked.

"I dunno," she said, giggling.

"You do too know."

"No I don't," she said, watching the TV screen.

He sat up and said, "Bring your legs up on the bed. That way we can get more comfortable."

She wasn't sure about this, but she did what he asked. Then he pulled her body toward the foot of the bed so that she was lying on her back and kissed her again. At first he lay on his side, but he finally maneuvered his way on top of her. She kissed him back, but she hoped he didn't want her to go any further. She'd thought it would be cool to have sex for the first time, but now she was afraid to.

When he heard the doorbell again, he pulled away and sighed.

"I hate this, but duty calls," he said, standing up. Alicia saw his thing bulging through his jeans and almost choked. It looked so big, and she prayed that he wasn't going to try and make her do it with him. Maybe she would think about it some other time, but she just couldn't do anything like that today.

He pulled the door closed, and soon after she heard him in the next room again. He was talking to some guy, but she couldn't make out what they were saying.

Over the next two hours ten other patrons came by to pick up CDs. But now Julian was back in bed with her, kissing her again. They kissed for a while, and then Julian removed her jacket and pulled her shirt outside her pants. He unbuttoned them and reached for her zipper, but she stopped him.

"What's wrong?" he asked.

"Nothing."

"Then why did you stop me?"

"I dunno," she said, wishing he would leave her alone.

"Look, sweetheart, I'm only trying to make you feel special. All I want is to make you feel like a real woman the way I promised. Now lie still and let me take care of you."

She tried not to resist, but before she knew it, she pushed his hand away from her zipper again.

"Alicia?" he said, sounding frustrated.

"What?" Her voice was soft and worried.

"All I wanna do is caress you. That's all."

She didn't want to make him angry, and if all he wanted to do was touch her, maybe that wouldn't be so bad.

Julian pulled down the zipper and then worked her pants below her butt.

He moved to the side of her, all the while kissing her and

rubbing his hand between her legs and inside her bikini underwear.

She moved her lips away from his and moaned. He'd been right when he'd said he could make her feel better in person. Julian kissed her neck. Then he took his middle finger and tried to penetrate her.

"Ouchhhh," she yelled.

"I know. But I've gotta get you used to this."

"Please don't, Julian. It hurts."

"Look, it's just my finger. So stop tryin' to fight me."

"But it hurts," she repeated.

"Look, girl, I'm gettin' tired of all this whining. Now stop it and be still."

Alicia burst into tears and wondered why Julian was being so mean. He was being downright cruel.

"Pull your pants all the way off," he said, stripping every stitch of his own clothing. His thing was enormous. It was aiming straight toward her. She was scared to death.

"No, Julian. I wanna go home."

"So what are you saying? That you've been teasing me all these weeks?"

"No," she said, sniffling.

"Well then, take all that shit off like I told you."

When Alicia curled into the fetal position, Julian snatched her legs toward him and forced her jeans down to her ankles. Then he removed them, dropped them on the floor, and ripped off her panties.

"Oh my God, Julian, why are you doing this?" she asked, scooting away from him.

"You said you were in love with me, didn't you?"

"Yes . . . but . ."

"Well then, stop complaining and take this like a woman."

Julian climbed back in bed on his knees and pulled her shirt and bra over her head at the same time. Then he spread her legs with his right hand and cupped the back of her neck with his left one.

"No, Julian," she screamed, trying desperately to tear away from him.

But he was too strong for her.

"Look, girl, I *said* open your legs."

"But it's gonna hurt," she explained.

"It hurts every woman the first time, so get over it."

"But I don't wanna do this. I wanna go home."

"For right now you *are* at home. And after I get what I want, you can go wherever you want to."

Alicia tried to push him off her, but Julian slapped her hard.

She felt dizzy, deranged even. And she wondered who this animal was, because it certainly wasn't the Julian she'd been communicating with on-line and by telephone. He wasn't the Julian who was in love with her.

"If you try to stop me one more time, I'm gonna fuck your little ass into next week, and you won't ever get to go home. You hear me?"

Alicia wailed loudly and hysterically.

"Do you want me to slap your little young ass again?" he said, forcing her legs open. "Because I really don't wanna do that." He kissed her forehead.

Alicia wished she could crawl into her mother's arms and never leave. She was sorry for all the problems she'd been causing and for sneaking off to be with Julian. Maybe if she told him how old she was, he would stop groping on her and would drive her back in front of her school.

"I'm . . . only . . . fourteen, Julian," she stammered, trying to catch her breath. "I'm just a freshman in high school."

"You think I don't know that? After listening to that little weak-ass conversation of yours? But I'm okay with that, because if you were any older, I wouldn't have wanted you in the first place."

"I'm . . . sorry . . . I . . . lied . . . to . . . you . . ."

She tried to say anything that would cause him to have mercy on her.

"Yeah, I bet you are," he said, stroking her hair. "But that's okay, because I lied, too, when I said I was in love with you."

Alicia felt like dying, but started struggling again.

"If you move one more inch, you're going to make me hurt you. I don't want to, but I hate it when you little bitches tease me on-line and then come over here actin' like you don't wanna fuck."

Alicia saw that she had no choice except to surrender.

Julian forced himself inside her, and she cried out like a small child. The pain was excruciating, but Julian moaned and told her how good it felt. He told her that she was everything he'd hoped she would be and then some.

When he finished, he told her to get her clothes on, that he never wanted to hear from her again, that if she ever told a soul, he would kill her parents.

He showed her a gun to make sure she understood him.

Alicia tried to remember what day it was.

'cause I would [illegible] try other [illegible] wouldn't have wanted to in the first place."

"I'm so sorry [illegible] I didn't [illegible] you."

She tried to say anything that would cause him to have mercy on her.

"Well, I bet you do," he said, stroking her hair. "But that's only because I let you know [illegible] and I was in love with you."

Alena shut her eyes [illegible] but started struggling again.

"If you make me more mad, I'm going to make [illegible] hurt you. I don't want to hurt [illegible] I hate it when you little bitches tease me on [illegible] and then come over here again and say you don't wanna fuck."

Alena saw that she had no choice except to surrender.

[illegible] forced himself inside her, and she cried out like a small child. The pain was excruciating, but Lithium moaned and told her how good it felt. He told her that she was everything he'd hoped she would be and then some.

When he finished, he told her to get her clothes on, that he needed [illegible] wanted to hear from her again, that if she ever told a soul, he would kill her parents.

He showed her a gun to make sure she understood him.

Alena tried to remember what day it was.

Chapter 18

"Hi, Mariah," Tanya said. "I'm sorry to bother you, but is Curtis home?"

"No, he's not," Mariah answered, and wondered why Tanya sounded so upset. "Is everything okay?"

"No . . . Alicia didn't come home from school, and now it's well after nine and—"

"Oh my God. Have you spoken to any of her friends?"

"Yes, but she's not with any of them. We even spoke to Danielle, but she doesn't know where Alicia could be either. I even called the school, some of the neighbors, and two hospitals."

"Okay, look, I'm going to try to get Curtis on his cell phone, and then I'll be right there."

"Thanks, Mariah. I really appreciate it."

Mariah pressed the flash button and dialed Curtis immediately. His phone rang again and again and then she heard his voice mail connecting. She threw the phone on the base and muttered to herself, "Curtis, where in the world are you?"

She grabbed her keys, rushed out of the house, and dialed Curtis again while she was driving. But all she got was his recording.

"Curtis, I really need you to call me. I'm on my way over to Tanya's because Alicia hasn't come home from school and nobody seems to know where she is. So you need to get over there as soon as possible."

Mariah cringed at the thought of where he might be and, worse, who he was laying up with. How dare he not be accessible when his daughter might actually be missing. She prayed that Alicia was safe and had merely lost track of time, but what if there was more to it? What if she'd run away or been kidnapped? Mariah erased every one of those thoughts and tried to pull herself together. What she needed to do was have faith that God would bring Alicia home before the night was over.

"Baby, what am I going to do with you?" Curtis said, lying on his back, trying to catch his breath. He and Adrienne had just finished round two of some of the best lovemaking they'd had, and he was completely spent. Although it still couldn't compare to the show Charlotte had put on for him two nights ago. After all these years, she still had it. She still drove him wild, and did things Adrienne and Mariah would never even consider.

"It *was* good, wasn't it?" Adrienne agreed, snuggling closer to him.

"That's an understatement. I'm totally worn out."

"You know, Curtis, I hate not being able to see you whenever I want."

"I hate it, too, but right now it can't be helped."

"I know, but I just wish we could somehow end our marriages tomorrow and not have to wait so long."

"I do, too," Curtis said and wondered why she was doing this again. Why did she always commence to whining about the same old thing every time they made love? She was starting to sound like an annoying parrot, and he was tired of having to explain what she already knew.

"I know you've promised me that you're going to divorce Mariah, but I won't sit right with this until it happens."

Curtis didn't even bother responding. He didn't have any new information, so he didn't know what she wanted him to say.

"You know what I mean, Curtis? Because what if something goes wrong?"

"What could go wrong? I'm going to divorce her, and there won't be a thing she can do about it."

"I don't know. I guess I can't get over what happened when you were married to Tanya. You kept promising that you were going to leave her, too, but it never happened. And on top of that, you were seeing someone else."

Curtis tried to think before he spoke, so he wouldn't say the wrong thing.

"But, baby, we've been over this a thousand times, and I told you it won't be like it was before. I'm not seeing anyone except you, and I don't want to spend my life with anyone but you."

"I hear you loud and clear, but you have to understand why I'm so worried," she said, pausing. "And I guess what I'm trying to say is, you need to speak now or forever hold your peace."

"Meaning what?"

"That if you have any doubts about divorcing Mariah or about marrying me, then you need to tell me. I'll be hurt, but I'll be okay with it," she said, sitting up and gazing at him.

"So are you saying it would be that easy?"

"No, but if you have any doubts, I need you to be honest with me so I can move on."

Curtis slid out of the bed and walked over to the window. Then he looked back at her. "You know, I'm not sure where this is coming from, but I don't need this right now."

"You don't need what?"

"I don't need you questioning my integrity like this. I know

I betrayed you in the past, but I can't keep going over the same thing every time we're together. We just made love like we never have before, and now you've ruined it."

"But it's because of how good you just made me feel that I need to get an understanding from you. I need you to make a final commitment to me once and for all."

"Well, what exactly do you think I've been doing for the last few weeks? I've been lying to Mariah and being with you almost every other day, so whether you realize it or not, I've *already* made a commitment to you. But if you still don't have faith in me, then maybe we need to go our separate ways."

"But that's not what I want, because I'm completely in love with you. But I won't be able to handle any surprises down the road, and that's why I'm giving you an opportunity to end this if you're not sure about us."

"But I am sure. I love you more than I've ever loved any woman, and I would never string you along if I didn't mean what I'm saying."

"Then I'll never bring it up again," she said, walking over to him. She hugged him from behind and rested her head against his back.

Curtis felt like a prisoner sentenced to solitary confinement. She was placing far too much pressure on him and now he knew he had to come up with something to buy time. He had to make her believe that he was in fact going to leave Mariah the way he'd promised. He could tell that Adrienne was deeply in love with him again, but for the first time he knew she wasn't going to accept being lied to.

And then there was Charlotte, whom he couldn't stop seeing even if he wanted to because he needed to meet his son. He needed to start being the boy's father. But Charlotte had placed pressure on him, too, right after they made love. She'd told him that the only way she could allow him to see his son on a regular basis was if he left his wife and promised to marry her. She told him their agreement would be a verbal contract, and that if he didn't keep it, he would never see Matthew again. Curtis hadn't believed the ultimatum she was giving, and hated that she'd taken those law courses so seriously. She'd even gone on to tell him that it was the only way her parents would accept the situation and the only way she could continue sleeping with him. So Curtis hadn't seen any other choice except agreeing to her terms. He'd told her that she was going to be his next wife. That was why she'd been hugging him so tightly in that hotel parking lot—the night Mariah had caught them.

So now he was trapped among three women, the same as he'd been five years ago. The only difference was he had a son who was part of the scenario. Which meant he might have to divorce Mariah after all. It also meant he would have to marry Charlotte like she wanted. Which actually wouldn't be so bad, because he'd have a beautiful young wife who could satisfy all his sexual needs. A beloved little boy who could carry on his name. He wasn't in love with Charlotte, but he was sure he could learn to love her in time. And as far as Mariah was concerned, he'd tell her to leave and that would be the end of it.

So the only issue was Adrienne. There was no way he could marry her, but he didn't want to give her up either. For the longest time he'd been thinking his attraction to her was only sex, but now he realized that maybe he *was* tied to her emotionally. He wouldn't necessarily call it love, but it was definitely something. If he could only get her to see how dull their relationship would be if they were married, maybe she'd back down. Maybe she'd realize that all the sneaking around they were doing was the reason they never tired of each other. Maybe she'd see that the sneaking was what kept all the fire alive in their relationship.

Curtis turned and faced Adrienne and pulled her into his

arms. He held her close and thought about his dilemma. He wished he could be honest with her and let her go. But he just couldn't. She understood him, and they had too much history to simply end what they had together.

He wondered why his life was becoming so complicated. It wasn't quite as bad as when he was married to Tanya, but it was complicated nonetheless. He wondered if he would still have all these problems if he hadn't decided to return to the ministry. But the truth was, he was a pastor again and couldn't imagine being anything different. He had a lot to offer his congregation, and they proved all the time that they loved him. They needed him and respected him, and he knew they would support his decision to end his marriage to Mariah. They would understand him wanting to marry the mother of his son. He would also become a better father to Alicia in the process.

He would call Alicia as soon as he and Adrienne left Tyler's condo. He hoped she would be happy to hear from him.

Curtis headed east on the Dan Ryan and dialed into his voice mail system. He had two messages and the first was from Deacon Taylor.

"Hey, Pastor. Hit me back when you get a chance, because I just found out some information for you. I was told by a very reliable source that Deacon Winslow wasn't always on the up-and-up a few years ago. And I also learned something about Deacon Thurgood that will make your head spin. Anyway, call me when you get a minute."

Curtis smiled and deleted the message. He couldn't wait to hear what Taylor had to tell him about his two favorite deacons. But first he listened to the next message. He listened to every word that Mariah said and then played her message again to make sure he'd heard her correctly. Unfortunately, he had. His daughter was missing.

He dialed Tanya's phone number and floored the accelerator.

"Hello?" Tanya answered on the first ring.

"Hey, it's me."

"Curtis, where are you? Mariah called you over an hour ago."

"I know, but is Alicia home yet?"

"No."

"Have you called the police?"

"Yes, but they can't do anything because she hasn't been gone long enough."

"Hasn't been gone long enough?"

"No. They said children her age run away or come home late all the time."

"That's just ridiculous. And you wait until I call them."

"What you need to do is get over here and help us figure out what to do about this. Especially since this is all your fault."

"My fault? How is it my fault?"

"Because you're nothing but a little whore, Curtis," Tanya yelled.

"What? What are you talking about?" Curtis said, frowning.

"You know exactly what I'm talking about. If you hadn't been out messing around on Mariah, you could have taken your daughter to that dance on time."

"Tanya, please. I don't even want to hear that. Our daughter is missing and that's all I want to discuss with you."

"Then we don't have anything else to talk about," she said, and hung up.

Curtis threw his cell phone on the floor of his car. Tanya still knew how to bring out the worst in him, and he couldn't believe she was trying to blame all of this on some dance. She'd probably been filling Alicia's head with that same insanity, and if he found out, he would never forgive Tanya. Maybe he didn't spend enough time with Alicia, but he wasn't a terrible father. He paid way more child support than the court had ordered him, so he didn't know what Tanya was complaining about. He took care of his daughter, and Tanya wasn't about to make him feel guilty about anything.

He pressed on the accelerator with even more force and said, "Lord, please let my baby girl be okay. Lord, please take care of her, and bring her home safely."

Chapter 19

"Hey, man, how's it going," Curtis said to James, and walked into the house. Curtis couldn't stand him and was only being cordial because of the current situation.

Tanya rolled her eyes at Curtis when he walked into the family room, so he went over and hugged Mariah. "Hi, baby. I'm sorry I didn't get your message right away."

"I'm just glad you're here now," Mariah said.

"So, still no news yet?" Curtis asked.

"No," Tanya snapped. "But it's not like you care, anyway."

"Look, Tanya. I know you're upset, but let's not do this."

"Let's not do what? Tell the truth? Because the truth is the reason we don't know where Alicia is. The truth is that you are a poor, pathetic excuse for a father."

"Whatever you say, Tanya," Curtis dismissed her.

"You're right, and if you don't like it, you can just get out."

"Now, baby, come on," James said to Tanya. "He's right. Let's just all try to be civil so we can concentrate on getting Alicia back home."

Curtis looked at James and said, "I hope when you say 'we,' you're including me, because that's *my* daughter. I know she lives here with you, but don't you ever start thinking you're her father."

"Man, I know who Alicia's father is. And I would never try to take your place."

"I'm just making sure you realize that her well-being is nothing you need to be concerned with."

"Well, the thing is, Curtis, her well-being has been my concern since the day I married Tanya. I'm the one who's here when she's sick, when she has a bad day, and when she needs a parent to take her places."

"Are you also the one who's been trying to brainwash her into thinking she doesn't need me anymore?"

"That's just ludicrous," James said, folding his arms.

"No, I don't think so, because just last night she was bragging to me about wanting to use your last name."

Tanya looked surprised.

Mariah was equally shocked.

Curtis wanted to hurt James—physically.

"Well, if she told you that, I didn't have anything to do with it," James said.

"Yeah, right," Curtis said.

"I love Alicia as if she was my own child, but like I said, I know who her father is."

"Well, a few years ago you also knew who Tanya's husband was, but that didn't stop you from sleeping with her," Curtis shot back.

"This is going too far," Tanya interrupted. "Alicia is who we need to be worrying about."

"I agree," Mariah said. Curtis looked at her disapprovingly and hoped she realized she was in the same boat as James and didn't have any rights or opinions when it came to Alicia.

They sat tensely for another forty-five minutes, mostly in silence. Everyone was worried sick, but there was nothing they could do. At one point Curtis told them to bow their heads in prayer. After that, he suggested going to look for her, but everyone wanted to know where he was going to begin his search. But he didn't care where because anywhere would be better than all this waiting they were doing.

Tanya walked into the kitchen, poured a cup of coffee, and heard the phone ringing.

"Hello?" she quickly answered.

"Hi, Mrs. Howard," Danielle said. "Did Alicia come home yet?"

Tanya closed her eyes. "No, sweetie, she hasn't."

"Oh. Well, yesterday . . ." Danielle said, and paused.

"Yesterday what?" Tanya said, sitting down at the table.

"Yesterday she told me that she'd been chatting on-line with this guy and that he wanted to meet her in person."

"What was his name?"

"I think it was Julian."

"Did she say she was going to go see him?"

There was a pause again.

"Danielle, sweetie, please. You have to tell me what she was planning to do."

"But she's going to be so mad at me." Danielle started to cry.

"Maybe she won't. Not when I tell her we were so worried about her that you *had* to tell us."

"She said she was going to meet him this week, but she didn't say what day."

"Did she say how old he was?"

"He's nineteen."

Curtis watched tears fall from Tanya's face.

"Is there anything else? Did she say where he lived or what kind of car he drove?"

"No."

"Did she tell you what they talked about?"

"He said some nasty stuff, but she said she wasn't going to do anything like that."

"Is there anything else you can think of? Anything at all?"

"No, that's it. That's all she told me."

"Well, if you think of anything, please call me back, okay?"

"I will, and, Mrs. Howard, I'm sorry I didn't tell you what I knew when you first called."

"That's okay, honey, and we'll let you know when we hear something."

Tanya pressed the off button, held the phone close to her chest, and walked back into the family room. She explained to everyone what Danielle had told her. Curtis, Mariah, and James were in shock. They all wondered how this could possibly have happened.

"You mean to tell me you don't monitor who your own daughter is on-line with?" Curtis accused Tanya.

"No. Not really. Do you monitor her when she's on-line at your house?"

"She would never chat with a grown man at my house," Curtis boasted. "She would know better than to even try it."

"I don't know how you can say that, because she doesn't even respect you. And if she was chatting with him here, you can believe she was doing the same thing when she was with you."

"Well, we need to call the police and tell them what we know," Curtis suggested.

"But they've already said she has to be gone twenty-four hours," Tanya said.

"I don't care what they said, I need them to get out there and look for my baby girl," Curtis said, standing up. He paced back and forth in the hallway and thought about the day Alicia was born. He'd been so proud and so happy. She'd been the cutest baby he'd ever seen in his life, and he would never forgive himself if something happened to her. He would never admit it to

Tanya or anyone else for that matter, but he couldn't help wondering if his lack of time with her was in fact the cause of her disappearance.

"Maybe we should try to go sign on to her computer to see if there are any old messages from this Julian," James said.

"That's a good idea," Tanya said. "I'm sure her password is saved on her computer, so it should be easy enough to sign on and check her messages."

But just as she started up the stairs, the phone rang again.

This time James answered it.

"Hello?"

"Hi, is this the Black residence?"

"No," James said. "I mean, yes, Alicia Black is my stepdaughter."

"Well, this is Linda Baldwin calling from South Suburban Hospital in Hazel Crest."

"Yes," James said, beckoning for Tanya to come to the phone. "Hold for one minute and I'll let you speak to my wife."

"Hello?" Tanya said in an anxious tone.

"Mrs. Black?"

"I'm Mrs. Howard, but Alicia is my daughter. Is she okay?"

"Well, a very nice couple found her walking along the street and noticed her clothes were torn. But when they couldn't get her to come with them, they called the police and they brought her here to the emergency room."

"Oh my God, is she all right?"

"She's going to be fine, but she won't let us come near her. And the only time she spoke to us was when she asked us to call you."

"We'll be right there," Tanya said, and hung up the phone. "Oh no, I forgot to ask which hospital."

"It's South Suburban in Hazel Crest," James said.

"That's only a few miles from here," Curtis said.

"It's also one of the hospitals I called earlier," Tanya said.

They all hurried out to their cars; James and Tanya drove in theirs and Mariah and Curtis traveled in his. Curtis thanked God that his baby girl was alive and safe.

As soon as they arrived at the hospital, they rushed through the emergency room entrance.

"We're here for Alicia Black," Tanya told the receptionist.

"Straight through there," she said, pointing toward the examination area.

A nurse led them to Alicia's room. Tanya broke down when she saw how swollen the side of her daughter's face was. Alicia's hair was tangled all over her head and black makeup streaked down her cheeks.

"Oh, baby," Tanya said, leaning over to hug her.

"Mom, I'm so sorry," Alicia said.

They held each other, mixing their tears together.

Mariah shook her head and looked at Curtis. James held the sides of his face with both hands. There wasn't a dry eye in the room.

"Alicia, sweetheart," Curtis said, walking around to the opposite side of the bed.

Tanya stepped back.

"Daddy," she said. "I'm so sorry."

"That's okay, baby girl, Daddy is just happy we found you."

When Curtis moved back from the bed, James leaned over and kissed Alicia on the cheek.

"I didn't mean to upset everybody," Alicia explained, and then looked over at Mariah.

"I'm glad you're safe, Alicia," Mariah said, smiling.

"Thanks."

"Who did this to you?" Curtis asked.

Alicia didn't say anything.

"Did you hear me?" Curtis raised his voice. "Because we want to get the police on this right away."

"I don't know," she finally said.

"Did someone force you into their car?"

"No."

"Then what happened?" Curtis was losing his patience.

Alicia burst into tears.

"Was it that Julian?" Curtis continued.

Alicia looked as if she'd just seen a ghost.

"Well, was it?" Curtis wasn't letting up.

"Alicia, your father is right," Tanya said. "We need to know who did this to you so the police can start their investigation."

"I don't know who it was. It was just some guy."

"Well, what did he look like?" Tanya asked.

"I don't know," Alicia said evasively.

"So you didn't even see his face?" Curtis asked.

"No."

"Of course you did, and I want you to stop lying to us right now," Curtis said, raising his voice higher than before. "We need to know who this clown is, and I don't want to have to ask you again."

Alicia was becoming hysterical.

"Curtis, please," Tanya said. "Why don't you step out and let me talk to Alicia alone."

"No, I want to know who did this to her," Curtis demanded.

"Curtis, can't you see how terrified Alicia is, and we're not going to get anywhere with all this yelling you're doing."

Curtis hesitated but finally stormed out. James and Mariah followed behind him.

"Now, Alicia," Tanya began. "I know you're afraid, but you have got to tell me what happened today. We need to know as soon as we can so the policemen can do their jobs."

"But he said he would kill you and Daddy if I told," Alicia

said, sitting up. "And I believe him, Mom, because he showed me his gun."

"He had a gun?" Tanya asked, sitting down.

"Yes."

"Well, regardless of what he said, you have to tell me who he is and what he did to you."

"But you're going to be so mad at me, Mom. And Daddy is going to be even madder."

"No I won't, Alicia. All I want is for you to help the police find this boy."

Alicia turned away from her mother and stared at the wall.

"Alicia, please?" Tanya begged. "You have to tell me everything."

"His name is Julian, and I met him on-line."

"And?"

"He lives right here in Hazel Crest, and his AOL name is JMoney1."

"Do you know what street?"

"No, but it was a tan apartment building."

"How did you get over there?"

"He picked me up in front of the school."

"In what?"

"One of those black Cadillac pickups."

"What did he do when you got to his apartment?"

Alicia's eyes filled with tears again.

"Come on, honey, you have to tell me."

"Mom, I told him I didn't want to, but . . ."

"It's okay, Alicia," Tanya said, sitting on the bed holding her daughter.

"Mom, he hurt me so badly when he did it . . . I mean it really, really hurt. And then he told me he never wanted to see me again."

"We have to tell the police."

"No, Mom," Alicia cried, reaching for her mother, trying to stop her from moving away from the bed. "He said he would kill you."

"Honey, we have to. And the police will protect all of us when we do."

Tanya asked one of the nurses to get one of the police officers, but two of them came to Alicia's room. One tall and one much shorter. Tanya told them everything, but when they attempted asking Alicia more questions, she refused to say a word. She wouldn't even give them a physical description.

"We have all of your information, ma'am," the taller one said to Tanya. "And we'll be in touch as soon as we have something."

"Thank you, officers."

Tanya turned to Alicia. "Let me go out and get everybody, and I'll be right back."

"No, Mom, please don't leave me."

"Honey, it will only take a minute."

"No, let the nurse go get them."

And that's what Tanya did. But as soon as Curtis heard the entire story, he lost it.

"I'm going to kill that little bastard," Curtis said. He was so furious, and while he knew that of all people, a minister shouldn't consider murdering anyone, he couldn't help it. That little thug had violated his daughter, and he was going to have to pay for it. It would be better for this Julian if the police found him first.

"Daddy, just leave him alone," Alicia begged. "He said he would kill you and Mom if I told."

"He's not going to do anything. I promise you that. Because if any killing goes on, I'll be the one doing it."

"I know how you feel," Mariah finally said. "But, Curtis, nobody is worth killing or going to jail over."

Curtis looked at her like she didn't have a brain in her head. She knew better than to disagree with him in front of people, so he wondered why she was opening her mouth now. He gave her a dirty look, though, and she focused her eyes back on Alicia.

"Mariah is right, he's not worth it," Tanya added. "The police are going to handle this, and they'll probably have him locked up by morning."

"I agree, because there can't be that many Julians who own a black Cadillac pickup and who also live in Hazel Crest," James said.

Curtis was sick of all of them.

"Mrs. Howard," a thirty-something Asian nurse said. "We really need to examine Alicia now."

Curtis saw the nervous look on Alicia's face.

"That will be fine, but will it be okay for me to stay with her while you do it?" Tanya asked.

"Sure, but everyone else will have to step back out to the waiting area."

"I love you, baby girl," Curtis said, kissing his daughter. "And I'll be right here when they finish."

"I love you, too, Alicia," James said, and Curtis wanted to backhand him.

Mariah looked like she'd swallowed a canary, and Curtis knew it was because she didn't know what to say. She knew Alicia couldn't stand her, so telling Alicia she loved her wouldn't have been the best choice of words. Instead she said, "I'll be back to see you when they say it's okay."

When they left, two nurses and a resident physician did a thorough examination. Tanya swallowed hard when she saw all the dried-up blood and thought she would have to leave the room when she saw Alicia jerking in pain. She couldn't help picturing the way Julian had raped her baby. Alicia was only fourteen, but now she'd lost her virginity in a violent and devastating way. Tanya wondered what she could have done to prevent it, and wished she had monitored Alicia's daily Internet usage. She'd seen a story on one of the nightly news programs about how dangerous Internet chatting could be, but she'd never imagined that her own child would become a victim. The reporter had discussed teenagers and how easy it was for certain predators to gain their trust. He'd even talked about a sixteen-year-old who'd gone to meet a man in his fifties, even though he'd told her he was twenty. But that little girl wasn't as blessed as Alicia, because when the police had found her two months later, she'd been raped, beaten, and strangled to death.

So now Tanya knew she'd taken the story much too lightly and that from now on she was going to pay attention to everything Alicia was doing. She was going to make sure their lines of communication were more open so that Alicia wouldn't be afraid to come to her about anything. She was hoping that Alicia would never have to resort to meeting on-line strangers again.

When the examination was complete, the doctor spoke to Tanya and Curtis alone.

"I don't know if you're interested, but just to be on the safe side, you might want to consider giving Alicia what we call *the morning-after pill*," the resident said.

"I've heard about it, but I'm not that familiar with what it actually does," Tanya said.

"It's a method of contraception that will not end an existing pregnancy, but it does reduce a woman's chance of getting pregnant by seventy-five to eighty-nine percent. So, basically, she would take a series of pills and would have to begin doing so within seventy-two hours of the incident. I suggest starting right away, though."

"Are there any side effects?" Curtis asked.

"She might experience some nausea, may start vomiting, and she might have some irregular bleeding, but she should be okay in general."

"Well, unless you have a problem with it, I think we should do it," Tanya said to Curtis.

"No, I agree, because the last thing we want is for her to end up pregnant by some rapist. And on top of that, she's just a baby herself," Curtis said, realizing he and Tanya hadn't agreed on much of anything in years and he was glad they hadn't argued about this.

When they arrived back at Tanya and James's house, Curtis and Mariah came in to make sure Alicia was settled. But Curtis couldn't help grilling her.

"Alicia, just tell me one thing. Why did you have that boy pick you up when you know you're supposed to come straight home from school?"

"I dunno," she said.

"You do know, and I also want to know why you let him rape you."

Alicia fell into her mother's arms.

"Curtis, we're all upset, it's been a very trying day, and I think it would be best if we all get some sleep."

Curtis wanted Alicia to answer his questions tonight, but against his will, he decided to let her rest.

"I'll be over here first thing in the morning," he promised. "Let's go, Mariah."

"Tanya and James, please call if you need anything," Mariah offered. "No matter what time it is."

"We definitely will, and thanks for being with us all evening," Tanya said, smiling at her.

Curtis and Mariah walked out of the house, got into their respective vehicles, and drove home. After a few miles, Curtis realized he'd forgotten to call Deacon Taylor. It was too late now, but he would call him first thing in the morning to see what information he'd been able to find.

He continued driving and his thoughts came back to Alicia. He didn't know whether to be sad, mad, or thankful that she wasn't hurt any worse. During the course of the evening he'd felt all three emotions, but now he was leaning toward fury. He hadn't understood how she'd been so naïve as to become mixed up with the likes of this Julian person. Especially since she had everything any child could want. No, she didn't have both parents living under one roof, and no, he hadn't been there for her as much as she wanted. But still, none of the above justified her recent behavior.

He would let her know that tomorrow. He would make sure she never did something this stupid ever again.

[illegible] he'd forgotten to eat. The son, Taylor. It was too late now, but he would call first thing in the morning to see what information he'd been able to find.

He continued driving and his thoughts came back to [illegible]. He didn't know whether to be sad, mad, or thankful that she wasn't hurt any worse during the course of the evening. [illegible] all have [illegible], but now he was coming to [illegible] couldn't understand how she'd been so naive as to become mixed up with the likes of that Julian person. [illegible] since she had everything any child could want. [illegible] have [illegible] living under [illegible] and [illegible] shoes for her as much as she wanted [illegible] justified her recent behavior.

He would let her know that tomorrow. He would make sure she never did something this stupid ever again.

Chapter 20

Alicia cuddled the teddy bear her father had given her years before and flipped through the channels on her television. When she arrived at the Nickelodeon channel, she sat the selector down. She couldn't remember the last time she'd watched anything so childish, but already she felt a sense of comfort. She felt like a small child and not at all like the seventeen-year-old she'd pretended to be. It had been such a mistake, her allowing Julian to pick her up from school, but he'd seemed so friendly each time they'd chatted. He'd seemed even nicer when she'd spoken to him on the phone. He'd even told her how beautiful she was and that he was in love with her. So she couldn't understand at all how everything had gone wrong. She couldn't understand why he'd forced her to have sex with him. She could still feel his body weight on top of her. She could feel the awful stinging and the actual tearing between her legs. She'd trusted him like she'd known him all her life.

Alicia was so embarrassed, and she was very sorry that she'd ever gone into that singles chat room. But she'd needed someone to talk to. She needed someone who was paying attention to her. She needed someone to give her the love her father wasn't giving. She told herself over and over again that this was the reason, and it was.

She was gazing at the TV when she heard knocking. She knew it had to be James, because her mother had already come in to check on her. Plus, her mother never waited. She always knocked and walked in simultaneously.

"Yes?"

"Hey, pumpkin, it's me. Can I come in?" James asked.

"Yes."

"So how are you feeling?" He walked toward her with his arms folded, already dressed for work.

"Not that good," she said.

"But you do know we're going to get through this, right?"

Alicia nodded yes.

"And no matter how bad things may seem and no matter what happens in the future, I want you to know that I'll always be here for you. I know I'm not your real father, but you will always be able to count on me."

Alicia believed every word he said and tears rolled down her face.

James hugged her. "I love you, pumpkin, and I'll see you this evening."

He strolled to the doorway, looked back at her, and smiled.

"I love you, too, James, and I'm glad Mom married you," she said, and was relieved he wasn't angry with her. She knew he was disappointed, though, but just hadn't showed it. Now she was even more embarrassed.

When he left, Alicia painfully eased out of bed and walked over to her window. The sun was shining brightly, but it did nothing for her depression. Still, she stood there, replaying the day before and wishing she could talk to Danielle. Alicia hadn't been very nice to her when Danielle said she didn't want to cover for her, and Alicia wanted to apologize. She hadn't found the nerve to call her this morning, but she would try to after school. Maybe Danielle would even come over to visit her.

After Alicia slipped back into bed, Tanya walked in with orange juice and oatmeal.

"They caught him, baby. I just hung up from the detective, and he told me they picked him up this morning."

"How did they find him?" Alicia asked, since they didn't know what he looked like or exactly where he lived.

"One of the officers took a chance on running the license plate JMoney1, and sure enough it was registered to Julian Miller."

Until now Alicia hadn't known what his last name was.

"So we can all thank God that that boy was foolish enough to use his on-line name for his personalized plates," Tanya said.

"Will they wanna ask me more questions? Because I don't wanna have to talk to them again."

"Honey, they need you to come identify him."

Alicia felt a wave of terror.

"But what if he gets out and comes looking for me?"

"He won't. At least not for a very long time, because when I asked the detective what he thought would happen to him, he told me he couldn't say for sure, but that he did know Julian will be charged with a felony. And it's all because he's more than five years older than you."

"But I'll be fifteen next month, and he's only nineteen."

"No he's not," Tanya said, sitting down on the bed. "He's twenty-one."

Twenty-one? That meant he'd lied about his age, too. It also meant she'd been with more of a grown man than she'd thought.

"Will they make me come to court?"

"They can't make you because you're a minor, but, Alicia, I really think you should go. You need to do whatever you can to help the state put Julian in prison."

Alicia didn't know if she could do that. She didn't know if she could face the man that she'd trusted—the man that had raped her. What she wanted was to forget that any of this had happened, but now the police wanted her to come identify him, and her mother wanted her to testify. She'd seen a lot of testifying in movies, but she still didn't want to do it herself.

Tanya rubbed Alicia's back and said, "I know you're afraid, but I'll be with you every step of the way. We'll all be there with you until this is over."

"I'm so sorry, Mom. I'm so sorry I snuck behind your back to go be with him."

"Well, I just hope you realize how serious this is and how much you let all of us down. We're all very hurt by what happened."

"I know, Mom, and I won't ever do anything like that again."

"I'm happy to hear that, because you could have been killed, and we still have to pray that you're not pregnant."

Alicia felt like dying. As soon as they'd given her that first pill at the hospital, she'd pushed the idea of being pregnant completely out of her mind. There was no way she could have a baby. Her friends would drop her, the same as they did that girl Robyn when she had hers in eighth grade.

"But what if I am, Mom? What am I going to do?"

"We won't even think about that right now."

"Well, when do the police want me to come in?"

"As soon as we're dressed. I know you're not feeling up to it, but the sooner we can get this over with, the better. Okay?"

Alicia nodded.

"And I'm also going to call your father to go with us."

Alicia dreaded seeing him. Especially since he'd seemed so angry with her before going home last night. She hoped he wasn't planning to yell at her again, because she couldn't take it.

"So why don't you eat your oatmeal and then go take a shower," Tanya said, standing up.

"Okay," Alicia said, but she still wasn't hungry. She didn't know if she'd ever be able to eat again.

"Oh, and another thing." Tanya turned to look at Alicia. "Even though I'm disappointed about what happened, I want you to know how much I love you. And you will *always* be the most important person in my life. I don't quite understand why you did what you did, but—"

"I did it because I felt all alone," Alicia interrupted.

"But why?" Tanya said, sitting back down on the bed. "James and I always try to do things with you. We always try to make you happy."

"But Daddy doesn't. He always says he's gong to do stuff with me and then he never does. I don't even get a chance to talk to him that much anymore."

"Maybe not, but confiding in a stranger wasn't the answer."

"But Julian didn't seem like a stranger. He listened to me, and he told me he loved me. He made me feel important."

"Well, as much as I wish I could, I can't change the way your father is."

"But why does he treat me like that when I love him so much?"

Tanya was speechless.

"I don't know, honey. Sometimes life isn't fair, and all we can do is pray for things to get better."

Alicia had already tried that, but it hadn't worked. She'd even tried messing up in school, but that hadn't worked either. Although she wondered if being raped by a twenty-one-year-old man would make him finally pay attention to her.

"Things won't ever get better with him," Alicia said.

"Well, even if they don't, you're still going to be okay. And from now on I want you to start coming to me whenever you feel sad or lonely or when you're having any problems at all. I don't ever want you to feel like you can't tell me everything."

Tanya hugged Alicia, and Alicia felt protected. The same as when she was a little girl.

"Alicia, do you realize how senseless this was?" Curtis lectured. But Alicia sat quietly in the leather chair with her legs resting on the ottoman, trying to tune him out. Tanya was across from her on the love seat and Curtis sat on the sofa. They'd just returned from the police station, and now Alicia wished he would leave her alone.

"Do you realize how serious this could have been?" he continued. "Do you realize we could be arranging your funeral right now or that he could have killed all of us? And on top of that, Alicia, we find out this thug is a drug dealer."

"But I didn't know that," she finally said.

"Well, from what I can see, all the signs were right in your face. You said yourself that people kept ringing the doorbell."

"But I already told you, I thought he was selling CDs."

"Well, you thought wrong. And if you couldn't simply look at that Negro and tell he was a drug dealer, you have a lot to learn. I knew what he was as soon as he walked in for that lineup."

"Daddy, I said I was sorry, so what else do you want me to do?"

"I want you to tell me why you made such a reckless decision."

Alicia looked at her mother, silently begging for help.

"Honey, why don't you tell him exactly what you told me," Tanya said.

"I've already told him that a hundred times," Alicia said, looking toward the window.

"Told me what?" Curtis asked.

"That you don't care anything about me. That you act like you don't even have a daughter."

"Now, Alicia, you know I love you more than anything in this world, and I would give my life for you if I had to. But I also have a church to run, too."

"Daddy, why do you do that? Why do you make excuses for *everything*?"

"I don't, Alicia. It may seem like that, but I don't do that on purpose."

"You couldn't even pick me up for my dance on time."

"I know I messed up with that, but I told you I would make it up to you. And that's still beside the point, because that has nothing to do with this Julian situation."

After all that had happened, he still didn't get it. But Alicia wasn't going to keep whining and complaining about something that was never going to be. She was starting to sound like a broken record, a pitiful little child who had nothing, and she didn't like it. But it was just that she loved her father so much and truly wanted a relationship with him. She'd always been a daddy's girl, but it was finally time to accept things the way they were. Which wasn't so bad, because she still had her mother and James. She still had two people who genuinely loved her.

She looked at her mother and regretted every smart comment she'd ever made to her. She was sorry for every time she'd come home later than she was supposed to. Sorry for purposely skipping class and not doing homework. Sorry for not cleaning up her room when she was told. She was sorry for being raped.

Her father ranted for another twenty minutes and then made more fake promises. Today Alicia took all of his words with a grain of salt. She'd been doing that all along, but this time his lies didn't matter so much.

As soon as he left, Alicia went over and lay in her mother's arms.

She closed her eyes.
She mentally asked God to forgive her.
She prayed she would get past what had happened to her.
She thanked God for James and her mother.
She thanked God for making them a family.

Chapter 21

At Curtis's request, Whitney had scheduled an impromptu meeting that afternoon with Deacon Thurgood and Deacon Winslow, and now Curtis couldn't wait for the next hour to pass. He'd finally spoken to Deacon Taylor this morning and learned that both Deacon Thurgood and Deacon Winslow weren't the holiest men alive. They talked a good talk, but Curtis was sure they would never want some of the incidents from their pasts exposed to the congregation. And if they played their cards right, Curtis wouldn't tell a soul what he knew. His lips would be sealed. That is, if they dropped their opposing views. They would have to agree with everything Curtis proposed from here on out.

He walked out of his study and told Whitney he was on his way over to the educational center but would be back in plenty of time to meet with the deacons. Each week he tried to drop in and speak to the members, mostly women, who volunteered in the soup kitchen, the food pantry, and the clothing bank. They loved seeing him, and he wanted them to know how much he appreciated their efforts. All three programs were extremely important to him, because he knew firsthand what it was like, going without food and clothing. He rarely thought about his childhood, though, and hadn't called his mother in years. Sometimes he wanted to, because he truly loved her, but he'd decided a long time ago that it would be better if he didn't. Better if he tried to forget how poor they'd been and how his father had spent all his money on other women. It was better because when he didn't talk to his mother, he didn't have to blame her for not taking him out of that horrible situation.

But Mother's Day was just over two weeks away, and the one thing he did do every year was send her a card and a check for one thousand dollars. Maybe this year he would even call to talk to her.

When he went into the clothing bank he saw ten homeless men over in the men's section and twenty or so women on the other side of the room.

"Hi, Pastor," Sister Waters said. She was seventy-something, the oldest of the volunteers and the best cook at the church.

"How are you, sister?" he said, kissing her on the cheek.

"I'm just happy to be alive and in my right mind," she said, smiling.

"I hear you. So am I."

"And how's Sister Black?"

"She's good. She'll be here later for her YGM gathering."

"I heard from Sister Fletcher that Sister Black has really motivated her foster daughter. She says that girl has a whole new attitude since she started meeting with Sister Black's ministry."

"It really is a blessing, isn't it?" Curtis said, and realized Mariah was going to be missed by many when he divorced her. But they would just have to get used to his son's mother instead.

"How are you, Pastor?" Sister Davis, a fifty-something wealthy widow said.

"I'm fine, sister. And you?"

"I can't complain. And this is Sister Harris," she said, introducing a woman who looked to be in her early thirties and whom Curtis hadn't seen before.

"It's good to meet you," Curtis said, shaking her hand, but had to catch himself when he realized he was staring at her. She was tall, shapely, and had perfect skin. She was beautiful, and he didn't have to ask her or anyone else if they were attracted to each other. The chemistry between them was immediate.

"It's good to meet you, too," she said, smiling.

"Are you a member here?" Curtis asked, and for the first time recognized the disadvantage of having so many members. It prevented him from seeing and meeting gorgeous women like Sister Harris. But maybe it was best because he didn't need any other temptations. He had to stick to his new policy about only dating women outside of the church.

"Yes, but I've been traveling pretty extensively on the weekends for my company and usually only get to church maybe once a month. But since I decided to take off a couple of weeks, I promised myself I was going to volunteer at the church a couple of days."

"Well, I'm glad to hear that," he said, checking to see if there were any wedding rings, but there weren't. "We truly need more people like you in the church."

"I'm just glad to be helping out," she said, folding some shirts.

"Well, I do hope to see you again, sister . . ." Curtis said when Sister Davis stepped away to answer someone's question.

"It's Leah Harris, and I'm sure you will," she said.

Curtis made his way around to all the volunteers and took one last look at Leah before walking out.

Lord have mercy, was all he could think. He wanted her badly, but he knew he had to focus on this situation with Charlotte. He had to stay focused on being with his son. He already had too many irons in the fire, but maybe Leah could take Adrienne's place. Especially since it sounded like she traveled a lot. Which probably meant she would never be interested in a permanent relationship. But then there was the problem of her being a member of the church. He just couldn't violate his new strategy, but maybe she'd be willing to leave Truth and attend somewhere else if he asked her to. He'd have to give all of this serious consideration.

When he walked back up to his study, he saw the two deacons waiting outside his office. Whitney looked up at him, and Curtis knew she was wondering why he'd asked to meet with them. It wasn't that he didn't trust her, but he'd decided it was best that only he and Deacon Taylor knew about this particular scenario.

"Come on in, Deacons," Curtis said, walking near them. "And, Whitney, please hold all my calls."

"Of course, Pastor," she said. "Just let me know if you need anything."

Curtis closed the door and both Deacon Thurgood and Deacon Winslow sat down in front of his desk. Curtis sat behind it and leaned back in his chair.

"Well, I'm sure you're both wondering why I called you here," Curtis began.

"As a matter of fact, we are," Deacon Thurgood answered.

"Yeah, because you usually don't call individual meetin's without the rest of the board," Deacon Winslow said.

"No, but I really don't think you want anyone else to be here for this one," Curtis said.

"Well, I guess you know best," Deacon Thurgood said.

"I do. But ever since I came here, the two of you have been acting like I don't. You've been acting as if I don't know anything."

"That's not true, Pastor," Deacon Winslow said. "Because we wouldna agreed to hire you if we felt that way."

"That's a fact," echoed Deacon Thurgood.

"Maybe, but at the last meeting the two of you shot down all three of my proposals. The ATMs, direct deposit, and the financial planners."

"But no one else agreed with you either," Deacon Thurgood explained.

"Only because the two of you influenced them."

"That's just not true," Deacon Winslow said. "Those men all know how to speak for themselves and we never try to stop 'em."

"Well, I really didn't call you here to argue, and the bottom line is this: I want you both to stop opposing everything I have to say. And at the next meeting I want you to tell the board that you've reconsidered your positions, and that you think it would be smart for us to install ATMs, set up direct deposit accounts, and hire financial planners."

"Man, you can't be serious," Deacon Thurgood said. "You must think we little boys or somethin'."

"No, but this is the way it's going to be," Curtis said.

"No it's not," Deacon Thurgood argued. "We don't believe in all this mess you trying to get us to do, and nothin' is going to change that."

"You got that right, Fred!" Deacon Winslow exclaimed.

"No, *Fred* doesn't have anything right, but I'll tell you what he does have," Curtis said. "Fred Thurgood has a criminal record. Fred Thurgood killed a man down in Clarksdale, Mississippi, back in 1958."

"That was self-defense," Deacon Thurgood admitted.

"Not according to some of the people who lived down there. No, according to them, you went looking for that man when you found out your wife was sleeping with him. And then you made it look like self-defense."

"Now that's a lie," Deacon Thurgood said, sliding to the edge of his chair.

Curtis was loving every minute of this. He knew he had the deacon just where he wanted.

"Whether it's a lie or not, how do you think the rest of the board and the church as a whole are going to feel once they hear about this?"

"This just ain't right, Pastor," Deacon Winslow interrupted. "You know it ain't."

Curtis clasped his hands together. "And Deacon Winslow, it wasn't right when you stole all those envelopes out of the collection plate at that church you used to attend on the West Side. I hear you had a real good time, until somebody busted you."

"The Lord done forgave me for that," Deacon Winslow tried to defend himself. He looked like he wanted to crawl out of his skin.

"I'm sure he has, but you never can tell how church people are going to react to something like this. They don't like thieves handling their hard-earned money," Curtis said. Deacon Winslow was weak, and Curtis enjoyed taunting him.

"I just can't believe you would do this," Deacon Thurgood said. "Not a man of God."

"Well, it's not like I have to. Not if you do what I ask. If you agree with everything I propose from now on, your little secrets will be safe with me. You won't ever have to worry about anything."

"Pastor, I'm really disappointed in you," Deacon Thurgood said. "I just wouldn't have expected you to try and blackmail us like this."

"And I wouldn't have had to if you would've recognized from the beginning that this is my church. You and the rest of the deacons help govern what goes on, but I'm the head Negro in charge around here. There's only room for one chief, and I'm it. I'm the chief until I leave here."

"Lord, Lord, Lord," Deacon Winslow said. "I just don't know what to say."

"Well, you'd better figure out something before our meeting tomorrow," Curtis promised.

The two deacons sat quietly. Curtis could tell they were in a definite state of shock. He could also tell they didn't understand who they were dealing with, but Curtis wasn't about to let two old-timer deacons stand in his way. He'd tried to be polite to the entire board, but with his one-year anniversary less than three months away, it was time he took charge.

"Unless you have something else, that'll be all," Curtis said.

Deacon Thurgood stood and walked toward the door. Deacon Winslow followed behind him. Curtis knew they would never debate him again. Not now, not ever.

Curtis highlighted some scriptures he wanted to use during next Sunday's sermon. He wrote a few additional notes and then smiled when he thought about the deacons. He'd phoned Deacon Taylor right after they'd left, and the two of them had laughed about the whole situation. Curtis had told him how surprised the deacons were and how they'd hightailed it out of his office without looking back. Curtis knew Deacon Thurgood would die if he found out his own sister-in-law was the one who'd told about him killing a man. Deacon Winslow would be mortified if he knew another deacon had blabbed about his former theft practices.

Curtis took a sip of water and heard his cell phone ringing.

"Pastor Black," he said, even though he recognized Charlotte's number.

"How are you?" she asked.

"Great, now that I'm hearing from you."

"Is that right?"

"You know I wouldn't lie to you. Especially not after last night."

Charlotte laughed. "I wore you out, didn't I?"

"That you did. But you always do."

"So how is Alicia?"

"I called her again this morning, but she didn't have much to say. And that argument we had after coming back from the police station yesterday didn't help things."

"Well, she's really been through a lot, but I'm sure she'll eventually come around."

"I hope so. And soon, because I don't like this wedge we have between us."

"I can imagine. But hey, the reason I'm calling is because I thought tonight might be a good night for you to meet Matthew. But only if you meant what you said."

"Of course I meant it. I would never joke about something like that."

"Curtis, I hope you are, because that's the only way I can let you meet him. And if you change your mind about leaving your wife and you don't marry me like you're claiming, you won't ever get to see your son again. I hate giving you an ultimatum like this, but I have to protect both him and me."

"And I understand that," Curtis said.

"Then where do you want to meet?"

"The same place as Saturday?"

"No, because the last thing I want is for your wife to show up there again."

"She won't, but if you don't feel comfortable, we can go somewhere else."

"I think that would be better."

"Then why don't we meet over in Barrington. It'll be a little bit of a drive for you, but a friend of mine has this nice condo he entertains at sometimes. But I need to call him to see if it's okay."

"Well, just let me know as soon as you can."

"I'll call him now. And, Charlotte?"

"Yes?"

"Thanks."

"For what?"

"For giving me a son."

"I'm sure he'll be just as happy as you are when he sees you."

Curtis hung up, wishing there was another way. But he knew Charlotte wouldn't accept anything less. He almost had to laugh at how strangely the tables had turned, though. She was so different now that she was in her twenties. She was a woman who knew what she wanted and knew how to get it. But what she didn't know was that he couldn't have cared less about her new way of thinking. What she didn't know was that he was only going along with her little arrangement because he wanted to be in the same household as his son. In return, she would have to become the perfect first lady of Truth Missionary Baptist Church. She would have to recognize that his son and church were his priorities.

Curtis checked with Tyler to make sure the condo was available and then called Charlotte back. But now he had to call Adrienne, because he'd promised her they could spend the evening together. He wasn't sure how he was going to break the news to her, but he would figure out something as he went along.

"Adrienne Jackson," she said.

"Hi, baby," he said.

"Heyyy. How are you, sweetheart?" she said, and Curtis dreaded canceling on her.

"Well, I sort of have this schedule conflict," he said.

"Uh-huh."

"I thought one of my associate ministers was going to lead Bible study and prayer service tonight, but it looks like he can't. And I've even tried to contact some of the others, but most of them have other obligations I've already assigned them. So it looks like I won't be able to see you until tomorrow."

"Curtis, not again."

"Baby, I can't help it. You know I went to an evening service on Sunday, I saw you on Monday, and then I was with Alicia all yesterday. I even stayed with her last night at the hospital, and Tanya and I brought her home this morning."

He hated lying about his own daughter being admitted to the hospital, but he couldn't think of anything else to tell Adrienne.

"I don't have a problem with that, but why was she there that long?" she asked. "Was she severely beaten? Because they don't usually keep rape victims for two nights. A coworker of mine was raped a few years ago, and she was treated and released the same evening."

"Everybody's different, and he did hurt her pretty badly," Curtis said.

"Maybe. But you mean to tell me you have all those associate ministers and all those deacons and not one of them can stand in for you?"

"No, so please try to understand."

"I'm trying, but it's hard when I have memories of how it used to be before. You would cancel on me and go places with Tanya. Remember the time I followed you and wanted to know why you were sneaking around behind my back? And you told me that you didn't have to sneak to do anything with your own wife?"

"Baby, why are you bringing up the past? I thought you said you weren't going to do that anymore."

"I know. But when you cancel on me, it makes me wonder."

"Well, I'm not doing it because I want to. I just don't have a choice."

"Then what about after prayer service?"

Curtis wondered why she was so adamant about seeing him. Especially since he'd been with her just two nights ago. Plus, she never wanted to meet him too late on weeknights because of the deacon.

"I won't be finished until around nine or nine-thirty," he said.

"That works for me, so are we meeting at Tyler's or somewhere else?"

Ohhh Lord. Definitely not at Tyler's. That's where he was meeting up with Charlotte and Matthew. He knew he wouldn't be having sex with Charlotte tonight, not with his son being there, but he still didn't want to take the chance of Adrienne bumping heads with them. It was too risky.

"Why don't we just wait until tomorrow? I have a meeting with the deacons, but I can meet you after that."

"Fine. If that's what you want."

"It's not, but it can't be helped."

This time she didn't respond.

"I'll call you first thing in the morning, okay?"

"Fine."

That was two too many "fines" in one conversation, but he was sure she'd get over it soon enough.

"I love you," he said.

"Talk to you later," she said, and hung up.

She was still angry, but after he bought her something special and made love to her, everything would be okay again.

[illegible] wondered why she was so [illegible] over seeing him. [illegible] she hadn't been with her for nights [illegible] never wanted [illegible] had too late on Wednesday [illegible] at the door.

"I won't be [illegible] until around nine-thirty [illegible]," he said.

"That works for me. So we're meeting at Peter's house [illegible]?"

"Uh, [illegible]. Where. That's where he [illegible] up with [illegible] and Matthew. He knew he wouldn't [illegible] with Charlotte tonight, not with the son being there, but he still didn't want to take the chance of [illegible] bumping heads with them. It was too risky.

"Why don't you just wait until tomorrow? I have a meeting with the [illegible] but I can meet you after that."

"Sure. If that's what you want."

"It's not, but it can't be helped."

This time she didn't respond.

"I'll call you first thing in the morning, okay?"

"Fine."

[illegible] was too [illegible] "Fines" into the conversation, but he was sure she'd get over it soon enough.

"I love you," he said.

"Talk to you later," she said, and hung up.

She was [illegible] after he bought her something special [illegible] everything would be okay again.

Chapter 22

Curtis was on pins and needles waiting for Charlotte and Matthew to arrive. He felt the way most children feel on Christmas Eve. He could still remember how excited Alicia used to be when he and Tanya were still together. The memory of it all sort of saddened him since he and Alicia were so far apart now. He tried to believe that it wasn't his fault, but he knew he had to accept most of the blame. He just hadn't found enough time for her since he'd become a pastor again. It was no excuse, but the church and gaining control of it, little by little, had become his priority. But he did feel guilty about all of the nights he'd been spending with Adrienne, and now the two nights he'd spent with Charlotte. Three if you counted this evening. He also hated admitting another truth he knew he couldn't deny. Their relationship wasn't the same now that Alicia wasn't living with him. He'd tried to spend as much time with her as possible when Tanya first married James, but he could never accept the fact that James was the one in the house with Alicia. James was the one who saw her every day and took her places, just the way he'd told Curtis the night Alicia was raped. Curtis knew it was wrong of him, but to a certain degree he also envied James and Tanya's relationship. He could tell they were in love with each other and that they were genuinely happy together, and he had a problem with it. Tanya was his first wife and not ever had he planned on losing her to someone else. He'd never planned on her sleeping with someone else while they were still married. How dare she do that to him. How dare she break her marital vows like they were nothing. Yes, he'd done the same thing, but the difference was he would never have left her for anyone. He'd planned on being married to her for the rest of his natural life. He knew they'd had problems, but what couple didn't?

Curtis turned the TV to the Disney Channel and left it there. He didn't know what channels his son enjoyed watching, but Disney had to be one of them.

He felt like loosening his tie, but he wanted to impress Matthew. He'd removed his jacket, but he still wanted to look fairly dressed up. Curtis couldn't wait to take Matthew to his tailor, too, and have him fitted for a couple of suits. He was only five, but he deserved the best of everything. Curtis wanted him to learn at an early age the difference between quality and the lack thereof. He never wanted Matthew to go without anything. He didn't want his son living the way he once had.

He heard the doorbell and took a deep breath. He walked over to the door and opened it.

"Hello, my name is Matthew," the boy said, reaching out his hand to shake Curtis's and stepping into the condo. "What's yours?"

"Curtis Black."

"It's nice to meet you, Mr. Black."

"Well, it's good to meet you, too, Matthew."

"How are you?" Charlotte said, hugging Curtis.

"I'm good. Both of you come in and have a seat. I think I've got on the Disney Channel, but you can watch whatever you want, Matthew."

"Okay," he said, dropping down on the floor as close to the television as possible.

Curtis and Charlotte sat down on the sectional. "He's the most handsome little thing I've ever seen," Curtis said.

"I told you he looks just like you."

"I just can't believe he's right here in the same room with me. Right here with both of us."

"Look, Mommy, that's the remote control truck I asked Paw Paw to get for me," Matthew said, pointing at a commercial.

"I know, sweetie," Charlotte acknowledged.

"Who's Paw Paw?" Curtis asked her. "Your dad?"

"Yeah, that's what Matthew calls him, and he calls my mom Nana."

"Oh," Curtis said, not able to take his eyes off the miniature "him" sitting just a few feet away.

"So who did you tell him I was?" Curtis spoke softly.

"I told him you were someone real special and that you wanted us to come visit you. But that's it."

"Man," Curtis said, blinking back tears.

"It's five years later, but you're still a proud father, aren't you?"

"That I am. And I'm so sorry I missed so much of his life. But as God is my witness, I won't miss any more of it. Not as long as I'm alive."

Matthew turned around when the credits rolled for the program he'd been watching.

"Mr. Black, can we turn to the Cartoon Network?"

"Of course," Curtis said. "But you'll have to tell me what channel."

"On our TV it's one seventy-six.

"We have Dish Network," Charlotte added.

"I think that's the same satellite system on this one, too."

Curtis switched it to the channel his son told him.

"Thank you," Matthew said.

"You're welcome."

"So are you sure this is what you want?" Charlotte asked him again.

"Yes. I'm positive."

"Matthew, sweetie," she said. "Come sit up here for a minute."

Matthew stood, walked over to the sofa, and sat between his parents. He looked at his mother, clearly wondering what she wanted.

"Honey, remember when you asked me if you had a dad?"

"Uh-huh."

"And I told you that you did, but that I hadn't seen him in a long time?"

"Yeah."

"Well, sweetie, this is your father," she said, pointing at Curtis.

Matthew looked at Curtis but turned away, blushing. "He is?"

"Yes. He's your dad."

"I always wanted a dad," Matthew said, looking at Curtis. "Just like all my friends."

"Well, now you have one," Curtis said, tears dripping from his eyes.

"Why are you crying?" Matthew wanted to know.

"Because I'm so happy to see you."

"Oh," Matthew said, looking back at his mother, smiling.

"Why don't you give your dad a hug," Charlotte told him.

Matthew reached toward Curtis, and Curtis squeezed him extra tight, trying to recapture all the lost years. He didn't want to let go of his little boy.

But when he did, Matthew asked him a question.

"So does this mean I can call you Dad?"

"That's exactly what it means," Curtis answered.

"And does it mean you're going to take me to baseball games this summer just like my friend Terrance's father does?"

"Yes, if that's what you want." Curtis had never gone to see the White Sox or the Cubs, but he was going to see what tickets he could get tomorrow.

"Do you want to play my Game Boy with me?" Matthew wanted to know.

"Yeah, but you'll have to show me how."

"Mommy, can I see it?"

Charlotte pulled out the purple Game Boy from her purse and gave it to him.

"It's Super Mario, and I'm real good at it," Matthew boasted.

Curtis looked at Charlotte and said, "Thank you."

"No, thank you. My baby really needed his father."

Curtis and Matthew talked about what he liked, what he didn't like, his friends, what he wanted for his birthday, and the fact that he loved school but always got in trouble for talking too much. He told Curtis that preschool was kind of boring, and that he couldn't wait to be in kindergarten this fall.

They talked about a lot of things and Matthew tried to teach Curtis how to play Super Mario. Curtis still didn't quite have it, but Matthew told him he'd get better and better every time he played.

When it was half past nine, Curtis told Charlotte he wanted to talk to her.

"Sweetie, I need to talk to your dad, so we'll be right back, okay?"

"Okay," Matthew said without looking up from his game.

Curtis and Charlotte walked into Tyler's master bedroom. Curtis pulled Charlotte toward him and held her.

"I'm speechless," he said. "For the first time in my life I really don't know what to say."

"Just say you're going to do everything you can to make us a family as soon as possible."

"There's no doubt about that. Mariah and I haven't spoken much over the last few days, but I'm going to apologize to her and tell her that I think it would be best if we end our marriage. And if everything goes okay, maybe she'll go with me before the deacons when I tell them."

"How long do you think this will take?"

"I don't know, but after seeing that beautiful little boy out there, it won't be long. But I don't want to push Mariah, so you've at least got to give me a month to work this out with her and the church."

"That's not a problem."

"You know, you've really done a wonderful job with him. He's such a good kid, and he's so outgoing. And he has a whole lot to say, too."

"Well, I wonder where he got that from?"

They both laughed.

"So when are you going to tell your parents?" Curtis asked.

"Not until you and Mariah have filed for a divorce. My father is going to be angry no matter what, but if he knows that you really are going to marry me, it will definitely soften the blow. My mom will be upset, too, but she'll be fine with it in the long run."

"Do you think Matthew is going to say anything?"

"I'm going to tell him not to, but you still need to be prepared just in case."

"This is going to be a tough road for all of us, but Matthew is the person we have to keep happy."

"I agree."

Curtis tilted her chin upward and kissed her. They kissed intensely, and while Curtis couldn't say he was *in* love with her, his feelings for her were a lot stronger than a few hours ago. He couldn't explain it, but there was a certain love he had for her because she was the mother of his son. He felt connected to her.

"I don't know if you'll ever love me the way I want to be loved," she said as if she was reading his mind. "But even if you don't, my main concern is Matthew. I want him to know what it's like to grow up with both his parents, I want him to be loved, and I want him to have every opportunity in life we can give him."

"Trust me when I tell you that you won't ever have to worry about his well-being. I realize I just met him, but I love him from the bottom of my heart."

"I'm really glad to hear that."

When they walked out of the bedroom, Charlotte told Matthew it was time to go.

"Do we have to, Mom?"

"Yes, because it's way past your bedtime, young man."

"I'm sorry for keeping you here so late, Matthew, but it was good to finally see you," Curtis said.

"It was good to see you, too, Dad."

"Can you give me another big hug?" Curtis leaned down and held him closely. "I love you, son."

"I love you, too," Matthew said, but Curtis knew he was probably only saying it because he thought he should. Which was fine, because Curtis would accept those words any way he could get them.

"Let me walk you guys out," he said, opening the door.

Matthew climbed into the backseat of Charlotte's car and buckled his seat belt. Charlotte pecked Curtis on the lips and told him she would call him tomorrow.

He watched them drive away. They were hardly out of sight when Adrienne blasted into the driveway.

Curtis jumped onto the grass.

She jumped out of her car, leaving the door open.

"Why, Curtis? Why couldn't you just leave me alone?"

"Look, Adrienne, I can explain. It's not what you think."

"It's not what I think? What the hell do you mean, it's not what I think?"

"It's not."

"First you lie to me about being at the church tonight, and then I come over here and find that girl Charlotte walking out with you and your son. Because I know you don't think I've forgotten what she looks like."

"No, but, Adrienne, I had to see him. But I didn't have sex with her if that's what you're thinking. I just wanted to see my son, and I couldn't tell her no when she called to say I could see him."

"You think I'm a fool, don't you? You think I'm the same fool I was the last time we were together?"

"No, I don't. And if you come inside with me, I'll explain everything to you," he said, hoping he could make her believe him.

"I'm not coming anywhere, Curtis," she screamed. "You make me sick. I hate that I ever even met you, and I'm not about to let you get away with this. If it means my life, I'm going to make sure you never hurt another woman ever again."

"Adrienne, please," he said, looking around to see if any neighbors had their doors open.

"No. Just leave me alone," she said, walking back to her car.

Curtis followed her and grabbed her arm.

"Don't." She spoke deep from her throat. "Don't . . . you . . . ever . . . try . . . to . . . touch . . . me . . . again."

"Baby, you're really blowing this way out of proportion."

"No. I'm not. I saw what I saw, and no matter what you say, I know you've been sleeping with that girl. You probably had to in order to see your son."

Curtis didn't say anything.

"And just a couple of days ago I gave you ample opportunity to tell me if you wanted out, but you lied the same as always."

"That's because I—" he tried to get a word in.

"Just save it, Curtis," she interrupted. "Save it for someone who truly gives a damn."

"Adrienne, all I'm asking you to do is come in for a few minutes," he tried again.

"You know, Curtis," she said, ignoring his plea. "People get killed for less than this every day. So if I were you, I would be very careful. I would watch every single thing I did, and I would pay real close attention to my surroundings."

She got back inside her car and drove away at normal speed, acting as though nothing had happened.

Curtis stood there for a few minutes, wishing she hadn't followed him. He'd known she was capable of it, but he'd been so caught up in the excitement of meeting Matthew, his judgment had become cloudy.

He wasn't sure if he should take Adrienne's threats seriously or not, but either way, their relationship was over. He hadn't wanted it to end this way, but at least she was one problem he no longer had to deal with.

So now all he had to do was handle Mariah.

Chapter 23

Right after leaving the church, Mariah had driven home, done a Pilates tape, and taken a hot bath in the Jacuzzi. But now she was leaning against a stack of king-size pillows reading the *Tribune*. She was also wondering where Curtis was and who he was with.

She was so tired of shedding tears, tired of living in fear, tired of being married to him. Which was why she'd decided tonight that she wasn't going to take it anymore. She wasn't going to keep pretending. Not about their happiness or about Curtis being a true man of God.

It was time she told Vivian.

"Hello?"

"Hey, girl, how's it going?" Mariah said.

"I'm good. But the question is, how are you?"

"Actually, I'm feeling a little strange."

"Really? And why is that?"

"I finally decided to take your advice."

"About what?"

"I finally decided to leave him."

"Well, good for you, Mariah."

"I know he'll never allow me to move out while he's here, so as soon as he leaves the house on Monday, I'll be packing my things."

"Will you need any help?"

"Yeah, if you don't mind."

"You know it's not a problem. All I have to do is request a vacation day."

"I really appreciate that."

"Nothing happened tonight, did it?" Vivian asked. "Curtis didn't try to hurt you, did he?"

"No. Actually, I haven't heard from him since he left this morning."

"Then what made you decide all of a sudden?"

"I'm just tired. I can't explain it, but I'm really tired."

"And you should be, because no one should have to put up with the shit Curtis is doing."

"I know, but the sad thing is, I still love him. Even after he said he didn't love me and that he could never be in love with me."

"But that's understandable, because you've loved him since the beginning."

"Maybe, but it's not a good feeling. And I hate being in love with someone who doesn't care one thing about me. Someone who doesn't care about anybody except himself."

"Well, I'm just glad you didn't stop taking those birth control pills."

"Yeah, I am, too," Mariah said, wishing things could have turned out differently between her and Curtis.

"So are you going to be okay until next week?"

"I'm sure I will. For the last two nights he's been watching television down in the family room and sleeping there until morning. So I'm hoping he keeps doing that until I leave."

"Okay, but you call me if you need me."

"You know I will."

"Take care, girl."

"You, too."

Mariah hung up and glanced over at all the cosmetics sitting atop her built-in vanity. She had a lot of packing to do, but for the most part she was only going to take what she needed. Especially since she didn't know if Curtis would eventually try to reconcile with her or if she'd be leaving here for good. But if the latter was the case, she would come back for the rest of her things later.

She leaned farther back onto the pillows and closed her eyes. She thought about the first day she'd met Curtis, the first time he'd asked her out, the day he'd proposed on Navy Pier. She even thought about the beautiful wedding gown and how proud she was to be wearing it. But none of those memories mattered now, because her marriage was practically over.

She thought about her life in general, but the more she did, the more pain she felt. The more tears she shed. The more times she wished she'd never met Curtis. She loved and hated him all at once, and for the first time in her life she wished harm on another human being. She wished it on her own husband and refused to apologize for it.

She was wiping her face when she heard Curtis coming up the stairs. She didn't want him seeing her like this, and she hoped he wasn't going to bother her.

"Mariah, we need to talk," he said, sitting down on the opposite side of her at the foot of the bed.

She looked at him but didn't say anything.

"Hey, what are you crying about?"

"Nothing."

"It's not about us, is it?"

"No," she lied.

"Good, because I know I haven't been the best husband to you lately, and I'm really sorry about that. I'm sorry for everything that I've put you through."

Mariah was baffled and wondered where he was going with this.

"And as much as I hate admitting it, I just don't think we should stay married," he said.

"What?" Mariah said. She knew she'd heard every word he said, but she was still shocked by it. And she didn't know how to feel, either.

"I thought about everything I was going to say when I was driving home, but I think it'll be best if I just tell you the truth."

Mariah sat up a little taller and braced herself. She didn't know what he was about to say, but she sensed it wasn't going to be good.

"You remember when I told you that I never loved you, and that I only married you because of the church? Well, even though I said it in anger, it's true."

He might as well have shoved a dagger through her heart. She'd heard him when he'd said it on Saturday, but the truth was a lot easier to take during an argument. It was a lot more painful when the person wasn't angry, because then you *knew* he was telling the truth. You knew he wasn't speaking illogically.

"I can't believe you did this to me," she said. "I can't believe you would use me like this."

"I know, and I'm very sorry."

"Well, what are you suggesting we do?"

"I think we need to file for a divorce. I know I told you I would never let you leave me because I didn't want to lose the church, but now I realize I don't have a right to control you like this. And I've also figured out a way to make it happen quickly."

"Meaning what?" she asked.

"Meaning, the only way the board will approve of me getting a divorce is if you admit you slept with another man."

"What?" she said, frowning. "But I haven't."

"I know, but it's the only way we can both get what we want. You can move out of here, and I'll be able to keep my position at the church."

"You can't be serious?"

"Of course I am. It's the only way."

"So you're saying you want me to ruin my reputation so that you can keep your church?"

"Not just that. Because you'll be able to go on with your life, too. And it's not like a lot of people will have to know about this."

"Curtis, there are over three thousand people at that church. And all of those people know other people here in Chicago and everywhere else."

"Yeah, but after a while it'll die down, and no one will even remember. I mean, even you didn't know I was ousted from Faith until I told you. So if that died down, this will, too."

"No," she said matter-of-factly.

"What do you mean, no?"

"I'm not doing that," she said, standing up and walking away from the bed.

"But you know it's the only way," he said, turning in her direction.

"Well, I'm sorry, but I won't lie about something I haven't done."

"Then what do you expect us to do?"

"You say you could never love me, so there's no other choice but to end this. But I'm not taking the blame for it."

"And I'm not losing my church either, Mariah. I told you that before."

"Well, maybe you need to tell them the truth."

"No, you're going to do what I told you." Curtis stood up.

Mariah didn't like the expression on his face and backed away from him.

"I told you that I would never let you or anyone else cause

me to lose another church, and I meant that," he said. "So you might as well get ready to meet with those deacons."

He grabbed her arm. "Do you hear me?"

"I told you I won't do that."

"Of course you will," he said, grabbing her tightly by her throat.

Mariah was terrified, and now she wished she'd made the decision to leave before today.

"Curtis, please stop it."

"Not until you do what I say."

She knew she could never lie about something this serious, but she told him what he wanted to hear so he would let her go.

"Okay," she said. "I'll talk to them."

"That's what I thought," he said, releasing her. "Crazy bitch."

Mariah wondered if he'd lost his mind.

"Curtis, you know this isn't right. You know I deserve to be treated better than this."

He laughed. "I see that big Amazon is still pumping you up, isn't she? But it doesn't matter. You know why? Because regardless of what you look like now, there's still a fat-ass woman inside you just screamin' to get out."

Curtis strode out of the room, totally dismissing her, but she heard him mutter, "Got me cursing in here like this."

Mariah had never felt more humiliated or more deflated in her life. She'd never had anyone speak to her so maliciously. She'd loved, honored, and, yes, obeyed him just like he wanted, and she despised him for doing this to her.

Then, to add insult to injury, he wanted her to go to the deacons. He wanted her to lie to them.

It would be over her dead body.

Chapter 24

There were two people Curtis needed to speak to this morning. Alicia, to see how she was doing and to tell her he loved her. Adrienne, to apologize and make sure she wasn't planning to do anything foolish.

He called his daughter first.

"Hello?" Tanya answered.

"Hi. You mean Alicia is actually letting you answer her phone?" Curtis said as amiably as possible. He'd had confrontations with both Mariah and Adrienne last night, and Lord knows he didn't want one with Tanya.

"She's in the bathroom, but she still wouldn't have answered it because she's not feeling too well," she said.

"Is she in pain or something?"

"No, she's just not feeling well emotionally. She had another nightmare about that Julian."

"What do you mean another one?"

"She had the first one two days ago, and I'm sure it's because she had to see him in that lineup. And then it happened again last night."

"Why didn't you call me?" he asked.

"No, the question is, why didn't you call me?"

"Because I spoke to Alicia directly yesterday morning."

"Well, you should be calling me, Curtis, if you want to know how she's doing. Alicia is only a child, and she's not going to tell you anything she doesn't want you to know."

"Have you heard anything else from the detective?" he asked, changing the subject. He just couldn't argue with Tanya today.

"He called a while ago to see if Alicia could tell him anything else that might help their case. Because what they're trying to do is find other girls he met on-line and may have raped."

"Well, I don't know why they keep bothering her, because they already have more than enough proof to convict him for statutory rape and drug possession. They told us that when we were in there."

"Maybe, but since that Julian has hired one of the best defense attorneys in the city, they want to charge him with as many counts as they can."

"So do you think Alicia needs to go to counseling for this?"

"As a matter of fact, the social worker at the hospital gave me a list of psychologists and Dr. Pulliam was on there. So I called and scheduled an appointment for this afternoon."

Curtis was fuming. He was sure that if he hadn't called, Tanya never would have told him about the call from the detective, the nightmares, or the counseling appointment. But he was willing to bet that James knew about everything.

"Well, you will let me know how it goes, won't you?" he asked.

"Of course. And Alicia just came out of the bathroom if you want to speak to her."

"I do."

"Honey, it's your dad," Curtis heard Tanya say.

"Hello?"

"Hi, baby girl."

"Hi."

"I heard you're not feeling too well today."

"No."

"Is there anything I can do for you?"

"No."

These one-word answers were trying his patience.

"You are praying to God, asking for strength, aren't you?" he asked.

"Yes."

"And you do know how much He loves you, right?"

"Yes."

"You're not just saying that, are you?"

"No." She sounded irritated.

"Well, if you need me, call me. And I'll try to get by there after I leave the church, okay?"

"Yes."

"I love you, baby girl."

"Bye," she said, and hung up the phone.

Curtis felt a tug in his heart. He'd tried to play down this whole rape situation so he wouldn't fall to pieces. He'd also tried not to be angry with God. Because no matter how he analyzed it, he couldn't understand why God had allowed this to happen. Why He'd allowed something so demoralizing and unsettling to happen to his daughter. But he knew this had nothing to do with God and everything to do with Satan. Satan was angry because he hadn't been able to keep Curtis out of the ministry and was now trying to attack him from a different angle. He was even attacking Mariah and Adrienne, and that's why they were suddenly being so difficult. But what Satan didn't seem to realize was that Curtis was a child of God and that he would never be able to compete with that.

Curtis signed a few letters for Whitney, made a few business calls, and contemplated how he should approach Adrienne. When he'd figured out what to do, he called her.

"Baby, please don't hang up," he said quickly when she answered.

"Why would I do that, Curtis? I love you, remember?"

He didn't know whether to take this bubbly tone of hers seriously or not.

"All I want is a chance to explain."

"It's really not necessary. You told me that you wanted to see your son and that you didn't sleep with his mother, and I'm fine with that. As a matter of fact, I apologize for blowing up the way I did. I was wrong for not trusting you."

He couldn't tell whether she was being genuine or sarcastic.

"And I was wrong for lying the way I did," he finally said.

"Don't even worry about it. I forgive you, Curtis."

"I'm glad to hear that, because you were pretty upset last night."

"I know. But let's not talk about that anymore, because I want to hear about your son."

This was simply too good to be true.

"I can't even explain it," he said, beaming.

"I'll bet it was an experience you won't ever forget."

"I won't, and he's such a good kid. And so handsome, too."

"Just like his father, huh?"

"If you say so."

See, that's what he loved about Adrienne. She was always so supportive of everything he did. She'd always been that way, and he was sorry that he was going to have to disappoint her again by marrying someone else.

"So tell me," she said, "are we still on for tonight?"

"You're serious?"

"Of course. Why wouldn't I be?"

"I don't know."

"So, are we?" she repeated.

He knew the best thing to tell her was that they couldn't see each other anymore, but without hesitation he said, "What time?"

"You still have your meeting with the deacons, don't you?"

"Yeah, I do. But I should be out around seven."

"Then what about eight?"

"That'll be fine."

"At Tyler's?"

"No, I think he's going to be there himself tonight, so unfortunately we'll have to meet at the hotel."

"Okay, well, I guess I'll see you then. Take care," she said, and hung up.

This was certainly a turn of events, and Curtis was thrilled about it. He didn't know why she'd had such a change of heart, but who was he to question it? Who was he to question any blessing that God had bestowed upon him?

He smiled at his latest thought and picked up a copy of the meeting agenda Whitney had typed earlier. This time things were going to be different, and he could hardly wait. He looked forward to hearing how supportive "Andy" and "Barney" were going to be when he re-presented his ideas. They would agree to everything he said or Curtis would sing like a Grammy winner. He would tell everything he knew about both of them, and they would regret ever knowing him.

Curtis leaned back in his chair and went to work on his next sermon.

"Good evening, everyone," Deacon Gulley the chairman said, and everyone greeted him in unison.

"Deacon Taylor, would you like to lead us in prayer?"

Curtis would have to thank Deacon Taylor properly for getting him that information so quickly.

"Sure. May we bow our heads," Deacon Taylor said, doing the same. "Dear Heavenly Father, we come right now just thanking You for another day. We thank You for waking us up this morning and for keeping us safe. Lord, we thank You for all the blessings You've given this great church and for making Pastor Black such a dynamic leader. So, Lord, today we just thank You for everything. We thank You for all that You've done and all that You're getting ready to do. And, Lord, if you would, please open our hearts and our minds during this meeting. Please let us work toward doing Your will and not the will of our own. Father, these and many other blessings I ask in your son Jesus' name. Amen."

"Amen," everyone said.

"It looks like we have a few items to cover on the agenda," the chairman began. "But before we do, I have a package here that is addressed to me and the deacon board of Truth Missionary Baptist Church. It was in my mail slot, but it must have been dropped off because there's no mailing address or postage on it."

Curtis wondered which member was unhappy now. The last anonymous letter they'd received had complained about how much time announcement reading was taking at the end of service. The one before that had complained about the location of the church picnic. Curtis hoped this one wasn't going to be just as petty.

"So let's see here," Deacon Gulley said, opening the envelope and pulling out a letter.

Curtis thought he would faint when he saw him pull out a cassette tape right along with it. Everyone else either frowned in surprise or leaned forward to get a closer look.

"Well, I don't know what this is, but I'm sure this letter is going to tell us," Deacon Gulley said, preparing to read it out loud. "Dear Chairman and other members of the board, It is with great regret that I write you this letter. Please know that I am not proud of what I have been doing, but I now feel obligated to tell you that I have been sleeping with your pastor for the past few weeks. Yes, I have been sexually involved with the man you appointed senior pastor of Truth Missionary Baptist Church. I have slept with him at hotels as well as other locations, and he has even made a commitment to marry me. He told me that he was going to divorce his wife so that we could be together permanently. But yesterday when I saw him with the mother of his illegitimate son, I realized that your pastor is the same manipulative, lying hypocrite he was when he was pastor over at Faith. And while I do not mean any disrespect to you as a church, I must say I was very shocked that you would hire a minister who has a reputation like Curtis Black. But at the same time, I do understand how easy it must have been for you to believe in him, because Lord knows I did. I believed him when he said he loved me, I believed him when he said he couldn't live without me, and I almost believed that he actually was going to marry me—this time. And I wasn't sure why until I finally had to admit that Curtis has this insane emotional hold on me. It's so insane that I can't even explain it to myself. But by now you must know how smooth and slick he is. Because based on what he's told me, your board gave him a deal of a lifetime. Five thousand per week, a huge housing allowance, and that Cadillac he proudly drives around in. It's almost as if no one has the ability to say no to him. But even though I still love Curtis, the good news is I'm finally finished with him. I know what he's capable of, and that he will stop at nothing to get what he wants. Which is why I took the liberty of recording our little reunion. A tape has been enclosed for your listening pleasure."

"This is totally outrageous," Curtis blurted out.

The board members looked back and forth at one another. Then they all fixed their gazes on Curtis.

"Can't you see that this is from some crazy woman?"

"Well, if that's true, then what do you think is on this tape?" Deacon Gulley asked.

"I don't know. Probably more lies."

Curtis was beside himself. He wanted to murder Adrienne.

"Well, I think we need to hear what's on it," Deacon Gulley said, standing up and walking toward the portable stereo system on the other side of the room.

"I'm telling you none of this is true," Curtis protested.

"But now that we have the tape in our possession, I think it's only right that we listen to it," Deacon Evans said.

"I agree," Deacon Pryor added, but neither of them looked at Curtis.

It was amazing how he'd had to force comments from them at the last meeting, but now they were willingly speaking up.

Deacon Gulley pressed the play button and all twenty-four men gave their undivided attention.

The first thing they heard Curtis say was, "Oh dear God. That's what I'm talking about." Then they heard lots of moaning and groaning and Curtis telling Adrienne that he didn't want her having sex with her own husband anymore.

At least ten of the deacons tried to muzzle their laughter. The others looked gravely disappointed. Deacon Taylor looked as though he'd entered the Twilight Zone.

Curtis tuned out the next few lines of dialogue and tried to decide if he should flee the room. But he realized it was best to stay put and act natural. He gazed toward the ceiling as if he was bored.

"No one has ever come close to giving me the pleasure you do," Curtis's voice rang out from the tape. "And Mariah has got to be the worst I've ever had."

Curtis scanned the room to see how everyone was reacting and then heard Adrienne continue.

"Curtis, I ask you again, what are we doing? What am I doing to myself?"

"You're spending time with the man you love, I'm spending time with the woman I love, and that's all that matters."

"I hate this. I hate that we're about to start all this sneaking around again. I almost lost everything last time, so you have to be very sure about this. You have to be positive that you're going to divorce Mariah in six months, and that I'm going to be your wife."

"Baby, all you have to do is trust me, because I'm really serious this time. I'm really going to marry you."

That was the end of the tape and Deacon Gulley stopped it and returned to his seat.

"Pastor, what were you thinking?" he asked.

"I wasn't thinking anything, because that wasn't me."

"But you know that that was clearly your voice we just heard."

"No. It wasn't. I'm not sure who it was, but it certainly wasn't me."

"You must think we're just plain idiots," Deacon Thurgood said.

"Look, Deacon, don't make me tell this board about your little mishap back in '58," Curtis threatened.

"Boy, you go right ahead and tell 'em whatever you want, 'cause I'm not about to be bullied by some jackleg minister."

"Pastor, you make me ashamed to even know you," Deacon Winslow said.

Curtis felt himself losing leverage, and now he knew he could forget about trying to blackmail the two deacons.

"I just don't wanna believe this," Deacon Pryor said.

"But I keep telling all of you, that wasn't me."

"Then who was it?" Deacon Evans asked. "And why did it sound just like you?"

"I have no idea. And all this means is that somebody is trying to set me up. They're trying to do the same thing they did to me when I was still over at Faith."

Most of the deacons exchanged blank stares and Curtis knew they didn't believe him.

"This is all a little too much for us to digest right now, so I say we adjourn and plan on meeting again tomorrow," Deacon Gulley said. "I know we don't usually meet on Fridays, but I think this meeting is very necessary."

"This is so uncalled for," Curtis said. "And I can't believe that any of you would sit here and take some outsider's word over mine. Some lunatic female."

"Well, it's not like we can just overlook something like this, and I think it would be best if you stayed out of the pulpit until further notice."

"Are you saying you're suspending me?"

"We really don't have any other choice. And the most I can say is that we'll try to get to the bottom of this as soon as possible. It would help if we could meet with this woman."

Curtis searched the room trying to find one of those able lieutenants Cletus had talked about, but he knew he didn't have any. He could tell by their faces. Some looked shocked, some looked angry, some looked as if they didn't care one way or the other. Curtis was also disappointed with Deacon Taylor. He hadn't said one word in Curtis's defense. Which wouldn't have been so terrible except, he was supposed to be Curtis's friend. He was supposed to be his partner in crime and loyal confidant. But it just went to show, a person really couldn't trust anyone except himself.

Curtis stood and walked out of the conference room.

He couldn't believe how caring Adrienne had sounded on the phone this morning when she knew she was planning to betray him. He was disappointed in himself for allowing her to do it.

He wasn't sure how he was going to convince the board of his innocence, but he would. He would find a way, because he had no intention of losing another church.

He had no intention of starting from scratch all over again.

betray him. He was disappointed in himself for allowing [illegible] to occur.

He [illegible] how he was going to confront the board of [illegible]. He would find a way, because he had no intention of losing [illegible].

He had no intention of starting from scratch all over again.

Chapter 25

Man, how am I going to handle this?" Curtis asked Tyler. He'd tried to keep his cool, but the farther he drove away from the church, the more nervous he became. Normally he would never discuss his relationship troubles with anyone, because he was his own man. But he knew he had to be very careful this time and needed all the advice he could get.

"First of all, you have to stay calm," Tyler said. "You can't let them think for one minute that you're afraid of them."

"I'm trying, but you should have seen the looks on their faces when they heard that tape. I mean, they actually heard me having sex with Adrienne. And I have to tell you, man, I *never* would have expected something like this from her."

"Maybe, but it's always been my experience that you can't trust any woman you're having an affair with. It's even worse for men like you and me because we're ministers. And unfortunately, most people thrive on trying to bring us down. They have no respect for God's disciples."

"You're right about that, because look at all the books and magazine articles that do nothing except bash ministers. It's almost like they've been hired by Satan."

"Well, you know the devil is always busy, and he'll do anything to stop the preaching of God's Word."

"That he will."

"But what I think you should do is first go home and tell Mariah about everything that happened, but stick to your story. You have to categorically deny everything, no matter how much she or the deacons try to corner you. You have to deny that tape recording until the end."

"I'm already a step ahead of you on that, because I will never admit that I've been seeing Adrienne again."

"And then the next thing you have to do is beg Mariah to forgive you. You have to stay married to her or this thing with Adrienne will look even more credible."

"But, man, that's my biggest dilemma, because I refuse to be without my son. The church is important to me, but I won't rest until he's in the same house with me. And the only way to make that happen is to divorce Mariah and marry Charlotte."

"But why do you have to marry her? Why can't you just be a father to your son?"

"Because Charlotte won't have it any other way. She's made it very clear that if I even want to see him, these are the conditions."

"Then that's a problem. Because the last thing you want right now is to end your marriage to Mariah and then immediately bring another woman into the picture. Those deacons at Truth just won't go for that. Especially not after hearing that tape."

"Well, there's got to be another way out," Curtis said, but didn't bother telling Tyler about his deal with Mariah and what she was going to tell the deacons.

"There is," Tyler said. "We just have to find it. But even putting all of that aside, the one thing you have to do is ignore this so-called suspension they're talking about. You have to walk right into that church on Sunday morning, business as usual."

"That's what I'd like to do, but I'm not sure how they'll react."

"I wouldn't worry about them, and as soon as I got there, I would walk into the pulpit, ask for everyone's attention, and I would tell the congregation that any rumors they've been hearing are all lies. Because if you can get the majority of your members to support you, the deacon board will keep quiet. At least during service."

"Yeah, I think you might have something."

"Because, see, the thing is, you have to let everyone—not just the deacons—but everyone know who's running that church. Remember we told you before. That's your church. And you have to treat it as such if you want them to back down and respect you."

"Well, we'll see what happens, but I'll definitely be there on Sunday morning with Mariah. I'm not sure what I'm going to do about Charlotte, but maybe for the time being she'll be willing to wait for me."

"Maybe, but I wouldn't tell her the reason why, because it's like I just told you. You can't trust *any* of these women."

But Curtis really did think he could trust Charlotte. He didn't know why exactly. But even though she was giving him an ultimatum and basically forcing him to marry her, he felt he could trust her.

"Well, man, thanks for listening," Curtis said. "And I'm sorry I had to call and bother you with this, but I really needed someone to talk to."

"Don't even think twice about it. This pastor, deacon, congregation thing is a war, and ministers like us have to stick together. If we don't, we'll all be out on the street."

Both of them laughed.

"I'll give you a ring tomorrow or the next day," Curtis said.

"You take care, man," Tyler said. "And be careful."

What a day. First it was another cold shoulder from Alicia, then Adrienne had played him for a knucklehead and dropped off that horrific tape. He cringed at the thought of his entire deacon board listening to the way he made love and the things he'd said. It was the worst thing that had ever happened to him—even worse than when the deacons at Faith had watched that videotape. Because at least then he wasn't there to view it with them.

Curtis drove into his driveway earlier than he had in weeks. He coasted into the garage, shut off the car, stepped out of it, and went into the house. Mariah was pulling out what looked to be some leftover spaghetti. Curtis threw his jacket on the chair, loosened his tie, and walked toward her. Mariah gathered her food and left the kitchen. She was candidly ignoring him. Now, he wondered if he should do what Tyler had suggested. He would still find a way to get rid of her, but for now maybe reconciling with her was the answer.

She sat on the sofa, pulled her legs under her body and turned the TV to Lifetime Movie Network. Curtis deplored that channel, because all he ever saw were women being abused by a man. Either that or they were being cheated on. It even seemed like they used the same actors for every story. What he'd like to see was a channel that condemned women. One that proved how terrible women could be—specifically those like Adrienne.

"So you're not speaking?" he said, sitting opposite Mariah.

"Hello," she said, chewing and staring straight ahead. Then she looked down at her plate and forked up another helping.

"That's all? You don't have anything else to say to me?" he said.

"Curtis, why are you doing this? Last night you physically abused me, you called me a fat-ass, and now you're acting like you're happy with me again?"

"I'm sorry about all that. I don't know what came over me, and my actions were totally unacceptable."

Mariah turned back toward the television.

"Something real terrible happened at the meeting tonight."

"Yeah, I know," she said, glancing at him.

"Who told you?"

"Deacon Thurgood's niece called me right after she spoke to her uncle."

Unreal. If the deacon's niece already knew, how many other people had been told?

"Well, you do know I'm being set up, right?" he said.

"I don't know anything. I wasn't at the meeting, and I certainly wasn't with you and your woman when she made that tape."

"But I was never with her. She called me over a month ago, trying to get me to meet her, but I told her no. I told her I was married, and that I wasn't the same man I used to be."

"Uh-huh. So what's her name, Curtis?"

"Adrienne."

"Not the Adrienne you messed around with on Tanya?" she said, setting her fork on the plate.

"Yes. And the only reason she's doing this is because I married you and not her."

"So you were never with her?"

"No. But now the deacons are saying they don't want me in the pulpit on Sunday."

Mariah raised her eyebrows, and Curtis could tell she didn't have much sympathy for him.

"So, Mariah, you have to stand by me. I know I don't deserve anything from you, but—" Curtis was saying when the doorbell chimed. "Are you expecting someone?"

"No."

Curtis stood, walked down the hall past the living room, and opened the front door.

"You lying no-good son of a bitch," Adrienne said.

"What are you doing here?" Curtis yelled.

"Because I have every right to be. I'm your next wife, remember? You *love* me, remember?"

"I think you'd better leave before I call the police."

"Huh. And you think I care about that?"

"Who is that, Curtis?" Mariah said, coming toward him.

"Nobody," he said, closing the door.

But Adrienne stuck her foot in the way of it.

"Hi, Mariah. I'm Adrienne."

"If you know what's good for you, Adrienne, you'll get back in your car and leave here," Curtis ordered.

"Not until I talk to Mariah."

"What do you need to talk to my wife about?"

"The fact that you're planning to divorce her and marry me. The fact that you've been sleeping with me every chance you get. The fact that you went on and on about how terrible she is in bed."

"Curtis, is this true?" Mariah asked.

"No!" he exclaimed. "I told you she's trying to set me up."

"Now why would I do that, Curtis?"

"Because you're jealous of my marriage to Mariah, and because you know I don't want anything to do with you."

"Whatever. But, Mariah, I really need to talk to you. You and I need to compare notes."

"Curtis, how does she know where we live?" Mariah asked.

"I don't know. She probably followed me."

"You're damn right I did," Adrienne admitted. "I followed your ass because I'm sick of you playing games with me."

"Look. That's it. I'm closing the door, and if you don't leave, I'm calling the police. Or better yet, I'm calling your husband."

"What husband?" Adrienne said, laughing. "I don't have a husband, remember? He kicked me out years ago because of you."

Curtis didn't know what she was talking about.

"Yeah, that's right, I lied to you, too. We're divorced. And the only reason I told you I was still married was so you wouldn't think you could be with me anytime you wanted. And I definitely didn't want you thinking I've been waiting around for you all these years."

"You're sick," he said. "You need professional help, and I suggest you try to get some."

"No, I'm perfectly sane. You're the sick one."

"I'm calling the police," Curtis said.

"Mariah, please call me. I work at KTM Corporation, and all you have to do is ask for Adrienne Jackson in marketing."

Curtis slammed the door shut.

"I told you she was crazy," he said.

"So is that why you all of a sudden wanted to divorce me?" she asked.

"No. I keep telling you, she's lying. I don't know why she's doing this, but none of what she's saying is true."

"Then where did that tape come from? Because Deacon Thurgood's niece told me that everyone in the meeting agreed that it was your voice they heard."

"I can't explain that, but you know how advanced technology is now. And for all I know, Adrienne called my cell phone, somehow recorded my outgoing message, and then had some professional put that tape together."

"Well, if that's true, how did she get your cell phone number?"

Curtis could kick himself. It was so unlike him to slip up like this.

"I don't know that either," he said. "Maybe she knows somebody at the phone company."

"Curtis, you are so unbelievable," she said. Her tone and smile were sarcastic.

"But, baby, I'm telling you the truth, and you have to stand by me. I'll do anything you want, but you have to help me convince the board that Adrienne is schizo."

Mariah dropped back down on the sofa.

"You know the other thing that Deacon Thurgood's niece said was that the letter Adrienne wrote talked about your five-thousand-dollar weekly salary and your housing allowance. So how would she know about that?"

"Because it's public information. Everybody at the church knows what I earn, so it would be pretty easy for her to find that out."

Mariah was quiet.

"Baby, I'm sorry that this is happening," he said, sitting down next to her.

She still didn't look at him.

"You do believe me, don't you?" he said, and didn't know how much more begging he could do. Especially since he didn't feel the need to beg any woman.

"Curtis, I can't think about this now. So, please, just leave me alone."

He thought about making one more plea, but decided he would go upstairs. He would talk to Mariah in the morning when things had settled down. Because he needed her to back him up on this thing. He needed her to stand by her husband.

He thought about Alicia and the fact that he didn't go see her today as planned.

He thought about Charlotte and Matthew and how he wanted to be with them.

He wondered if Mariah would have the nerve to call Adrienne.

Chapter 26

"Whitney, if you have a moment, I need to see you," Curtis said.

"Sure, I'll be right in."

Curtis had tossed and turned all night and hadn't slept more than two consecutive hours. Outside of that, he'd done a ton of catnapping. He'd watched the clock on and off the entire time: 12:40, 1:10, 1:40. He'd awakened every twenty minutes until he'd finally had enough. He'd gotten up at five, but unbelievably, he wasn't tired. Probably because his mind was still racing. He was trying to figure out what had come over Adrienne and how he was going to explain this to everyone.

Whitney walked in and shut the door.

"You sure came in late today," she said. "And you're wearing a jogging suit, too."

Curtis knew she was only trying to break the ice.

"I went to see Alicia this morning, and I know by now you've heard the news."

"Yeah, I sort of did."

"So what is everyone saying?"

"That they believe it's you on the tape."

Curtis sighed and leaned his head back, staring at the ceiling.

"I know this really isn't my business, Pastor, but is there any truth to what that woman said in the letter?"

Curtis debated whether he should confide the entire story to Whitney or only part of it. Tyler had told him not to tell anyone, but Whitney had proven her loyalty since day one, and he knew whatever they discussed would never leave his office. But the problem was, he felt ashamed and didn't want her thinking badly of him.

"As much as I hate admitting it, yes, I was seeing her, and I did tell her I was going to marry her. But the truth is, I was never going to do it."

"Then why did you tell her you were?"

"Because I knew she wouldn't keep seeing me if I didn't."

Whitney's expression pronounced that she didn't understand.

"Go ahead," he said.

"What?"

"Tell me how stupid it was for me to make that sort of promise."

"You said it, I didn't."

Curtis couldn't help laughing with her.

"So how are you going to deal with this?" she said.

He could tell she was genuinely worried about him and he appreciated that.

"I don't have a clue. The board has already asked me not to preach on Sunday, and they're having another meeting this evening."

"Gosh, Pastor, this is so unfortunate."

"Yeah, but it's my own fault."

"Maybe if you go before the church and apologize, it will make a difference. Maybe you need to take your chances and tell the truth."

"Oh, how I wish it could be that easy. But I just don't think they'll go for that. Not after what happened at Faith, because one-third of our members were also members over there when I was ousted. And now that they've placed all this trust in me again, I don't think they're going to be very forgiving."

"What will you do then?"

"At this point all I can do is pray. And I'll definitely be here on Sunday morning. I can't tell them the whole truth, but I will ask them to try and forgive me."

"I really hate that this is happening."

"Imagine how I'm feeling."

"I'm sure."

"So is there anything else you've heard?" he asked.

"The truth?"

"Yes," Curtis said, and dreaded what she was about to tell him.

"Well, the word is you've been a money-hungry womanizer ever since you came here, and most people are surprised you're just now getting caught."

"Whoa. Maybe the truth is not what I needed to hear."

"Sorry."

"Well, I did ask you. And is there anything else?"

"There have been quite a few members calling because they want to know why you haven't already been fired. They don't feel another meeting is necessary."

"This is worse than I thought. It sounds like they've already convicted me without a trial."

"I know."

"Which means I'm going to have to say and do whatever it takes to convince them that I'm innocent."

"I realize you have to make the final decision on this, but I still think your best bet is to tell the truth. Because people have a lot more respect for the truth than they do a lie."

Curtis heard what she was saying, but if he confessed to everything he'd been doing, they'd string him up and hold a witch hunt right in the sanctuary. So, no, that wasn't the route for him to take. He was good at lying. He was good at making people believe him. It was better to stick with his area of expertise. He didn't want to deceive them, but if he could just get past this one major catastrophe, he'd be home free.

"Well, you know I appreciate your honesty," he said.

"No problem. But is there anything I can do for you?"

"Pray. Pray for me every time you think about it, because I'm really going to need it."

"I've already been doing that. And no matter what happens, just remember that God loves you, and there are a lot of other people here who still love you, too."

"Thanks, Whit. It really means a lot."

"I don't even know how to tell you this," Curtis said. He and Charlotte were sitting on a picnic table, and Matthew was playing on the slide with his little cousin Daniel. Curtis had met them an hour ago at a secluded park near Evanston, right after Charlotte picked the boys up from school. Now Curtis was trying to tell her what was going on.

"What's wrong?" she said, caressing his back.

"I might be losing the church."

"You what? Why?"

"You remember Adrienne Jackson, right?"

"How could I forget?"

"Well, she wrote this off-the-wall letter and gave it to the chairman of the deacon board."

"When?"

"Yesterday. So, of course, he read it in the meeting."

"What did it say?"

"That I've been sleeping with her, and that I promised to marry her. Pretty much just a whole lot of nonsense."

"Well, did you?"

"Did I what?"

"Did you sleep with her and promise to marry her?"

"Over five years ago, but not recently."

Charlotte looked over at the boys, watching them climb to the top of the slide.

"Hey," Curtis said.

"Yeah," she responded, but didn't look at him.

"I haven't been sleeping with her, if that's what you're thinking. And the only woman I've promised to marry is you."

"I hope so, Curtis, because I have no intention of being caught in some love triangle. I said I could deal with you not being in love with me, but I won't tolerate other women. I won't tolerate being unhappy. So if you plan on seeing anyone else once we're married, we need to end this now."

"But I don't want anyone else, and slowly but surely I am falling in love with you."

He knew she didn't believe him, but he truly was. He wasn't head over heels, but it was still love.

"So what's going to happen now?"

"They've asked me not to preach again until I hear from them."

"Then this is pretty serious."

"Yeah, it is, and I have no idea what the outcome will be."

"But if you haven't been with her, it's her word against yours."

If only it were that simple. If only Adrienne hadn't seen a reason to record what they were saying and doing to each other. It was still so inconceivable to Curtis, and he wondered how many other tapings she'd done. He even wondered why she'd lied about still being married to the deacon. She'd been telling him for weeks how miserable she was with *Thomas*, how she didn't want to hurt *Thomas*, and how *Thomas* was starting to question her whereabouts. So either she was one great actress or she wasn't dealing with a full deck. She had to be nuts in order to fabricate something like that.

"There's more," he said.

"Can it get any worse?"

"Yes. She also sent a cassette tape."

"But why?"

"Because she wants them to think she has proof."

"Well, does she?"

"No, but when they played the tape, it sounded like she and I were having sex and talking to each other. Which means she must have used some sort of high-tech equipment to make it."

"What high-tech equipment are you talking about?" Her voice was rising.

Curtis had assumed Charlotte would be upset, but not to this extent.

"I don't know, but she had to use something because the voice on the tape sounds just like me."

"And you expect me to believe that?"

"Yes, because if I wasn't going to tell you the truth, why would I even bring it up?"

"Well, it's not like you couldn't not tell me either, because I'm sure this is going to cause some sort of delay with you getting a divorce. Am I right?"

"Maybe, but it won't be long. It'll just be until I can calm down the deacons and get things back in order. After that, we're good to go."

"I really hope that's true, Curtis, because I have something I need to tell you, too."

"What's that?"

"Matthew told my dad that he met you."

"And how did he respond?"

"You don't even want to know. I mean, he was so furious with me. But I told him the reason I allowed you to meet Matthew was because I want him to know his father, and because you promised to marry me."

"And?"

"We argued back and forth, until finally I was able to make him see that this is what I want. But he did say you would be sorry if you didn't keep your word."

"Which means?"

"That he's prepared to press charges if he has to. I tried my hardest to reason with him, but he's very serious about it. He's even spoken to an attorney."

"About what?"

"To see what the statute of limitations is for Illinois."

"And?"

"You won't like it."

"That's beside the point."

"It's ten years after a minor rape victim turns eighteen. And he made it very clear that he has until my twenty-eighth birthday to have you arrested."

"This is crazy."

"I know, but my dad doesn't think so."

Curtis didn't like the sound of this. He didn't like the idea of anyone having that much control over him. He knew he'd been wrong for sleeping with Charlotte back then, but God had already forgiven him for that. God had forgiven him for every sin he'd committed, so why couldn't everyone else? Why couldn't they all just leave him be and mind their own business? It was almost as if there was some sort of conspiracy against him.

"You know what?" Curtis said. "I don't mean any disrespect, but right now your father is the least of my worries."

"Well, he shouldn't be, because he's not someone to be played with."

"Maybe he isn't. But, baby, if I don't keep my focus on this Adrienne situation, I'll end up losing everything."

"I understand that, but just so you know, I won't wait around for you forever. Because whether it ends up being you or someone else, Matthew will have a good life, and he will have a father."

Curtis didn't know what else to say. She was clearly upset, and he hoped she wasn't planning to keep his son from him. He hoped she would try to hold on for just a short while longer. If she did, they would both get what they wanted. He would keep his church and get his son, and she would have the life she always dreamed of.

Curtis smiled when he saw Matthew and Daniel running toward them.

"Dad, come get on the slide with us," he said, pulling Curtis away from the table.

"C'mon, Auntie Charlotte," Daniel said, grasping her hand.

"I think I might be a little too old for this," Curtis told his son.

"I know, but it'll still be fun."

Curtis grabbed Matthew and tossed him over his shoulder.

Matthew squealed with sheer enjoyment.

Curtis turned to look at Charlotte and smiled at her.

She smiled back, but Curtis knew she wasn't happy. She wasn't nearly as happy as when they'd first arrived at the park. Before he'd told her the news. Before he'd lied to her about Adrienne. But whether she realized it or not, things would work out for them. He didn't know exactly how, but they would.

There just wasn't any other alternative.

Chapter 27

Mariah and Curtis had just arrived at church, and she was happy he'd gone straight to his study. She was happy she didn't have to look at him for at least the next hour. It had been three days since Adrienne dropped that bomb on the deacons and then paid Mariah and Curtis a surprise visit at their home. At first Mariah had despised the fact that Adrienne had been bold enough to ring their doorbell, but once she'd called Adrienne, she realized it was a blessing. She realized God always allowed everything to happen for a reason. She'd known about some of the things Curtis had done and said about her, but Adrienne had told her everything. Everything from the way Curtis had talked about Mariah's ghetto family to how he dreaded lying in the same bed with her. Adrienne had also told her how she'd caught Curtis, Charlotte, and their son walking out of Tyler's condo. She'd told Mariah how this had been the ultimate slap in the face for her. Partly because Curtis had lied to her about why he couldn't see her that night, partly because she'd known for sure he was sleeping with Charlotte again, and partly because she'd seen a little boy she might've had herself if Curtis hadn't talked her into having that abortion. Mariah had learned more about her husband from Adrienne in one day than she'd known the whole time she'd been married to him. She'd been totally in the dark about everything, but she had to admit she hadn't gone out of her way to find out much of anything. She'd been happy just to be with him and happy that he'd chosen her as his wife. But now she knew she'd been living some ridiculous fantasy and it was time to accept reality. Thanks to Adrienne and her friend Vivian, her eyes were now wide open, and she wasn't afraid of Curtis anymore. She'd been worried about leaving him, because of the way he'd threatened her, but now she didn't care what he said or tried to do to her. Not after finding out about Charlotte and her son, not after discovering his affair with Adrienne, and certainly not after he'd had the audacity to demand that she tell the deacons she'd been unfaithful to him. Because it was then that she knew for sure that Curtis didn't care a thing about her, and that he clearly thought she was stupid. He thought she was some child who would do and say anything as long as he told her to. But she knew it was her own fault, because she'd been completely submissive from the very beginning. Unfortunately for him, though, his good thing with her was quickly coming to an end.

Mariah walked into the sanctuary and smiled at Sister Fletcher.

"How are you, Sister?"

"I'm fine, Sister Black," she said, hugging Mariah.

"Wonderful. And where's Miss Carmen at today?"

"She's here somewhere," Sister Fletcher said, looking around for her. "Probably looking for some of her little girlfriends to sit with."

"Well, tell her I asked about her, and that I'll see her on Wednesday at the ministry meeting."

"I will, and by the way," Sister Fletcher whispered, "I'm so sorry about that woman and what she's accusing Pastor of. That poor man must be a nervous wreck trying to explain all these lies that woman is telling."

"Thank you," was all Mariah could say, and was amazed at what she was hearing. She didn't understand how anyone could believe Curtis was innocent of anything. Not when there was audible evidence to prove that he wasn't. Now Mariah wondered how many other people were planning to support him until the end.

Over the next half hour Mariah greeted one parishioner after another and finally saw Vivian walking down the aisle.

"So you made it," Mariah said, embracing her.

"I did. But as you can see, I'm running a little late."

"You're fine. Service doesn't start for another fifteen or twenty minutes."

"I'm loving that turquoise blouse you have on," Mariah said, waiting for Vivian to slide before her into the second pew.

"Well, thank you," Vivian said, smiling. "A real good friend of mine bought it for me. And this skirt I have on, too."

Mariah sat down next to her and smiled. Vivian didn't come to church very often, but Mariah was always glad when she did.

A few more minutes passed and finally Deacons Gulley, Thurgood, Winslow, Taylor, and Evans lined up across the front of the church for devotion. Mariah still hadn't seen Curtis come in, but he'd told her he wasn't planning to make his entrance until devotion was over with. He'd decided that this would be the best time to address the congregation. Mariah knew it would be more like an interruption, since the board had told him he was suspended. They'd held another meeting on Friday as planned, but had decided they didn't want to make any decisions until after they held a churchwide business meeting in a couple of weeks. They wanted to hear from the people and possibly take a vote. They'd hoped to interview Adrienne but hadn't been able to contact her.

After the deacons led the congregation through a scripture, hymn, and prayer, they took their seats, and one of the associate ministers stood at the podium. But when he did, Curtis walked into the sanctuary and into the pulpit. He shook hands with the young minister and the young minister took his seat again. There was noticeable stirring and whispering throughout the building. Most of the deacons looked annoyed and disturbed.

"Good morning, church," Curtis began, and Mariah and Vivian looked at each other. Mariah wondered if he was still planning to tell all those lies she'd heard him practicing yesterday. He'd even asked her to listen to a few lines of this pathetic speech he was about to give because he wanted to know what she thought about it. But she'd told him she didn't have any opinion one way or the other, and he'd become irritated with her.

"First of all, I want to apologize for all the rumors that most of you have been hearing. And I'm sure by now you know the board has suspended me indefinitely. And while I was a little upset about it in the beginning, I now realize the board was only doing its job. Because the truth of the matter is, there have been some very serious allegations made against me. They are all lies, but still, they are very serious and cannot be overlooked."

Curtis looked at Deacon Gulley and a few others on the board and saw that they weren't happy about him being up there.

"Deacons, I know you probably don't approve of my being here today, but I'm hoping you'll just bear with me for a few more minutes. I'm hoping you'll allow me to explain my situation to the people of this great church," he said, looking over at Mariah. But she never directed a smile at him.

"It's true that I did have some problems when I was pastor

at another church, but I'm here today to ask one question. How many of *you* haven't had problems? How many of *you* haven't done something you're not too proud of? How many of *you* don't have skeletons you wouldn't want anyone to know about? And don't get me wrong, because I'm clearly not trying to place blame or trying to justify my past transgressions. I'm simply trying to make everyone in here realize that I'm no different than any of you. I'm just as human as the next person, and I've learned from my mistakes.

"But what I want to talk about more than anything else is this current situation. I want to tell you that I'm innocent of all these slanderous accusations. The woman who has made them is very disgruntled and obviously unstable, and she's gone out of her way to set me up. I'm not sure why she's doing it, but I can only assume it's because Satan is very, very busy in her life. And he's using her to try and stop my ministry. He's trying to turn all of you good people against me. He thought he'd destroyed my spirit and my faith in God when I stopped preaching a few years back, but when all of you great people offered me a position here, it made him angry. It made him realize he had to double his determination if he wanted to get revenge on me.

"And, church, I tell you, he's been working on every person who is special in my life," he said, looking at Mariah again. "He tried his hardest to turn my wife against me through this woman and her lies, but thank God she's not allowing him to do it. Thank God she told me she knew Satan was a liar, and that these allegations are all lies, too," Curtis said, wiping tears from his cheeks. "And he's even been trying to drive this wedge between my daughter and me. He's attacked her in the worst possible way, and he's trying his best to turn her against me, too. He's even got her thinking that the church and the work I'm doing for the Lord is the reason I can't spend as much time with her. Oh, I tell you, church, I need all of you to pray for me. I need you to stand by me and ignore all that you've been hearing. I need you to open up your hearts and see that this is all Satan's doing. I don't know how this woman got a hold of my voice and made that tape, but it's like I told my wife, anything is possible with all this new technology."

"Amen," more than one person called out.

"So I'm begging you," Curtis said, crying openly. "Please don't believe these lies that are being told on me. Please tell your assigned deacon that you support me, and that you want me to stay on as your pastor. And if you would, please pray for my wife and me. Please pray for that woman and her insanity. Pray that she gets help immediately," he said.

"The only person who's going to be needing any help is you, Curtis," Adrienne yelled, strutting down the aisle directly toward him. She was decked out from head to toe. She wore a tight-fitting black dress and a wide-brimmed black hat which was pulled down over mafia-style sunglasses. A black shoulder purse hung past her waist.

"Father in heaven, I stretch my hand to Thee," Curtis said.

"Come down out of that pulpit, Curtis," Adrienne said.

Deacon Gulley and a few other board members stood up.

"Deacons, please," Adrienne begged. "I didn't come here to harm any of you or anyone else at this church. I only came here to deal with Curtis."

"But, miss, this isn't the time or the place," Deacon Gulley said. "This is the Lord's house, and we're going to have to ask you to leave."

"Not until I get what I came for," she said, pulling out a gun and pointing it at Curtis. "Now come down out of that pulpit before I have to make you."

"Lord have mercy, she's got a gun," someone yelled.

"She's gonna kill him," another shouted.

Mariah gasped and moved closer to Vivian. Adrienne hadn't said anything about bringing a gun. They'd spoken again on Friday night, right after Adrienne had come home from work, and then decided that the best way to stop Curtis was to re-create what happened at Faith. They'd decided Adrienne would do the same thing her husband, Thomas, had done five years ago when he'd gone before the church and disclosed all of Curtis's sinful secrets. So Mariah wondered why Adrienne was standing here now, placing everyone's life in danger. She wondered why there'd been such a drastic change in plans.

The deacons moved out of Adrienne's way and hundreds of people screamed and started to rush out of the church. But since Mariah and Vivian were sitting barely three feet away from Adrienne, they could hear everything she was saying.

"Curtis, don't make me ask you again."

"Why are you doing this?" he said, backing away from the podium.

"Because this is the only way to stop you. It's the only way to stop you from hurting so many people. Now, for the last and final time," she said, moving closer to him, "come down out of that pulpit."

The choir members scattered, seeming not to care that Adrienne might accidentally shoot any one of them. Mariah could hear others in the congregation steadily stampeding out. But she didn't dare look behind her. She didn't dare take her eyes off Adrienne.

"I want everyone else in the pulpit to leave, nice and slow," Adrienne instructed. "Because I *will* use this if I have to."

Curtis took a step forward.

"No," Adrienne ordered. "Don't you even think about moving. I gave you a chance to come out of there, but you wouldn't. And if you take another step, you won't even live to regret it."

"What is she doing?" Vivian whispered to Mariah.

But Mariah didn't respond. She didn't move, and she hoped Vivian wasn't planning to say anything else.

The other ministers followed Adrienne's order, and now Curtis was left in the pulpit by himself.

"Miss," Deacon Gulley said. "Please don't do this. I know you're upset, but nobody is worth going to jail over."

"Move out of the way, Deacon. Please," she said.

Deacon Gulley saw that she was serious.

Mariah could tell that the church was almost empty, and that the only people left were those sitting toward the front. Those who were afraid to move.

"Why don't y'all do something?" Curtis finally said.

"Shut up, Curtis," she said, holding the gun with both hands. Then she fired it.

"Ohhhhhh, Jesus," Curtis said, grabbing his shoulder and squeezing his eyes together. Blood forced through a bullet hole in his suit and he staggered to one side.

Mariah covered her mouth with both hands.

Adrienne fired another shot, and this time Curtis keeled over and slid down the stairs of the pulpit. She watched him and then, seemingly in slow motion, raised the gun to her own head.

Blood splattered everywhere.

Even on Mariah.

Chapter 28

Daddy," Alicia said, crying and hurrying toward her father's bed. Tanya walked in behind her and hugged Mariah.

Curtis had been rushed to the hospital by ambulance and was immediately taken into emergency surgery. The surgeons had removed the first bullet from his shoulder and then the other one, which, according to his doctors, should have killed him. The bullet had only missed puncturing his heart by a quarter of an inch. He was now resting in the intensive care unit, and the nurses were allowing only immediate family to see him for a few minutes.

"Baby girl," Curtis said, forcing a smile and reaching out his hand. There was an IV needle inserted in the center of it, so Alicia lifted it carefully.

"I'm so sorry," Alicia said.

"I am too." Curtis's voice was weak and groggy.

"Are you going to be okay?" Alicia asked.

"Of course," Curtis said, trying to smile again. "Daddy . . . is . . . going . . . to . . . be . . . just . . . fine."

"What's wrong with him?" Alicia asked Mariah, and Mariah could tell she was worried.

"They have him on a lot of pain medication, so he goes in and out from time to time. But he's okay," Mariah said, rubbing Alicia's back. But to Mariah's surprise, Alicia turned and laid her head on Mariah's shoulder and sobbed.

Mariah wrapped her arms around Alicia.

"Honey, he's going to be fine. I know all these monitors and tubes are scary, but he will pull through this."

"You know your daddy is a fighter," Tanya said, moving closer to where they were standing. She looked over at Curtis.

Mariah glanced over at Curtis, too, and felt sorry for him. She knew he'd brought the entire shooting and that whole scene with Adrienne on himself, but she still had sympathy for him. Although, she was sad to say, she didn't think she had enough sympathy to stay with him. Too much had been said, too much had gone wrong, too much had happened between them. She would stay with him until he recuperated, but that would have to be the end of it.

Alicia saw Curtis move his head to the side and open his eyes again. She went toward the bed and again stood over him.

"Where's your mom?" he asked.

"She's right here." Alicia reached past Mariah and pulled her mother's arm.

"Leave it to you to scare all of us like this," Tanya said, smiling. Curtis smiled back at her.

Mariah knew that shouldn't have bothered her because he and Tanya had been divorced for years. Not to mention Mariah was preparing to divorce him herself. But it was just the way Curtis fixed his eyes on his ex-wife. He gazed at Tanya in a way that Mariah had always wanted him to look at her. But he never had.

"Baby girl, I'm sorry about everything," Curtis said to Alicia.

"It's okay, Daddy. You just get better."

"No, it's not okay. I've . . . been . . . a . . . hor-ri-ble . . . fath . . ." Curtis dropped off to sleep again.

"We probably need to let him rest," Tanya said.

"I think so," Mariah agreed.

Alicia bent over and kissed him on the cheek. "I love you, Daddy, and I'll be back in here to see you in a little while."

One of the nurses came over.

"He really is doing well, considering what he's gone through," she said.

"I know," Mariah said. "He's very blessed."

"When will he get to go home?" Alicia asked.

"I don't know for sure, but over the next few days his doctor should be able to answer that," the nurse answered.

"Oh," Alicia said, sounding disappointed.

Mariah, Alicia, and Tanya walked toward the waiting area.

"Mom, can I use your cell phone to call Danielle?" Alicia asked.

"Sure, and when you finish you can go get me a diet soda," Tanya said, reaching into her handbag for money. She also pulled out her cell phone.

"Okay."

"Mariah, do you want anything?" Tanya asked.

"No, thanks."

Alicia took off down the hallway and Mariah broke into tears.

"I know this is hard for you," Tanya said.

"It is, and it's still hard to believe that Adrienne shot him like that. In the church. And I don't even want to think about her turning the gun on herself. It just didn't make any sense. I mean, why would she want to kill herself over Curtis?"

"Especially after all these years," Tanya said.

"Well, that's the other thing. He'd starting seeing her again almost two months ago."

"No," Tanya said.

"Yes. And he was seeing Charlotte again, too, just like we thought."

"Unbelievable," Tanya said.

"Yeah, but with Curtis, what isn't?"

"I know."

"He is who he is, and there's nothing anyone can do to change that."

"So what are you going to do?"

"I don't know exactly, but I definitely won't stay married to him."

"Well, no one can blame you, that's for sure."

Mariah waved at some of the church members walking toward them. There had been a few others who had followed the ambulance but had already gone home. Vivian had also left, but said she would be back in a few hours. Mariah suspected that over the next few days there would be a good number of people coming to visit Curtis. Because regardless of what had happened, she knew he'd still have loyal supporters.

Mariah wondered if she should call Curtis's mother, because she was sure she'd want to know about her son being in the hospital. But since Curtis was so adamant on not contacting her, Mariah would wait to ask him before doing so.

Mariah thought about a number of things as some of the members reacquainted themselves with Tanya. But mostly she wondered how Adrienne's family was handling the news. She wondered how they were dealing with such a terrible tragedy.

Chapter 29

It had been two months since that dreadful first Sunday in May, and Curtis was elated to be going home in a few days. He would have gone much sooner, but there had been major and unexpected complications. Internal bleeding, elevated blood pressure, and, worst of all, cardiac arrest. He couldn't remember ever suffering so intensely or feeling so much pain. But now his doctors were saying his prognosis seemed promising and that he should eventually start feeling normal again. His recovery period would still take a few more weeks, but he was thankful just to be alive. Although, emotionally, he felt like his life had been turned upside down and tossed around in circles, and he still had no understanding of why Adrienne had decided things were so bad she had to shoot him. Worse, he couldn't fathom why she'd killed herself.

He'd known she was in love with him, but never in his wildest imagination would he have anticipated her showing up at church with a gun in her purse. Except the more he looked back on it, the more he realized he actually should have suspected something. Specifically, that night she'd rung his doorbell and announced she'd been pretending she was still married. Before that, he hadn't noticed anything strange about her and never suspected she had mental problems, but now it was clear that she did. Curtis wished she'd chosen another route to take, though, something other than committing suicide, because now he worried about her soul. He wondered how a person could ask for forgiveness once they'd taken their last breath. Yet, on the other hand, there was the theory, once saved, always saved—by the grace of God. So who was he to judge anyone, especially since it was finally time for him to admit that he'd become the same sinful, conniving, manipulative person he used to be when he was married to Tanya. He hadn't wanted to mess around on Mariah, but his desire for a certain type of satisfaction had gotten the best of him. He just wasn't strong enough to fight the temptation. He'd told his congregation how they needed to do that very thing, but he wasn't capable of it himself. So now he had to ask God again why He'd ever called him to preach. Because no matter how many women he slept with, he couldn't deny that he truly *had* been called. He still remembered what it felt like, and how he'd even tried to ignore it. And the fact that God had given him another well-known church confirmed he was destined to be a minister. He was supposed to preach God's Word to as many people as possible.

But Curtis also had other concerns he was desperately trying to deal with. Mariah was preparing to divorce him, and the members of Truth had kicked him out. So once again he was losing a wife and a prominent church. Now he was glad he'd negotiated a few clauses into his contract that would protect him. Truth would have to continue paying his weekly salary and housing allowance for an additional three months. But after that, he didn't know what he was going to do, because it would take a lot more than that to maintain his current lifestyle.

Still, the money was the least of his problems, because he

still had two children to worry about. Alicia had come to the hospital every single day, and the two of them had spent hours trying to mend their relationship. But more importantly, he was happy to learn that she wasn't pregnant by that hoodlum. He was even happier when the state's attorney told them two other girls had come forward. Because with three charges of rape and another for possession with intent to deliver, Julian wouldn't be leaving prison for a very long time. Although Curtis still couldn't wait for the trial to start and be over with, because he knew it would be draining for Alicia. It would be difficult having to relive that horrifying incident, but Curtis would be there with her until the end. She'd have both her parents by her side the way she wanted.

He and Tanya had always had their differences, but not while he'd been in the hospital. She'd even come to see him the day he was shot and then a couple of times after, and she'd been very cordial to him. He knew she was in love with James, but she would always have a special place in his heart. He'd always hold a special place for his first love, his first wife, the mother of his first child. It was another truth he could no longer deny.

Then there was Charlotte, who was just walking in. She, of course, hadn't been happy about the whole Adrienne situation, but was still planning to marry him. Which meant he would finally be a full-time father to his son. He'd also decided that, from here on out, his children were going to be his priority. He didn't know what the future held for him in general, but what he did know was that nothing would ever come before Matthew and Alicia. No massive churches, no beautiful women, no anything.

"So how are you today?" Charlotte said, kissing him on the lips.

"Feeling stronger every day," he said, trying to reposition himself in bed. "And you?"

"I'm good."

"Matthew?"

"He's fine, too. Begging to come see you, of course."

"You are bringing him by after you pick him up from day camp, right?"

"He'll never let me rest if I don't."

They both laughed.

"Come here," Curtis said in a serious tone.

Charlotte lowered the side rail and stepped closer.

"I just want you to know how much I appreciate you being here. Because I know it's been difficult."

"Well, let's hope the difficult times are behind us. But there is something I need to make clear."

Charlotte sat down on the bed, facing Curtis.

"This sounds serious."

"Actually, it is. I've been wanting to talk to you ever since the shooting, but I figured it was best to wait until you were better."

"You haven't changed your mind about marrying me, have you?"

"No, but in terms of our relationship, I think it's important for us to be on the same page."

"I'm not sure what you mean." Her change in demeanor confused Curtis.

"Well, first I need you to understand that I won't be as tolerant as Tanya and Mariah were. I won't allow extramarital affairs. Not of any kind."

"I don't expect you to."

"Because if I ever find out you're sleeping around, you won't ever see Matthew or me again."

"We've discussed this before, and I promise you won't have to worry about that. This thing with Adrienne has made me totally rethink who I am and who I'm supposed to be. I've spent every day in this hospital begging God to forgive me. I know I was wrong on every count, and that I've hurt too many innocent people. So from this day forward, I'm going to live my life a lot differently. I'm going to live it the way God expects me to."

"I hope you mean that, Curtis, because it's the only way we can be happy. It's also the only way my father is going to forget about those charges."

Now Curtis knew for sure that he was a changed man. In the past, he never would have allowed anyone to threaten him, and he would have told both Charlotte and her father where they could go. He was proud of his newfound decency.

"Baby, I don't know how many more times I can say this, but I won't be unfaithful to you," he said. "I won't disappoint you or Matthew."

"I'm glad."

"Good."

"I'm also concerned about your financial situation."

"I realize that, and once I'm back on my feet, I'll do whatever I have to to take care of you."

"But before that Adrienne incident, you were going to give Matthew and me the best of everything."

"I still will. It might take me a few months, but I'll still make it happen."

All of these demands and high expectations were starting to irritate Curtis. But he was trying to give his future wife the benefit of the doubt. He was trying to understand how she felt.

"So does that mean you've been thinking about staying in the ministry?"

"Definitely. But the other day it occurred to me that I'll have to do things a little different this time."

"How is that?"

"You and I could start our own church. Start it from the ground up. That way, we can appoint the people we want on the board. It wouldn't be a deacon board, though. Possibly some kind of governing committee. But regardless of what it is, you and I would also sit on it. Because if we're the founders of the church and we're also sitting on the board, we'll still have control of everything."

"You've really thought this out, haven't you?"

"Not completely, but I do have a general idea of how this would work."

"Where would the funding come from?"

"The bank. Donations from potential members. Fund-raising."

"And where would you want to do this? In the city? One of the suburbs?"

"No, and this is the part you might not like. To be honest, I'm not thrilled because I don't want to leave Alicia."

"Are you talking about moving?"

"Yes, because I think it would be much better if we made a fresh start in a smaller city."

"Like where?"

"Six years ago I did this revival in a city called Mitchell. It's northwest of here and has no more than a hundred fifty thousand residents."

"You're kidding? My Aunt Emma lives there. But I haven't spoken to her in a while."

"Does she like it?"

"As far as I know."

"Well, maybe you could give her a call."

"If you're serious about moving, I will."

"I'd at least like to consider it. But the question is, will you be okay with leaving Chicago?"

"It'll be hard, because my parents are so close to Matthew. But if you think we can have a better life somewhere else, then I'm fine with your decision."

"I do think a smaller community is best, and I'm sure the

cost of living will be much lower than it is here. I won't be earning as much as I did at Truth, but as our congregation grows, everything will eventually fall into place. My plan is to create programs that the city has never seen before. Day care, drug addiction, Christian competitive sports, libraries. And all of it will be started by us. Then, slowing but surely, I want our services to become nationally televised. You see it all the time with churches in major cities, but I'm planning to make it happen in Mitchell. My vision is so great, and this time I'm going to do everything that God wants me to do."

Charlotte smiled. "Then sweetheart all I have is one question."

"What's that?"

"When do we get started?"

Acknowledgments

Kimberla Lawson Roby expresses much love and sincere thanks to:

God, for being my strength and for making my writing career possible.

My husband, Will, for being the love of my life and for ALWAYS encouraging me to pursue my dreams. What would I do without you?

My brothers, Willie Stapleton, Jr., and Michael Stapleton, and the rest of my family for so much love and support.

My girls, my friends, my sisters: Lori Whitaker Thurman and Kelli Tunson Bullard for the conversations we have every day of every week. You both make a tremendous difference in my life, and I thank God for you. Peggy Hicks for our friendship and for all the great publicity work you've done for me over the years. Words cannot express how much I appreciate that. Janell Green for our many years of friendship, for having so much enthusiasm about my work and for always making me laugh. You are a gem. Victoria Christopher Murray for being such a wonderful friend and for all the moral support you give so genuinely. You are the best.

My author friends, E. Lynn Harris, Eric Jerome Dickey, Patricia Haley, Brenda Thomas, Shandra Hill, Yolanda Joe, Travis Hunter, Jacquelin Thomas, Eric E. Pete, Tracy Price-Thompson, and so many others.

My agent, Elaine Koster, for just being you. I couldn't have chosen a more caring and hardworking person to represent my work, and I am totally indebted.

My amazing editor, Carolyn Marino, for being just that—amazing; her incredible assistant Jennifer Civiletto; my wonderful publisher, Michael Morrison; my very supportive publicity director, Debbie Stier, in-house publicist Diana Harrington Tynan, marketing director Lisa Gallagher, and their entire departments; the entire sales force and the rest of the HarperCollins/William Morrow family.

To my other publicist—the wonderful Tara Brown! Thanks for all your hard work.

To the developer of my web site, Pamela Walker Williams at Pageturner.net, for your spirit, compassion, and expertise.

All the radio and television hosts, every newspaper or magazine writer, every on-line organization or reviewer who continues to promote my work. Locally, I want to thank Mark Bonne at the *Rockford Register Star*, Steve Shannon and Stefani Troye at WZOK-FM, Michelle Chipalla at WREX-TV, Sean Lewis at WTVO, Andy Gannon & Eric Wilson at WIFR-TV, and Charlyne Blatcher Martin at Insight Communications.

Finally, I thank all of the bookstores nationwide who sell my books, the hundreds of book clubs that read and discuss them, and the thousands of individual readers who support each story I write. You truly make the ultimate difference, and for that, I am grateful.

Want More?

Turn the page to enter Avon's Little Black Book —

the dish, the scoop and the cherry on top from KIMBERLA LAWSON ROBY

Why I Made the Decision to Become a Writer

Well, for starters, I must say that writing really was not a lifelong dream of mine. I remember enjoying it but it was never my plan to follow a career in it.

Once I entered high school and neared graduation, I decided that the business arena was the real place to be—mainly because I'd discovered that business majors were earning a lot more money than those who majored in English or journalism. But this is also the reason I now tell students at high schools and universities to follow their hearts and that they should not allow money to be the deciding factor when making their career choices. I tell them that if they follow their purpose, the money will eventually come. I also tell them to pay close attention to what they enjoy doing as well as what others are telling them they are good at. I, unfortunately, never did that personally, but if I had, I might've seen the early signs, hinting that I was destined to be a writer.

For example, when I was nine, I wrote an essay on the dangers of smoking which was chosen by CBS to air on one of their Sunday morning segments of "In the News." My essay was one of only a few that had been selected nationally, but I don't remember thinking it was that big a deal.

Then, when I was eleven, Mr. Groff, my sixth grade teacher, wanted to know why, when he asked for the time, I always had to build him an entire clock. He would assign our class one written paragraph but I would write one to two pages. If he assigned two pages, then I would write four or five. He would constantly tease me about it but would then say that I really needed to consider a career in writing.

When I was twelve and thirteen, I wrote for my junior high school's newspaper and was chosen by my journalism teacher to serve as the morning anchor for a closed-circuit TV news broadcast that our class produced each morning for the entire student body. I remember writing my own scripts, but thought it was more fun than anything else. I know now that fun is a good thing to have when you are going to be doing something for practically the rest of your life.

In college, I took an elective course called Women in Management and the final paper we had to write was a case study. To my surprise, my professor asked me if I would authorize the university to use the one I'd written as a sample for her future students.

Still, I didn't think much about it and instead, I continued on my path toward business. I decided that I would work hard in marketing, finance or both and climb the corporate ladder at some major company. But even after giving it my all and receiving superior performance reviews, I was never happy. I didn't see myself excelling fast enough, so I was never satisfied with my current position—whatever it was. Hence, after several years, I would find myself preparing the next resumé submission campaign, hoping to find the perfect job.

But in 1995, I asked myself a life-changing question. "What would I enjoy doing even if I weren't being paid a single dime for it?" Soon after, I realized that writing was the answer. Then, once I determined what to write about, I walked around for weeks mentally creating my characters, allowing them to become real people. I wrote every evening, every weekend and every holiday all while working full-time as a financial analyst and at the end of seven months, I submitted my manuscript to fourteen agents. But what I received was one rejection letter after another.

Not to be defeated, I decided to, without representation, send query letters to eight editors at eight major publishing houses. But once again, I received one rejection letter after another. Some were very nice rejection letters, but they were rejections nonetheless. So, at this point, I did become somewhat discouraged because even though I really did want to be published, I wondered if maybe it wasn't meant to be and if it was time to move on to something else. I even considered going back to school for an MBA. But my mother, God rest her soul, said to me, "You know I support everything you do, and if you want to go back to school that's fine, but I really don't think you should give up on your chance of getting published. There are too many women reading your manuscript and saying that they can't put it down until they finish it and that has to mean something."

Then, there was my husband, Will, saying, "Well, your background is in business, so why don't you start your own company and publish the book yourself?" But the thing is, I had never entertained the idea of doing anything like that because I knew absolutely nothing about the publishing industry. Still, I heard what he was saying and I went out and purchased the most popular book on self-publishing. I read it from cover to cover and then did additional research to find out how we could promote the book on a national level. I decided that the sales would have to extend much further than just locally or regionally if we were going to invest thousands of dollars into the start-up process. So, after writing an extensive marketing plan, we decided to go for it and ended up selling just over 10,000 copies the first six months. I also signed with an agent after the first month of publication and then with a New York publisher for my second novel (my first hardcover) based on a nine-page synopsis.

But this was all after burning the candle at both ends and even in the middle. As a self-published author, you wear every hat imaginable. From hiring a cover designer to having the manuscript typeset to choosing a printer, you have a ton of items on your to-do list from the very beginning.

I will never forget the day a huge truck pulled up in front of our house with 3,000 copies of *Behind Closed Doors.* Will, my mom and my brothers assisted me with removing my first printing from the truck and then piling them into a guest bedroom. Then, when the orders started coming in, my mom would leave work each afternoon, come straight to my home office, write out labels and then attach them to the appropriate boxes. Will usually arrived home from work about an hour after she did and the three of us would load up two to three hundred books per day in three vehicles and haul them over to UPS. My mom was always so eager to help out and she even seemed to look forward to it. It was hard to believe that she was so determined since she'd just had brain tumor surgery only months before. She was definitely not as strong, but you could never tell it when we were packaging up books. She seemed more energized than I was. She would tell me that "all you have to do is double your determination." This was also something I had heard my grandmother say on more than one occasion.

But even after hearing about my journey in self-publishing and how favorably it turned out, many writers will still ask if I would have preferred having my first book published in the traditional way. And I guess I would have to say yes, because it would have meant a lot less work production-wise, but once I had gone through the self-publishing process, I soon realized how invaluable the whole experience had been for me. I learned the business side of publishing and how to promote my work, and I am thankful for that. I learned the ins and outs of the industry and even today, after writing seven novels, it is not unusual for me to purchase reference books on how to market my stories and how to improve my craft of writing. Self-publishing is a lot of hard work, but it truly is a great way to get your book out there and to show major publishers that you are willing to work side by side with them to sell as many books as possible.

Love and blessings,
Kimberla Lawson Roby

Book Club / Reader Discussion Questions for *Too Much of a Good Thing*

1. When you first began reading *Too Much of a Good Thing,* were you surprised that Curtis was deciding to return to the ministry?

2. Do you feel that Mariah is typical in terms of some women wanting to marry men with money or who have a certain amount of power?

3. In your opinion, was Curtis truly called by God to preach or did he decide on his own to become a minister?

4. Why do you think Alicia resorted to dating on the Internet?

5. Do you feel that Curtis and/or Tanya could have prevented Alicia from meeting J-Money J-Money on-line? What about in person?

6. Do you believe that real-life ministers in your own city spend social time together, discussing their corrupt ways the same as Curtis, Tyler, Malcolm and Cletus did?

7. When Adrienne was first re-introduced, did you think she would begin seeing Curtis again?

8. Do you feel that Mariah acted accordingly by staying with Curtis for as long as she did? Do you believe this is typical of most pastors' wives?

9. In your city, what is the most memorable and outrageous scandal involving a pastor or church congregation?

10. What do you believe can be done to stop pastors who are morally challenged and who have no respect for God or people as a whole?

11. In the end, do you believe that Curtis Black has finally changed for the better?

12. Would you like to see more of Curtis Black in the future?

Meet the Reverend Curtis Black

- He was ousted from his position as pastor of a large Baptist church in Chicago due to an obsession with money, power, and women—to put it plainly, he got caught.
- Now the charismatic Curtis is building a new congregation.
- He earns a certain percentage of all monies collected.
- He's been married twice . . . and counting.
- He has a difficult time resisting temptation, especially beautiful female parishioners.
- But he's trying to recover. . . .

Now turn the page and see for yourself.

Here's a sneak preview of
The Best-Kept Secret
by Kimberla Lawson Roby

Available in hardcover from
William Morrow
An Imprint of HarperCollins*Publishers*

Curtis turned on the television and then glanced at the fireplace mantle lined with photos. At first, he smiled, but when he saw the picture of Alicia, his sixteen-year-old daughter, his spirit dropped instantly. It was hard to forget about all the pain he'd caused for so many people. Seven years ago, he was ousted from a large Baptist church in Chicago due to his obsession with money, power, and women and, as a result, lost his first wife, Tanya, to her current husband. He'd also lost part of his daughter's love. Alicia had even witnessed one of the deacons telling the entire congregation that Curtis had been sleeping with Adrienne, the deacon's wife, and that Curtis had paid for Adrienne to have an abortion. Alicia had only been nine at the time and was devastated. Then, after leaving the ministry for five years, Curtis was offered another pastoral position at an even larger church and then married his second wife, Mariah. He could still kick himself for not being faithful to her. If he had, things surely would have turned out differently. He never would have started seeing Adrienne again, and she never would have shot him down from his own pulpit and then turned the gun on herself. It had been an absolute nightmare, and the reason Curtis had made the decision to relocate. He'd wanted to move to a city like Mitchell where there were only one hundred fifty thousand residents. That way, he and Charlotte could found their own church and start their lives afresh. He'd wanted to give his son Matthew a normal, decent life, and thus far, they'd been able to do that.

KIMBERLA LAWSON ROBY

Rich Andreoli

KIMBERLA LAWSON ROBY is the author of the national bestselling novels *The Best-Kept Secret, Too Much of a Good Thing, A Taste of Reality, It's a Thin Line, Casting the First Stone, Here and Now,* and *Behind Closed Doors*. She lives in Illinois with her husband.